THE PORNOGRAPHER

John McGahern was born in Dublin in 1934 and brought up in the Republic of Ireland. He trained to be a primary-school teacher before becoming a full-time writer and later taught and travelled extensively. He lived in County Leitrim. The author of six highly acclaimed novels and four collections of short stories, he was the recipient of numerous awards and honours, including a Society of Authors Travelling Scholarship, the American Irish Award, the Prix Etrangère Ecureuil and the Chevalier de l'Ordre des Arts et des Lettres. *Amongst Women*, which won both the GPA and the *Irish Times* Award, was shortlisted for the Booker Prize and made into a four-part BBC television series. His work appeared in numerous anthologies and has been translated into many langauges. In 2005, his autobiography, *Memoir*, won the South Bank Literature Award. John McGahern died in 2006. *Love of the World*, a collection of his non-fiction, was published in 2009.

by the same author

JOHN McGAHERN

The Pornographer

faber and faber

First published in Great Britain in 1979
by Faber and Faber Limited
Bloomsbury House, 74-77 Great Russell Street,
London WC1B 3DA
This Paperback edition first published in 2009

Printed in England by CPI Bookmarque, Croydon

© John McGahern, 1979

John McGahern is hereby identified as author of this work
in accordance with Section 77 of the copyright,
Designs and Patents Act 1988

A CIP record for this book is
available from the British Library

ISBN 978-571-22571-2

2 4 6 8 10 9 7 5 3 1

To Wil Albrecht

I watched the sun cross and recross the carriages as the train came in between the pillars, lighting the grey roofs; and then hands began to draw down windows, doors flew open, and the first figures met the platform with a jolt, and started to run.

By the time the carriages themselves had jolted to a stop the platform was already black. When eventually I saw his small round figure far down the platform, childishly looking around, the raincoat over his arm, "A wise man always carries his coat on a good day", I turned back to the bookstall one side of the gate, and started to spin the paperback stand. He had need of all his own space, without interference from my eyes, as he came up the long platform. He was the last of the passengers to come through the gate. As he did, I went forward and offered to take his coat.

"It's no weight," he said as we shook hands.

"You decided not to take the car?"

"Why should I take the car—when you can sit back and the train'll take you. Then the other fella has to do the driving."

"Which would you prefer—to go straight to the hospital or have something to eat first?"

"Maybe we might be as well to have something to eat," there was suddenly unease and apprehension in the eyes as they searched mine.

We had beef sandwiches with a bottle of stout in a bar across the road from the station. We sat at a table just inside the door, out of range of the television high in the corner which was showing horses being led round a parade ring before the start of some race.

9

"Well," he cleared his throat. "How is the patient?" in a voice that would have been equally suited to asking me if I thought the Great Wall of China was likely to be around for long more.

"She's not getting any better. She's not well."

"Well, when do you think there might be a change for the better?"

"I don't know if there'll be a change for the better."

He took a sip of the stout, but this time he hurried his words, the voice shaking, "You mean that the writing could be more or less on the wall?"

"I'm afraid that's what it more or less is."

We sat in silence, drank and ate in silence. On the small screen a jockey in blue and yellow silks, a whip tucked under his arm, crossed to the centre of the ring and smartly touched his cap to a man in a top-hat, binoculars on his chest.

"Jim must be head beetler at the mill today," I changed. As a boy Jim had come to work for him at the saw mill. He still looked on him as a boy, though only careful scrutiny could tell which of them was the older man now. They'd grown to look like one another, to take on the same grey, ageless look, into which neither happiness nor unhappiness entered— just a calm and even going about their narrow and strong lives.

"You should have heard him," he brightened and began to chuckle, easy again back in the familiar corridor. "You'd think the sky was about to fall because he had to be on his own for the one day. And all that has to be sawn is a few scrubs of beeches. And they're left ready."

"Is there any sign of Cyril coming up?" I asked about my aunt's husband, his brother-in-law.

"He didn't say. He's good for nothing anyhow."

"What's he up to now?"

"They say he's foolin' round with other women. He's drinking lots."

"Maybe it's just as well he doesn't come up." I remembered

10

her agitation the one time he did come. Her medical card had been clipped to the foot of the bed and it had her age written on it. Torn between terror of her husband discovering her true age and the doctors checking the card on their rounds, she tried to alter the figures but had only succeeded in drawing attention to the poor attempt. In the end, she had to unclip the card and hide it in the bed during his visit. Probably sometime late at night she had hung it back in its place. I winced as I thought of her lying there waiting to put the card back. It was the only time he'd come to visit her through the long illness.

"What do you think we should bring her out?" my uncle asked.

"Whatever you'd like."

"I know but you'd be better than me at knowing those sort of things."

"Bring her brandy then."

"She was never one for anything but a sip of altar wine or a sherry or two at a wedding, and then only if she had to," there was alarm in his eyes. The drink was one of the great greasers of the slope we'd slide down anyhow.

"I bring her brandy all the time. It seems she mistrusts the medicines and pills. She drinks brandy to kill the pain."

"How much will we bring?"

"We'll bring her a bottle each. That way she'll be all right for a few days."

The sun was so brutal after coming out of the dark of the bar that we stood on the pavement a moment blinded, the bottles parcelled in brown paper in our hands, the glass of cars glittering as they passed.

"We'll get a taxi. There's no use fooling with the buses at this hour," I said.

"That makes sense," he echoed. He'd put himself completely in my hands and shambled by my side towards the taxi rank outside the station, the raincoat over his arm, hand gripping the brandy bottle. Only once did he speak on the way to the

11

hospital, to remark on the stink of the Liffey as we crossed Butt Bridge. "The city would sometimes make you want to throw up," he said.

There was a long corridor from the lift down to the ward but we were in her eyes immediately we got out of the lift. She must have watched that small space outside the lift with the excitement of a hunter ever since the train had got in. I saw her lean towards her locker as we came up the corridor, frantically checking her hair and features in a small mirror. It would have been easier to walk down that corridor if we hadn't to pretend that we didn't know she'd seen us yet, imprisoned and awkward in the enforced deceit, as sometimes it is difficult to do some simple thing while being watched, and I was thinking we'd be better walking backwards down the ward when suddenly she waved to us and smiled, her theatricality betraying that she'd been already all too aware of our arrival. Now that we found ourselves in this switched-on light we began to grin and nod with equal grotesqueness.

"We brought you this," my uncle betrayed his nervousness by putting the bottle down at once, and it alarmed her.

"What is this?"

"It's not flowers anyhow," I tried to joke. "It's far better. And I brought another. It's brandy."

"I don't know what on earth yous want bringing the two bottles for. You'd think it was Sticks McCabe yous were coming in to see."

"Poor Sticks, beJesus," my uncle chuckled automatically, but before she'd time to light on him I said, "Nobody thinks you're Sticks. I've already told how you take a little against the pain."

"It's a good job there's somebody to tell him something."

"It's you that's touchy," I said.

"Nobody meant a thing," my uncle said cautiously, and she was mollified.

12

"I just take it for the pain. I don't trust those pills they give you. They're hardly gone down when you can feel them spreading the cold in you as well."

With that, my uncle began to slowly clear his throat, filling the hospital ward with the rude health of a tree of crows, and pitching his voice on to the firm security of high ground said, "By the way, Cyril sent you his best. He said he's terrible busy but he'll be up as soon as he's ever able."

"Poor Cyril," she said dreamily, going inward and protective, all criticism gone. "I know he's run off his feet. You must tell him that no matter what comes he mustn't worry. That I'll be all right," and I saw my uncle turn his face away to hide any true feelings that might show.

The visit was as predictably on its way as a train or plane journey that had begun. My uncle had looked to it with apprehension. I who had made the journey often in the past months and knew it would go this way could not have said to him, "It'll be all right. Nothing will happen. It'll be the same as everything. We'll get through it."

Now that it was taking place it amounted to the nothing that was the rest of our life when it too was taking place. It would become part of our life again in the memory. In both the apprehension and the memory it was doomed to live far more vividly than in the taking place. Nature had ordered things well in that we hardly lived our lives at all. Our last conscious moment was the moment when our passing nonexistence and our final one would marry. It seemed felicitous that our going out of life should be as similarly arranged as our coming in. And I was ashamed of the violence of the reflections my own emotional idleness during the visit had brought on : the dead of heart can afford to be violent.

"You were great to come up," my aunt was saying to my uncle now that the visit was ending.

"It was great to see you," he shook hands. "I'll be able to tell them all that you'll be home in no time."

"And you? Won't you be in soon?" she asked me anxiously.

13

"I'll be in the day after tomorrow."

"God bless you both," I heard her say.

He was diminished and silent as he came out, the raincoat over his arm, and as soon as we got a little way down the tarmacadam from the hospital he put his huge fists to his face and turned away. When I saw the body convulse with sobbing I moved across the road out of way of the traffic and started to move a white lawnblock about on the grass with my shoe as I waited.

She used to abuse him for trailing sawdust into the house on his boots. I could see him sitting at the head of the table, close to the black-leaded Stanley, hungry, while she carried over a plate of fried eggs and bacon and sausage.

"Look at the dirty sawdust all over the floor. You'd think you were still in a field," I could hear her complain as she put down the plate. "Some people put sawdust down to clean floors," he'd say half-heartedly, his mouth already full. "O they do, do they, on clean floors! And it'd be fresh sawdust, not soaked in dirt and oil and carried in on boots." He'd be happy to let the last word go with her in the peaceful sounds of his knife and fork on the plate. These chidings, and his acceptance of them, were but tokens of the total security they felt with one another. Nothing threatened. Everything was known. Within its protective ivy frightening affection must have grown. He must be about two or three years older than she, I was remembering, when I saw him straighten and turn, wiping his hand across his eyes. They'd lived together twenty years before she married. And five years after she had married he was still living with herself and Cyril.

"Would you have a handkerchief on you there?" he asked.

I gave him a white handkerchief. I saw how discoloured the back of his hands were with scars. He moistened the handkerchief as he wiped his face and eyes.

"Is it all right now?" he asked, dabbing at his eyes.

14

"There's just a streak there to the side," I showed him and he wiped it clear. "You're fine now."

His tiredness was gone. He looked completely refreshed, even happy.

"Is there anything you'd like to do?" I asked.

"The train goes at six?" He wanted to hear it again.

"That gives you almost three hours. Is there anything you'd like to do before then?"

"What about you? You may have to go about your own business now."

"I have the day off. Don't worry about me."

"I brought these few addresses with me," he drew a crumpled piece of paper from his breast pocket. "They're saw factors. There's a few parts I could do with and there's no use asking them for anything over the phone," the voice was suddenly so swollen with the charming self-importance of a child that all I could do was smile.

"We have plenty of time," I said. "We have so much time that we're as well to go round the corner and wait for a bus. A bus will take us in at this time almost as quick as any taxi."

There are many who grow so swollen with the importance of their function that they can hardly stoop to do it, but there was no such danger with my uncle. In him all was one.

The factor's office was a flat-roofed prefab, out beside the gasworks, islanded by disused arteries and locks of the canal which once joined it with the mouth of the river. We crossed it by a footbridge, water pouring through leaks in the great wooden gates. The smell of rotting waterweed mixed with the pervasive sulphur everywhere. Inside, the office was lit by a naked bulb screwed to the ceiling. A rodent-like little man looked up from behind the high plywood counter.

"We're lookin' for spares," my uncle boomed.

"We only supply the trade here, sir."

"We are the trade," my uncle pulled some billheads from his

15

pocket. "Mr McKenzie knows us well." Mr McKenzie was the chairman of the company and was certaintly as unaware of my uncle's existence as he was of his small red-haired clerk behind the counter who was now turning the billheads over in his hands. Suddenly he opened a door to his right and called, "Hi, Jimmy," and when Jimmy appeared he looked as if he might be a brother of the small man behind the counter. He handed him the billheads and said, "These gentlemen are looking for spares." When they opened the counter leaf we followed Jimmy into a large warehouse. It was lit by the same naked bulb that lit the office. The floor was soft and earthen but all along the walls the parts were neatly arranged on shelves. The saws and larger parts were stacked in the centre of the floor. It was what I imagined a wine cellar might be or a place where mushrooms might be grown. For a while, with affection as well as some amusement, I watched my uncle flower in the dankness of the warehouse, examining parts, displaying his knowledge, even going so far as to lecture the patient Jimmy; and when I lost interest I hung about in the boredom of childhood until my uncle was through. When he was, Jimmy carried the parts out to the office. He and the clerk made up the bill from a price list in a plastic folder, parcelled the parts, and my uncle paid from an enormous wad of notes he pulled from his trouser pocket. The evening sun seemed as harsh and blinding when we came out as it had been when we'd left the pub to go to see my aunt in the hospital.

"It's a great ease for me to have those," he said when I took the parcel to carry. "You can imagine the writing and tele-phoning you'd have. And do you think you'd have a chance of getting anything? You'd be as well idle. It was there under their noses and they couldn't see it unless you took them by the hand. You'd often wonder if there's anybody in this country that knows anything. Is there long before the train goes?" "An hour," I checked on the watch. "Is there anything you'd like to do before then?" it was his turn to ask now. He was positively expansive.

16

"We might as well get close to the station first. We can have a drink or a cup of tea, whichever you'd prefer."

"We might as well have a drink for ourselves. It's not every day of our lives that we have an outing."

We had the drink in the corner bar at the traffic lights across from the station. We had more than forty minutes left. He insisted on buying large whiskeys. He grimaced as the first gulp went down but put the glass firmly on the table.

"Does this city business bring you in much money?" he asked with all the confidence he'd won at the factor's warehouse.

"It brings in enough," I answered but when I saw his disappointment named in or around what I earned.

"That's money, all right," he was impressed and asked apprehensively, "Do you ever think the day might come when you'd think of selling up the place at home?" about the house and farm I had inherited from my parents.

"No. There'll never be any chance of that."

"I tauld them," he said in triumph. "Though they're that land-mad they'd not believe you. 'He'll hardly be keeping on that place now that he's in Dublin and you'll be sure to remind him not to sell without telling me first. Him and me are the best of friends and he knows I'd see him right,'" he mimicked. "I told them they'd have more chance of jumping in the river than you selling."

"There's no danger of me selling," I reassured him.

"I know. Selling a place like that is like selling your life. You'd never know when you'd want to go back to it. And it'll not move unless you move."

"That's true," I raised my glass.

"And that girl you used bring down in the summer, do you still see her?"

"No. I haven't seen her for almost a year."

"That must be a great relief to you."

"No." I was forced to laugh outright. "On the contrary, I loved her."

17

"I know. We all have to make those noises."

"I wanted to marry her and she wouldn't marry me. That was all there was to it," I said between laughter and an old catch of pain.

"I know, but isn't a relief to you now that she didn't take you at your word? You'd be in a nice fix now if she had. Your aunt had you married off the minute you appeared on the doorstep with the girl, but I've seen too much come and go. And I know you're no fool."

"It wasn't that way at all," I said.

"I know it's not easy to own up to it, but if you talk to the wall this weather—am I right or wrong—will the wall answer back?"

"No, I don't suppose it will."

"Now you see the light!"

I saw the light. The wall would not talk back, and it was perfect and it was dull, better not to have lived at all.

If my love had married me it might all by this time have dwindled to a similar dullness, but at least by now we would know the quality of that dullness, having tried to live in love. Now we would never know at all.

My uncle saw his own state as the ideal, and it should be the goal of others to strive to reach its perfect height. For me to disturb its geometry with any different perspective would be a failure of understanding and affection.

The long black hand of the pub clock jerked past six.

"Will you have one for the road?" I asked, adding, "A small one?" When I saw his hesitation, "We have nearly twenty minutes yet."

"You must want me to go rolling home. The train'll be travelling on its roof," he laughed.

"Well, you shouldn't have any if you don't want."

"I don't want," he said.

"I don't suppose you'd ever think of retiring from the mill and taking it easy," I said.

"I haven't seen anybody retire yet but they were six feet

18

under before they knew where they were or if they weren't they'd be as well off if they were—drooping about the place with one hand as long as the other. You're a burden to yourself and everybody else once you stop working."

"You've enough money?" I said to keep the conversation going. I knew him to be a comparatively rich man, having several times over what his modest needs would require.

"Nobody has enough money," he countered vigorously. "Money is life. And once you stop earning it soon gallops away."

When we got up to go to the train he found his feet were hurting. "When you're not used to the concrete it takes it out of you," and we went very slowly across to the station. I carried the parcel of spare parts but he kept the raincoat. For a time, as we waited on the platform and talked about the difficulty of getting spare parts down the country and how nobody in the city knew more or less one thing from another, I thought that he wasn't going to mention the real purpose of his visit at all; but then I saw his face pucker painfully, as if it could no longer avoid a darkness too deep for him, and he said abruptly, "If she wants for anything get it for her. I'll see it right. There's no use expecting anything from Cyril. And there's no scarcity of money on this side."

"Don't worry about it. I'll see to her. I'm not short of money either."

"Sure, I know that," he took my hand. "You'll be down soon?"

"As soon as I can."

I watched him go down the platform to the carriages, small and indestructible with his parcel and raincoat, "My uncle, you will live forever." I murmured the prayer with a force all the greater because I knew it could not be answered.

The last of the sun still mingled in the evening rush hour outside the station. All day my life had been away, in easy

19

attendance on the lives of others, and I did not relish its burden back, the evening stretching ahead like a long and empty room. It must surely be possible to be out of our life for the whole of our life if we could tell what life is other than this painful becoming of ourselves.

I saw a bus idle up to the distant traffic lights which were on red, and I had time to get to the next stop. It was too far off to make out its number. Like spinning a coin or wheel I'd let the number of the bus decide the evening. If it turned out to be the fifty-four-A I'd get on and go back to the room and do the work I'd been putting off; if it was any of the other buses I'd turn back into the city and squander the evening. With a calmness now that I was within the rules of a game I stood at the stop and waited. The lights changed. With a grinding of gears the bus drew closer. It was a fifty-four-A. I put out a hand and it stopped and I got on.

There was no sound when I opened the door of the house and let it close. Nor was there sound other than the creaking of the old stairs as I climbed to the landing. I paused before going into the room but the house seemed to be completely still. I closed the door and stood in the room. Always the room was still.

The long velvet curtain that was drawn on the half-open window stirred only faintly. A coal fire was set ready to light in the grate. The bed with damaged brass bells stood in the corner and shelves of books lined the walls. Books as well were piled untidily on the white mantel above the coal grate, on the bare dressing table. Beside the wardrobe a table lamp made out of a Chianti bottle lit the marble tabletop that had been a washstand once, lit the typewriter that rested on a page of old newspaper on the marble, lit an untouched ream of white pages beside it. I reflected as I always did with some satisfaction after an absence that the poor light of day hardly ever got into this room.

I washed and changed, combed my hair, and washed my

20

hands again a last time before going over to the typewriter on the marble, and started to leaf through what I had written.

We used to robe in scarlet and white how many years before. Through the small window of the sacristy the sanded footpath lay empty and still between the laurels and back wall of the church, above us the plain tongued boards of the ceiling. It seemed always hushed there, motors and voices and the scrape-drag of feet muffled by the church and tall graveyard trees. Kneelers were no longer being let down on the flagstones. The wine and water and hand linen had been taken out onto the altar. The incessant coughing told that the church was full. The robed priest stood still in front of the covered chalice on the table, and we formed into line at the door as the last bell began to ring. When it ceased the priest lifted the chalice, and we bowed together to the cross, our hearts beating. And then the sacristy door opened on to the side of the altar and all the faces grew out of a dark mass of cloth out beyond the rail. We began to walk, the priest with the covered chalice following behind.

Among what rank weeds are ceremonies remembered, are continued. I read what I had written, to take it up. My characters were not even people. They were athletes. I did not even give them names. Maloney, who was paying me to write, effectively named them. "Above all the imagination requires distance," he declared. "It can't function close up. We'd risk turning our readers off if there was a hint that it might be a favourite uncle or niece they imagined doing these godawful things with"; and so Colonel Grimshaw got his name and his young partner on the high wire joined him as Mavis Carmichael.

This weekend the Colonel and Mavis were away to Majorca.

"Write it like a story. Write it like a life, but with none of life's unseemly infirmities," Maloney was fond of declaring. "Write it like two ball players crunching into the tackle. Only feather it a little with down and lace."

21

Mavis had come straight from the typing pool where she was working to the Colonel's flat.

"That bastard McKenzie knew I wanted to be away early. He made me go right back over the last two letters. You could feel his breathing as he pushed up to me to point out the errors," Mavis declares as she flings off her coat.

"It's perfectly ridiculous, darling, and all your own fault. I've always said you should give up that filthy job and come to work for me full time."

"I know what working full time for you would mean. It'd mean I'd never be off the job."

"I can't think of anything more delightful," the Colonel beams. "We've still almost three hours to the flight time. What would you like to have, darling? A g-and-t?"

"With plenty of ice," she says kicking her shoes off and stretching full length on the wine-coloured chaise longue. She has on a black wrap-around leather skirt and a white cotton blouse buttoned up the front and fringed with pale ruffles.

He lets his fingers dangle a moment among the ruffles and she smiles and blows him a low kiss but says firmly, "Make the drinks first."

When he comes back with the drinks he sits beside her on the chaise longue. "We'll have time for a little old something before going to the airport."

"I could do with a good screw myself."

As he sips at the drink, "It is my great pleasure," he slowly undoes the small white buttons of the blouse, and slips the catch at the back so that the ripe breasts fall.

Seeing his trousers bulge, she finishes the gin, reaches over and draws down the zip. She has to loosen the belt though before she can pull 'my old and trusty friend' free. The Colonel shivers as she strokes him lightly along the helmet, lifts it to her mouth. Uncontrollably he loosens the ties of the skirt, pushes the leather aside to feast his eyes on the

22

pale silk and softer, paler skin. With trembling fingers he undoes the small buttons, and the mound of soft hair, his pussy, his Venus mound, breathes free between the rich thighs.

"Why don't we go into the bedroom, I'm tired," she says.

He picks her up like a feather and carries her into the room, feeling as if he could carry her without hands on the very strength of his bayonet of blue Toledo.

"I want to see that gorgeous soft mound on high," he says and lifts up her buttocks and draws down a pillow beneath, and feasts on the soft raised mound, the pink of the inside lips under the hair. When she puts her arms round his shoulders the stiff pink nipples are pulled up like thumbs, and he stoops and takes them turn and turn about in his teeth and draws them up till she moans. Slowly he opens the lips in the soft mound on the pillows, smears them in their own juice, and slowly moves the helmet up and down in the shallows of the mound. As he pulls up the nipples in his teeth, moving slowly on the pillow between the thighs now thrown wide, she cries, "Harder, hurt me, do anything you want with me, I'm crazy for it."

She moans as she feels him go deeper within her, swollen and sliding on the oil seeping out from the walls. "O Jesus," she cries as she feels it searching deeper within her, driving faster and faster.

"Fuck me, O fuck me, O my Jesus," he feels her nails dig into his back as the hot seed spurts deliciously free, beating into her. And when they are quiet he says, "You must let me," and his bald head goes between her thighs on the pillow, his rough tongue parting the lips to lap at the juices, then to tease the clitoris till she starts to go crazy again.

"I have to shower," she says firmly, as much to herself as to him. "We haven't all that much time." "We'll shower together," he lifts her and carries her into the bathroom. She wraps her thighs round his hips as the iron-hard rod slips again within her. Once he pulls the switchcord they

23

can be seen in all the walled mirrors, and she watches herself move at the hips, over and back on the rod, feeling it hard and enormous within her. "We have to hurry," she says. Then, slowly, pressed back against the steamed mirror, she feels the remorseless throb within her, and gripping him tighter she opens and closes to suck each pulse until she shouts out, "O Jesus," as she feels the melting into her own pulsing go deeper and deeper, as gradually the world returns to the delicious scalding water showering down on them.

I am tired and flushed as I get up from the typewriter. Nothing ever holds together unless it is mixed with some of one's own blood. I am not able to read what I've written. Will others be inflamed by the reading, if there is flesh to inflame, as I was by the poor writing? Is my flush the flesh of others, are my words to be their worlds? And what then of the soul, set on its blind solitary course among the stars, the heart that leaps up to suffer, the mind that thinks itself free and knows it is not—in this doomed marriage with the body whose one instinct is to survive and plunder and arrogantly reproduce itself along the way?

I am impatient for the jostle of the bar, the cigarette smoke, the shouted orders, the long, first dark cool swallow of stout, the cream against the lips, and afterwards the brushing of the drumbeat as I climb the stained carpeted stairs to the dancehall.

I check myself in the mirror but I am already well groomed enough, except for a dying flush, for both the bar and the dance, and with a shudder of relief I go out, leaving the light burning beside the typewriter and pages on the still marble.

As soon as I came through the swing door I saw him against the smoked oak panel at the far end of the bar, his pint on the narrow ledge, puffing on a pipe and staring meditatively into space. Space mustn't have been all that absorbing for he woke and began to greet me with over-active flourishes while I was still feet away. He was in his all-tweed outfit, long overcoat and matching suit, gold watch-chain crossing the waistcoat which had wide lapels. The small hat was tweed as well, "English country", and much the same colour as the coat and suit, a dead briar brown. The bow-tie was discreetly florid and the highly polished oxblood boots positively shone.

"Ahoy, old boy," he mimicked an English accent quite unsuccessfully. "What's it to be?"

"A pint."

"Another pint when you have the time there, Jimmy," he called to the barman in his own voice.

"A Colonel Sinclair lived down the street from us. Every morning he'd come down for his *Times* and ten Kerry Blues. '*Times* and a packet of dogs,' he'd shout as soon as he'd come through the door. '*Times* and a packet of dogs.' "

I wondered if his imitation English accent or the ordering of the pint had triggered the story. "You look ridiculous in that gear."

"Tweeds are in, old boy," he was not at a moment's loss. "And besides, your good Harris, well treated, will last forever, unlike its masters."

"You'll get like Grimshaw," I countered poorly.

"I wouldn't mind a bit being the old Colonel. Very exhilarating, I should say. Except I have hardly his constitution. No matter. One of the reasons of art's supremacy is just because of the very limitations of life. There will be no art in heaven. You should know that, old boy, you university types. Did you bring the family jewels along?"

"As usual," I handed him the pages.

"Up to your usual high standard, no doubt," he flipped through the pages. "Ireland wanking is Ireland free. Not only wanking but free. Not only free but wanking as well."

It tripped out easily, like the well-worn shoe that it was; but once he began to read he was silent.

He, too, had ambitions to be a poet once, in the small midland town where we first met, he a reporter on the local

25

Echo, I just out of university, a temporary teacher of English at the Convent Secondary School. Such as he and I who worked in the town but were not from it were known as runners, and all runners of any standing lodged at Dempsey's Commercial Hotel—Maloney, myself, a solicitor, four women teachers, men and women who worked in the banks, a poultry instructress, the manager of the flour mill, and the whole of the A. I. station, its five inseminators and the two office girls.

All spring and summer Maloney had gone out with Maureen Doherty, a local postman's daughter who worked in Dr Gannon's office. Sometimes they came to the tennis club but more often they went for long solitary walks into the country or along the wooded bank of the river. Maloney seemed always to walk a few feet ahead of the girl, lecturing on the books he'd got her to read, quoting reams of deadening verse.

"Nothing sweetens pedagogy like a little sex. Nothing sweetens sex like a little pedagogy," Newman, the manager of the flour mill, nodded his sage head in Dempsey's. "Except usually it ends disastrously with the pupil coming of age."

Maureen was blonde and small and exceedingly pretty. Tiring of his strenuous self-absorption she threw Maloney over for a young vet who came to town that August and who had also taken up lodgings in Dempsey's. Humiliated and numbed Maloney went completely into his shell that autumn, spending all his evenings in his room and it was even rumoured that he was writing a novel. Down at the *Echo* office his rows with Kelly the editor increased in ferocity whenever Kelly insisted on removing some of the "rocks" or "jawbreakers" Maloney was fond of using in his column, which were clearly acts of aggression against his readers, whom he despised and was fond of describing as "the local pheasantry, crap merchants and bull-shitters".

And then one evening, drawing up to Christmas, he rounded us all up after the hotel tea—bank clerks, teachers, the solicitor, the poultry instructress, old Newman of the flour mill, the artificial inseminators, even the young vet, whose VW was seldom seen in the evening without a happy-looking Maureen Doherty, and shepherded us upstairs to the big lounge where he had already a fire lighted. With much nudging, low giggles, scraping of chairs and feet he read his poem, in rhyming couplets, of lost love, seemingly oblivious of the blatant discourtesies. And no matter how loud they might scrape or cough no one could boast of having escaped the reading. When he finished, everybody applauded, relieved that love's labours at last had ended.

Warmed by the applause he explained that there were two kinds of poets. One, having written the poem, would comment no further, insisting that the poem speak for itself out of its own clarity or mystery. While he respected the position he did not number himself among that persuasion. He was someone who was prepared to analyse every line or syllable, and he had no hesitation in admitting that the source of the poem was frankly autobiographical. He had been in love, had failed in love, and out of the loss had grown the poem.

He warned against the confusion between art and life. Art was art because it was not nature. Life was a series of accidents. Art was a vision of the law. Rarely did the accident conform to the Idea or Vision, so it had to be invented or made anew so that it conformed to the Vision. In short, it was life seen through a personality. Which brought us to the joyous triumph of all art. For, though life might be intolerable or sad, the very fact of being able to bring it within the law made it a cause for joy and celebration. Or, to put it more crudely, though in this particular autobiographical case the girl was lost, it was through the particular loss that the poem had been won.

Afterwards, impervious to laughter or ribaldry, he insisted on buying his whole audience a drink, even forcing the young vet who tried to make protestations that he had to be away to stay. With the same imperviousness, Maloney began his first pornographic paper, defied the obsolete censorship laws in much the same way as he defied the sense of embarrassment

27

provoked by poetry at Dempsey's—by simply remaining oblivious of it—and made it a success against all predictions. And he'd gone on from there to become the rich and fairly powerful man he now was. I suspected he paid me the higher rate he did as much out of affection for the old times as out of any belief that I could manufacture those sexual gymnastics any better than any of the several other hacks he hired.

I ordered two more pints, placing the fresh pint beside his unfinished one on the ledge. He made small notes or changes as he read and I knew they'd all be improvements. Time was suspended as I watched him. I watched his face register the world of the words, Colonel Grimshaw and Mavis Carmichael. It is a chastening sight to watch somebody totally absorbed in a world you yourself have made.

"It's good. As always. That's what'll juice them up. There's just these few changes."

He got curious pleasure from the changes, almost standing back to admire the line of the sentences, like someone admiring the true line of a wall he has just straightened.

"Nobody can stand anybody else, of course. You're one person who really knows that, aren't you? You just have to have someone you like stay in your house for a few days to find that out. It's all got to do with room. But we can all stand a lot of the Colonel and Mavis," and he began to tell me what to do in the next story. The couple should be split up in Majorca. Mavis should be given a bullfighter and the Colonel a brown-skinned Arab girl of fifteen or sixteen.

"You should write it yourself."

"No. I'm too busy. And I wouldn't manage it right," he handed me a brown envelope.

"Thanks," I could feel the notes in it as I took it.

"By the way, I'm expecting Moran any minute," he named the most powerful newspaper man in the city. "You don't mind meeting him?"

"Of course not. Why should I?" I was determined at once to deprive Maloney of his pleasure. One of his few new pleasures since becoming rich was to spring someone powerful or famous on his ordinary company and to stand back and observe.

"You should have seen her crawl to impress him, indecent ambition suddenly all over the place," he'd remark as if remembering a good wine. "One moment his feathers were all preened and the next completely drooped. It was like the effect a pike might have on a shoal of perch," I remembered hearing him boast.

"You don't seem very impressed. Or are you just hiding it?" he berated me now.

"I'm too old. And I know you too well. Besides, I have to go in a few minutes."

"Where are you going to now? You seem to be always going some place."

"To a dance. To the Metropole."

"All the young whores and the rich baldies."

"Do you want to come?"

"I have to go home after I see Moran. Dada has to say good-good night, tuck the hush-a-baby in, go to safe-safe sleep, or Mama will spank-spank," he mimicked before adding sharply, "You seem to have escaped all that crack?"

"It's just as bad without it," I had time to tell him as Moran pushed towards us at the end of the bar, a large florid man in thornproof tweeds.

"I see you're inflaming the people again. You better not get them too riz or they'll turn wicked on yez," it sounded so well polished that it was hardly the first time it had been put to use. "I was just on my way," I said, and with apologetic clasps on arms I left before there was time for protest. "I'll finish that for you in a few days."

I stood and breathed freely a few moments in the rain-washed air outside, and then moved towards the lighted dance-hall. As I drew near I saw three girls with overcoats and long dresses get out of a taxi and go in ahead of me through the swing doors.

The womb and the grave. . . . The christening party becomes the funeral, the shudder that makes us flesh becomes the shudder that makes us meat. They say that it is the religious instinct that makes us seek the relationships and laws in things. And in between there is time and work, as passing time, and killing time, and lessening time that'd lessen anyhow, such as this going to the dance.

There was a small queue in front of the ticket window when I went through the doors, the three girls in long dresses who had just got out of the taxi at its end. An even longer queue had formed by the time I was able to buy a ticket and a porter brought out a small easel and a pale red *House Full* placard, and left the placard one side of the easel, ready for putting up.

With the ticket I climbed the heavily carpeted stairs, running into another queue half-way up, which only moved every minute or so at a time, four or five steps, like disembarking from a ship. A man at the head of the stairs in full evening dress was the cause of this last queue, his black hair slicked back from handsome, regular features that had all the marks of an ex-boxer. As he tore each ticket in two, handing a half back, stabbing the half he kept on to a piece of wire, he stared into the faces like the plainclothes policeman beyond the barriers stare when a watch is being kept on the ports.

In the cloakroom a man was carefully hiding a bald patch with a comb and side of the hand. He was concentrating so hard that he did not even notice when I excused myself to get past him to the towels.

The band was playing to an empty floor, slowly, a foxtrot, the brushes caressing the drums. The four steps up from the bar left the dance floor just below eye-level. I sat in the bar, watched its pale maple on which some silver dust was scattered lie empty in the low light. After a while a blue dress swung past, followed by a steel-like trouser leg, the first couple started to dance.

None of the tables were completely free. I sat by the windows across from a young man with dark red hair and a winning smile who had already several empty glasses in front of him.

"You're enjoying yourself," I said to the red-headed man who was little more than a boy but looked more aged because of a weathered face. The hands were scarred and the nails broken.

"Just getting up some old courage," he was too involved with his anxiety or fear to want to talk and we just smiled and nodded back into our separate silences. Far below in O'Connell Street toy cars were streaming past, and most of the small figures on the pavements seemed somehow comic in their fixed determination to get to wherever they were going. I saw the boxer in evening dress leave the head of the stairs. The *House Full* notice must have gone up on the easel below. It was no longer possible to see onto the dance floor, the space at the head of the steps packed with men, and men on the steps below struggled to push through. Everywhere now there was the sense of the fair and the hunt and the racecourse, the heavy excitement of preying and vulnerable flesh, though who were the hunters and who the prey was never clear, in an opening or closing field one could easily turn into the other; and, since there were not many young people here, there must have been few in the dancehall who at one time or another hadn't been both, and early as it was in the evening, if we could scent past habits and tobacco and alcohol, in all the gathering staleness, there must be already, here or there, in some corners, the sharp smell of fresh blood on the evening's first arrowheads.

The redhead and I rose at the same time from the table which was immediately seized by the waiter for a large party of five or six couples who started to move vacant chairs away from half-filled tables.

"I suppose we better be making a start," the man smiled apologetically.

31

"I suppose if we're ever going to," I smiled back in the same way as we allowed the tables to part us, making our separate ways towards the dance floor.

Way had to be pushed through the men crowded in the entrance at the top of the short steps. The women stood away to the left of the bandstand, between the tables, some of them spilling onto the floor. It is not true that we meet our destiny in man or woman, it is those we meet who become our destiny. On the irreversible way, many who loved and married met in this cattle light.

I went towards her, the light blue dress falling loosely on the shoulders, the dark hair pinned tightly back to show the clean, strong features. She seemed not to be with anyone, and she moved nervously in the first steps of the dance.

"Did you come on your own?"

"Judy was to come with me. She works in the office with me, but she got a sore throat at the last minute. And I had the tickets. So I said—to hell—I'll come on my own," she explained.

"What sort of office do you work in?"

"The bank, the Northern Bank. It's boring but as my uncle used to say it's secure, and you can't beat security."

She was not as young as she'd looked in the light across the dance floor, there was grey in the dark hair, but she was, if anything, more handsome. The body was lean and strong against my hand.

"And do you come here often?"

"O boy, are you kidding? Some real weirdoes come to this place. The last person I was dancing with asked me if I slept with people."

"And what did you answer?"

"I was too shocked to answer and then I was angry. And then he asked me again, quite brazen-faced. And when I didn't answer he just walked off and left me standing in the middle of the dance floor."

"Not many people are young here," I said.

"I'm not young. I'm thirty-eight," she answered as if she'd been challenged.

"It wasn't that kind of age I was thinking of," I said.

All around us on the maple the old youngsters danced. The stained skin did not show in the blue light, but paunches did, bald heads, white hair, tiredness. People do not grow old. Age happens to us, like collisions, that is all. And usually we drive on. We do not feel old or ridiculous as we pursue what we have always pursued. Tonight, as any night, if we could anchor ourselves in the ideal greasy warm wetness of the human fork, we'd be more than happy. We'd dream that we were flying.

"What do you do?"

"I write a bit," I said.

"What do you write?" she asked breathlessly.

"Just for a syndicate," I said cautiously. "It's a sort of advertising."

"That's funny," she said. "I write too. It's not much, but I write nearly a whole magazine, it's called *Waterways*. It's the magazine of the Amalgamated Waterways Association, old dears and buffs who meet twice a year. Walter—he's my friend —he's the editor, but he's so lazy I wind up writing nearly the whole of every issue. You should see us the last two nights before we put it to bed—it's a panic. Luckily, it only comes out every two months," she was laughing and unaware that she was bumping some of the couples on the crowded floor.

"Do they pay you for this?"

"A little, but they don't have any money, just enough for a small salary for poor Walter, who'd work for nothing if he had to, he's that crazy about all rivers and lakes and even half filled-in canals. What I get, though, is plenty of trips and cruises."

Enough similar tags had been cast into the air to mark us off for one another, like a dab of dye on the markings of mallards.

"Why don't you come and have a drink with me?" I asked,

33

and when she hesitated, "It'd be easier and more pleasant for us to talk than in this bump-around. . . ."

For the first time she looked at me sharply, stepping instinctively back, taking stock of the whole. One of the few laws of the cattle light was that if you came off the floor with someone for a drink the sexual had been allowed in.

"All right," she said suddenly, without qualification.

The bar was jammed downstairs and when I found the waiter I'd had earlier he told me that there were some tables free at the far side of the upstairs balcony and that he'd bring the drinks there. "Bring large ones. Gins and tonics," I told him.

I pushed ahead of her through the crowd downstairs and then followed her through the women crushed together on the stairs outside the ladies' cloakroom. She had a magnificent strong figure beneath the light blue woollen dress, and when she turned her fine features, seeing the empty tables across the balcony, and smiled, "It's a wonder they've not been taken," she looked astonishingly beautiful, a wonderful healthy animal.

"Some prefer the milling downstairs. As well, they probably don't know that it's empty up here."

We got a table where we could lean against the balcony rail and watch. A fine dust was rising from the floor as well as the thick curls of tobacco smoke. The drummer had taken his jacket off and was sweating profusely as he launched into a solo. The waiter came with the drinks. He spooned in the ice from a jug he carried on the metal tray.

"Will you be wanting anything else, sir?" he asked.

"Bring the same again in a while. You might as well take for both now," there'd be no need to think again of the drinks.

"Do you live in a flat. . . ?" I asked when we lifted the drinks.

"No. I live in my aunt's house. I've lived there since I was six. Three of her daughters live there as well, my cousins. It is a house of women," she spoke excitedly.

"How do you happen to be there?"

"It's a long story. I have one sister but she's married to a solicitor down the country, where we come from. My father was a small builder. He struggled all his life, and when he was just beginning to do well—we had a bungalow in Clontarf—and mother and he could afford to go out together in the evening, they were coming from a dinner-dance in the Shelbourne, driving, and somehow missed the turn below Burgh Quay, and went into the Liffey. My sister and I were too young to know much about what happened except the bustle. We were shared out between two different aunts. The aunt and uncle I was given to already had eight children of their own. It was much stricter there than with my poor parents. My uncle taught chemistry. He was the Professor, a light of Maria Duce. He certainly wouldn't approve of this place," she was looking down on the dancers below. It was a slow waltz. Some of the couples were so wrapped round one another on the floor that except for the drapery of clothes they might be dancing in coitus.

"No, if he was like that I can't imagine he'd approve of it," I said idly.

The waiter came with the other tray of drinks.

"I don't think I'll be able for all this. Already I'm feeling a little tipsy," she said.

"Pour me what you don't want," and having established the intimacy we clinked our glasses.

"It killed my uncle having to retire," she went on.

"Is he long dead?"

"Two years. He suffered a terrible death. One Sunday I came into the room and found him crying. 'Josephine,' he said. 'I never thought anybody could go through this pain and still believe there is a God.' "

"Where are all his sons now?"

"They're scattered all round the country. They're all in professions. I guess they all got out of the house as fast as they could. Just the women stayed."

"It's odd that there wasn't even the ceremonial black sheep,"

35

these idle words mattered and did not matter. They mattered only in the light of where they led to.

"Johnny was for a while. There were some terrible scenes over his drinking. But he qualified. Now he makes more money than any of them but he never lost his old gaiety. You'd like Johnny."

"Why don't we dance?"

"I'd like to dance," she rose from the table.

We danced close. At first she held nervously and suspiciously back, but when I didn't press her she came naturally close. I could feel her hair brush my face. A hot, fierce burning ache—the Colonel and my Mavis again—grew to bathe in this warm living flesh beneath my hands. Across her shoulder I saw the gleam of a man's wristwatch as his hand crossed a neat pair of buttocks beneath their shimmering silk. And then our lips met.

"And are your aunt and cousins home this night?" I asked.

"They're sound asleep by now," she said.

"Why don't you come back to my place, then? We can have a quiet drink and talk."

"That's fine," she hesitated, and then added nervously, and too brightly, "We can talk far better there."

I waited for her in the downstairs bar, at the head of the stairs. The tired waiters were cleaning up but still serving drinks to what were now very drunken tables. It was the hour they usually cheated most. The bouncer in evening dress who had earlier taken our tickets was patrolling between the tables, his hands clasped behind his back. He'd pause where the petting at the tables was too heavy or where there were disputes over change. When he spoke his whole body went completely still, his lips barely moving. Beside me there was a solitary man at one of the small tables trying to shake salt from an empty saltshaker into a glass of tomato juice or Bloody Mary, growing visibly frustrated.

She had on an expensive brown leather coat and matching handbag when she came back, her walk intense and concen-

36

trated on anything or everything except what she was doing, like a man concentrated on the far trees while striking the golf ball at his feet; and she was smiling unnaturally hard.

"You look much younger than I thought," she said suddenly as we went down the stairs, her arm now in mine.

"I'm not young. I'm thirty," I said.

"That makes me ancient at thirty-eight."

"You don't look it. Anyhow after you leave twenty, age doesn't make much difference," I heard the phoney unction in my voice that I'd heard in others declaring that money counts for little in this life.

To escape any more of such conversation I put my arm firmly round her on the stairs : to hold this beautiful body, to enter it, to know it, to glory in the knowing, was age enough, or seemed no mortal age. Catching my desire, she looked at me, and we kissed. It was cold when we went through the swing doors but there was a line of taxis waiting for the end of the dance and we got into the first car.

The light from the Chianti bottle was shining so calmly on the typewriter and white pages on the marble when we came into the room that it jolted me far more sharply than the cold outside the dancehall. I took the leather coat and hung it on the back of the door. "You have a lovely place," she looked along the shelves of books and then went to the typewriter, touching the keys without pressing them deep enough to move the bar. I grew aware of the large bed in the room as I put a match to the fire in the grate.

"Is this what you write?" she asked.

"That's it. It's poor stuff. Sometime I'll show it to you. When you show me your pieces," I took the page away from her, the Colonel and Mavis might prove a rough overture. "What'll you have to drink?"

"What are you having?"

"A whiskey. I feel cold."

"A small one for me—a very small one, then."

37

I heard the pieces of coal shift in the grate as the fire caught. I was grateful for the whiskey burning its way down into the tension.

"Is it all right to put off the light?" I asked. "Soon the flames will be bright."

"It's nice to sit and watch the fire," she said and I turned off the light on the typewriter and marble. The flames bounced off the ceiling and walls, came to rest on the spines of the books, flashed again on the marble. We sat in front of the fire, and when I put my arm round her she returned my kiss, over and back on the mouth; but when I slid my hand beneath her dress she reacted so quickly that the whiskey spilled. Suddenly we were both standing, facing one another in front of the fire.

"Boy, you don't move half fast," she said.

"What did you expect?"

"You hardly know me."

"That's right."

"You couldn't love me or even care for me in this length of time."

"Love has nothing got to do with it. I'm attracted to you."

"You've. . . ." She paused, embarrassed.

"Slept with people without being in love with them? Yes I have."

"At least you're honest about it."

"That's no virtue. There's no way I can make you sleep with me if you don't want to."

"I'm sorry about the whiskey," she said.

"That doesn't matter. There's more. Will you have some?"

"I'll have a little," she held out her glass. We drank in silence. The fire had completely caught, the coals glowing, a steady, flickering flame dancing everywhere about the room.

"O why not," she said suddenly, and I felt no trace of triumph, only an odd sadness. "I want it too."

"Are you sure? We don't have to do anything," I said, but our kissing spoke a different language, and without a word we

38

started to slide out of our clothes. I was first in the bed and waited for her. For one moment I saw her stand as if to record or reflect, the flames flickering on the vulnerability of the pale slip with lace along the breasts, and then she slipped out of the rest of her things, and came to me.

"It's wonderful just to lie and bathe in another's body. You have a very beautiful body," I heard my own words hang like an advertisement in the peace of the firelight, the flames leaping and flaming on the brass bells of the bed, on book spines and walls and ceilings.

She was excited and yet drawing away in her nervousness.

"Is it safe?" I asked her in the play.

"It's the end of the month. I'm afraid I'm as regular as old clockwork."

"I won't hurt you," I said.

"Be careful," she answered. "It only happened once before," and she guided me within, wincing whenever I touched the partly broken hymen.

Within her there was this instant of rest, the glory and the awe, that one was as close as ever man could be to the presence of the mystery, and live, the caged bird in its moment of pure rest before it was about to be loosed into blinding light; and then the body was clamouring in the rough health of the instinct, "This is what I needed. This-is-what-I-need-ed." And we were more apart than before we had come together, the burden of responsibility suddenly in the room, and no way to turn to shift it or apportion it or to get rid of it.

"I'm sorry I hurt you."

"No, you were very gentle. You see, it only happened to me once before."

"When?" I was glad of this sudden opening to escape.

"Last summer. I have this friend Bridgie. She's a teacher. And she has this flat at Howth that I take over from her when she goes away on the long school holidays. It's just up from the harbour. Every Thursday evening I'd go down to buy fish off the boats when they'd come in. It was a Saturday it hap-

39

pened. It was awful. The man was a journalist and he was married."

"Had he anything to do with Amalgamated Waterways?"

"No, he wasn't from Waterways, in fact he's quite famous but I don't want to bring his name into it.

"A band was playing on the front that evening, where the grass and beds of flowers are, just before you get to the pier wall. He had come out to see me.

"We listened to the band. It was the Blanchardston Fife and Drum. They were playing 'Johnny I hardly Knew You'. There was the lovely smell of the sea mixed with cut grass and some of the children were playing in their bare feet. It's funny how clear you remember everything just because something awful is about to happen to you. Then we walked out to the very end of the wall where the small lighthouse is. We just stood there and breathed the sea air and watched the boats tack in and out of the harbour, some of them nearly colliding, till it started to get cold. We went into the Abbey on our way back. We had a plate of prawns and brown bread. He had stout and I had cider and we bought both evening papers from a small dirty-faced newsboy who came in. I have an almost total blackout about everything that happened as soon as we went back to the flat. Anyhow, we found ourselves in bed together. He was very gentle, it hardly hurt at all, but afterwards, O boy, that's when the trouble started, that's where it ended.

"There was I feeling all these emotions : So this is what it was like. It has really happened after all these years, I was no longer a girl, I wasn't a virgin any more, I must be a woman now at last at thirty-seven."

"That was just last summer, so?" I asked.

"That's right. It was the Saturday of the first week in August."

"What happened then?"

"O boy, that's when it happened. There was I with all these jumbled, mixed-up emotions racing all round in me, I had waited for this moment all my life, and now it had happened,

I had given myself to a man. And he reached across and looked at his watch and turned on the transistor, 'The racing results will be coming on in a minute,' he said, and I couldn't believe it. He got up, put on his clothes, pulled back the curtain. I saw him sitting in his shirtsleeves in the armchair, just socks on his feet, ticking off the results on the racing page as they were announced. I started to cry, stuffing the bedclothes to my face so that he wouldn't hear. And then when I heard the time signal for the news and saw him still sitting without the slightest movement in the chair, I stopped the crying, and I asked him what he was thinking. If he had made any reference to what had happened, just the barest word, I think it would have been all right, but you know what he said, all that he said was, I can still hardly believe it, 'I've just missed the crossed treble by a whisker,' it seems funny now but it sure wasn't funny at the time. I'd never felt so humiliated in all my life. Can you believe it, 'I've just missed the crossed treble by a whisker.' Then he heard me, and came over, but it was too late. I could never have anything to do with him again. It just made everything seem so ridiculous."

"You've never been with anybody else before tonight?"

"No. And I feel fine. I don't feel guilty or anything."

It was a long way from Colonel Grimshaw and Mavis, but there was Howth, the sea and the sunlight, masts of the fleet in the evening sun when they went down to the harbour. There was the band playing on the grass. Time stood still in the Abbey Tavern for an hour. And just before the racing results came over the air, her seal had been broken.

"I wish I had taken you back to the room that evening," I stirred with desire. "I wouldn't have said that I had missed the crossed treble by a whisker."

"I wish you had too. You don't think I'm too old for you?" there seemed to be tears on her face.

"No. It has nothing to do with it."

We played, cumbersomely: and yet, when her breathing grew heavy, and my fingers smeared the rich oil along the lips above the half-shattered hymen, I, sure in the knowledge that she could hardly turn back from her pleasure, might be a poor Colonel Grimshaw, and she, excited and awkward by my side, might be his Mavis.

When I heard her catch towards her pleasure I rose above her and she opened eagerly for me, guiding me within her. The Colonel should drive and shaft now and she be full of his thunder, but I lingered instead in the warmth, kissed her in case I would come and die.

We were man and we were woman. We were both the tree and the summer. There was no yearning toward nor falling away. We were one. It was as if we were, then, those four other people, now gone out of time, who had snatched the two of us into time. For a moment again we possessed their power and their glory anew, pushing out of mind all graveclothes. We had climbed to the crown of life, and this was all, all the world, and even as we surged towards it, it was already slipping further and further away from one's grasp, and we were stranded again on our own bare lives.

"Six or seven hours ago we didn't even know of one another's existence," she said.

"That's right."

"And you don't think you love me even a little?"

"No. Love has nothing to do with it. How do you feel now?"

"I feel great. I don't feel guilty at all or anything. Only I'm afraid I'm beginning to grow fond of you. Do you think you might grow fond of me?"

"I don't know. I don't think you can programme those things."

"And, you've done this with several?"

"With a few," I was growing irritated.

"Without loving them?"

"I loved one woman but love has nothing got to do with this. I don't think it is important now. It was blind. That was all."

"Who was she?"

42

"She doesn't matter now. Some other time I'll tell you."

The coal fire had almost died, throwing up the last weak flickers. In a tear in the curtain I could see the grey light outside.

"Will your aunt and cousins not notice that you are out so late?"

"I'll say that I was at a late-night party. I suppose though I should be making a move."

"I think it's close to morning. What I'll do is walk you to a taxi. There's no telephone to call from. And there's always a car in the rank at the bottom of Malahide Road."

"I don't feel guilty or anything. I feel great. What is it but what's natural," she repeated as she dressed. "How do you feel?"

"I feel fine," I said.

When she went out to the bathroom and I turned on the light the room seemed incredibly small and lonely and undamaged, like a country railway station in the first or last light.

"Are you ready?" I asked.

By way of answer she kissed me and we went out of the house in the early morning stillness. We walked in silence down the road empty except for a milkman and his boy delivering bottles from a float, the whine of the electric motor starting between the houses and the rattle of the bottles intensifying the silence.

"I suppose this is the usual. Now that it's over it's just good-bye," she said as we drew towards the end of the road.

"No. I was hoping we'd meet again."

"When?"

"What about next Wednesday?"

"What'll you be doing before then?"

"I have some writing to do. And there's this aunt of mine who's in hospital who I have to go to see."

"Where will we meet, then?"

"Do you know the Green Goose?" and when she nodded I said, "We'll meet up in the lounge at eight o'clock."

43

We kissed again as I held the door of the taxi open, the stale scents of the night mixed with fresh powder or perfume. I gave the taxi man the address and told him I wanted to pay him now. He looked cold and disgruntled in a great swaddling of an overcoat and counted out the pile of silver I gave him, only acknowledging it when he reached the tip. As the taxi turned in the empty road, the traffic lights on red, I saw her waving in the rear window in much the same exaggerated way as she had walked towards me at the head of the dancehall stairs.

After the sharp night air the room smelled of stale alcohol and perfume and sweat. I tried to open the window but it had been shut for too long and I was afraid the cord might break and wake people in the other rooms. I washed the glasses, bathed my face in the cold water, and when I drew back the crumpled pile of sweat-sodden clothes there were blood stains on the sheet. I shuddered involuntarily as the mind traced it back, and the grappling of the hours before stirred uneasily and did not seem to want to grow old.

I sipped at the coffee in the upstairs lounge of Kavanagh's the next evening, the two Marietta biscuits on the rim of the saucer, unable to free myself from the unease of the haphazard night, and I concentrated on the barman wrapping the bottle of brandy I had to take to my aunt in the hospital, thinking energy is everything, for without energy there can be no anything, no love and no quality of love.

For long I had limped by without energy, accepting what I'd been given, taking what I could get—deprived of any idea outside the immediate need of the day. Once the sensual beat had carried me on, careless of reason. Now I wanted to pause and turn and pause and stare and pause and idiotically smile. Colonel Grimshaw mounts his Mavis Carmichael and her ever-ready juices grease his ever-seeking bayonet, both rapturous as they hold the ever-rising tide of the seed on the edge of spurting free. They are in Majorca now. Blood dries on woollen sheets

44

in Dublin, salt and water unable to sponge it completely clear.

The barman searched for my eyes as he twisted the brown paper round the neck of the bottle and putting it on the counter called, "Now."

"It could pass for Lourdes water," I said as I counted out the money.

"Aye," he laughed agreeably as he rang up the price and said apologetically as he handed me the change, "only it's an awful lot dearer."

"There's nothing going down except ourselves."

I walked the hundred yards to the taxi rank at the bottom of the road. Two taxi men were playing cards on the stone drinking trough, their cars waiting by the curb. When I gave the name of the hospital, one of the men motioned towards the first car but I stood—"There's no rush"—to follow the short game to its close. When we pulled away into the green of the traffic lights I saw her face as she waved in the back of the turning cab of the night before, and wanted to turn away from it. Then I gripped the brandy bottle and sat back and listened to the ticking of the meter as the taxi took me like some privileged invalid through the fever of the city in its rush hour. When we turned in at the hospital gates, with its two white globes on the piers, the city gave way to trees and soft fields, and suddenly in the middle of the fields the concrete and glass block of the hospital rose like some rock to which we must crawl to die on when the blessed cover of these ordinary days is all stripped away.

I caught her sleeping lightly, some late sun on the pillows from the high windows facing home. Her hair had grown so thin that if I was to smooth her brow I felt the fingers would move back through the hair without disturbing the roots, and the last traces of gender seemed to have slipped completely away from the face. I touched the bedclothes above her feet and she was shocked to see me when she woke.

"I don't know how I dozed off. I was expecting you."

45

"It's good to see you."

Under cover of little trills and gestures, she made up her face, snapping a final glance at it in a small blue compact mirror before acknowledging the bottle of brandy.

"God bless you for bringing it. I never needed it more. Last night I wouldn't have got a wink of sleep without it."

"Do you want some now?"

"Are there any of those nurses looking?"

"No."

I cursed the barman's zeal as I unwrapped it, unscrewed the top, took a glass from the plastic-topped locker where both bottles from two days before were hidden away empty. I poured it slowly, waiting for her to call enough, but she let it rise to the brim.

"I don't trust those pills. They give you those pills to get rid of you. I know it costs a lot but I'll never forget it to you. It's the only thing that does any good for the pain now."

"Shush! Don't you want it now?"

"Is there anyone looking?"

"She's several beds away."

Turning towards the windows, she covered over the glass, covering the dark little act with a small bird's wing, and I winced as I heard her swallow, all that raw brandy burning its way down. Catching her guilt, I stirred uneasily at the foot of the bed, watching the nurse's long back bending over a patient, five beds away. The nearer beds were all encircled by their visitors. As soon as she finished I took the glass and filled it with water, but not quickly enough. She started to cough violently into the bedclothes. I put a hand to her back and held the water to her lips, saying silently, "Drink, for the love of God," as the nurse looked enquiringly in our direction. The coughing eased as she took some water. I nodded to the nurse that everything was all right and breathed easily when she turned back to her patient. I handed my aunt the blue packet of peppermints.

"In this place they have noses like whippets," she said.

"Maybe you shouldn't drink so much and so quickly."

"It's easier to get it done while you're here. It's all that does any good any more. I can feel it killing the old pain already," and reaching for control returned my scold with one of her own. "You should have known better than to bring in those two bottles with your uncle. You must know by now what he's like. He was never able to take anything up right. He'll have it rooted in his head now that I'm well on the way to being another Sticks McCabe, when you know I only take it for the old pain."

The three-thirty bus is climbing Seltan Hill on a hot July day. As it passes the monument of the stone soldier with his stone rifle at the top of Seltan, Sticks McCabe, drunk, rises from his seat and shouts, "Respect the memory of the dead. Everybody stand to attention," before falling backwards, bringing down a suitcase from the rack as he falls. Jimmy the conductor does not smile as he returns Sticks to his seat and crutches, making sure he has not hurt himself, and puts the suitcase disdainfully back in the rack. A boy on a motorcycle looks back to see why the bus has stopped on Seltan as he whizzes past towards Mohill.

"He'll not think that," I said and she hadn't even noticed that I'd been away in a more permanent day than this the day of the ward. "I told him you only took the brandy for the pain," God knows where she had been since, in what different permament, impermanent day.

"You'd never know what he'd think but as long as he doesn't go and tell poor Cyril. Cyril has enough to worry about. Where did he go after he left?"

"We went down the docks. He wanted some parts for the saws."

"Of course he went and hauled you down the docks, as if you hadn't a thing in the world else to do. All he thinks about is those old saws. There'll be plenty of saws when he's gone," and then the tone dropped. "Do you think will I ever get out of this place?"

47

"Of course you'll get out. You'll be out and around in no time. But you'll have to be patient. You'll have to wait till they have you better."

"I don't know. Sometimes I think they have you in here just to get rid of you," but her eyes searched mine eagerly, pleading for her words to be denied.

"That's just rubbishy talk. The brandy may be doing as much harm as good."

"Say nothing against the brandy," and I shifted uneasily as she began again to thank me profusely.

It was cut short by the nurse's arrival at the bedside. I made way for her and she asked, "Which of you has been boozing?" as she put light, tidying touches to the bedclothes.

"I'm afraid I have," I answered.

"Maybe you both have," there was far more a hint of challenge and even laughter behind the counter than any rebuke.

"It's not allowed in here."

"There are many things not allowed in here but they still go on."

She lingered, but when nothing more was said she asked professionally, "Are you all right?"

"If I was all right I wouldn't be in here," my aunt said belligerently.

The nurse left quietly and authoritatively, without the slightest response to the attempt at a joke.

"Who is she?" I asked.

"Nurse Brady," my aunt was more than willing to tell. "She's an awful ticket. Pure man-mad. Sings and dances in the ward."

"Why didn't you introduce us?"

"She'd like nothing better. The unfortunate that gets her will have his work cut out."

I spent the next minutes trying to talk myself out of having to come in for the next few days. I pleaded work, saying I'd fallen days behind in the work.

"But you'll come on the Tuesday," she said.

48

"I'll come on the Tuesday," I said as we kissed.

The tall, black-haired nurse was waiting at the end of the ward as I passed out.

"I hope I'll see you soon," I said as much out of simple attraction as to counter what I'd thought of as my aunt's rudeness.

"Why don't you come in to see us the next time," she laughed. "Auntie is well enough taken care of."

"Auntie is well enough taken care of. Why don't you come in to see us the next time?" echoed all the next morning as I tried to get to the typewriter.

I'd shaved, dressed, lit the fire, washed my hands several times, scraped fingernails, had cups of coffee . . . and each time I tried to move I'd hear, "Why don't you come in to see us the next time? Why-don't-you-come-in?"

I saw the ridiculous white cap pinned to the curly black hair growing thick and close to the skull, her strong legs planted apart, her laugh, its confident affirmation of itself against everything vulnerable and receding and dying.

To ring her. To go out with her into the evening, turning it into adventure, accepting whatever it brought; turning it into a great vital kick against all the usual evenings that seemed to fall like invisible dust. . . . But—there was still this work to do, this typewriter on the old marble of the washstand to get to.

If she came out with me and if the evening did not turn out well, and I was too old not to know its likely outcome, how would I be rid of her, having to risk running into her every time I went in with the brandy to the hospital. Caution and cowardice were getting me closer to the typewriter. It was the same caution that never allowed me to indulge in more than a passing nod or word with any of the other people who lived in this same house.

I sat and typed frivolously, like dabbing toes above steaming

49

water : *"There was a man and a woman. Their names were Mavis Carmichael and Colonel Grimshaw. They lived happily, if it could be said that they lived at all,"* and I x-ed it out and put a fresh page in the typewriter, and then started to work, the worm at last spinning its silken tent.

Several hours and blackened pages later I got up from the typewriter for the day when the barely audible turning of a key sounded from one of the upstairs rooms after a loud banging of the front door. I thought it could be only two or three o'clock and yet it must have been close to six if one of the office girls had got home. It had just gone six. Seldom is it given, but when it is it is the greatest consolation of the spinning, time passing—sizeable portions of time—without being noticed. Is it a promise of a happy eternity or just another irony, the realization of the unawareness. We feel that we have been freed of the burden of time passing, and the happiness is in the feeling and not in the blind forgetful play among the words.

I counted what I had written.

The Colonel and Mavis have had carnal knowledge of one another six times, fucked one another six times, not counting the time in the Colonel's flat before leaving for the airport. They show no signs of tiredness though Mavis sleeps late while the Colonel goes out to buy wine and fruit for the room, has a Campari and soda at a sidewalk café, and buys a spray of mimosa—my only extravagance—on the way back to the hotel room. As he sniffs it he promises to improve its scent with the even more delicious scent between Mavis's lovely waking thighs, "my honey".

I was tired and flushed, my flesh excited again by the play of Mavis and the Colonel in the mind's eye. How could it be otherwise? The words had to be mixed with my own blood. How could the dried blood of the words be turned back into blood unless they had once been bound by living blood? "Nonsense, rubbish, blackpudding, pig's blood," Maloney had countered not so long ago in the Palace. "That's poetry talk. And

50

you know what I think of that nowadays. Our average reader
—and the average is king and queen of circulation—is already
so inflamed that he or she would get a rise out of a green tree
in Gethsemane."

One more long day's work and he'll have his Majorcan story
and I'll be free for a whole week. I was tired enough to be
grateful that I hadn't to think what to do for the evening,
that it was already decided : I had to meet her at eight in the
upstairs lounge of the Green Goose. The memory of the
accidental night was already vague enough for me to be curious
again, and having driven Mavis and the Colonel from feat to
feat I had grown inflamed enough myself to want to lie down
with any warm body.

The Green Goose was grey and concrete and had a painted
green bird on an iron sign in the forecourt of the car park
that seemed to rattle its sense of not belonging in every sudden
gust. It had been built twenty years before to serve the lower-
middle-class roads and drives and avenues of brown-tiled semis
all around it, and had aged like them into an ugly mildness.
The upstairs lounge was heavily carpeted with blue peacock's
eyes, and green and red peacocks stared from the wallpaper.
A whole generation of young marrieds must have grown tired
of the flap of nappies on lines and summer lawnmowers under
those same unalterable eyes.

It was too early for the couples. There were just a few men
with evening papers who had not quite made it from their
offices to their front doors. I bought a drink at the counter
and took it to one of the corner tables.

She came at exactly five minutes after eight on the bar
clock, wearing an elegant tweed costume, its collar and cuffs
edged with dark fur. She walked quickly towards me, chin
raised, smiling so hard that her dimples seemed to rise and fall.
Her strong body was perfectly formed, the features clear and
handsome. She would have been beautiful, I thought, except
for this flurry of blue forget-me-nots she seemed to send quiver-
ing out with every step.

51

"O boy," she said as she sat down. "I was afraid you mightn't be here."

"Of course I'd be here."

"I thought coming up the stairs that you mightn't be here. I thought so much about you the last days you cannot know," her eyes shone with an overdose of sincerity.

"What will you have to drink?" I asked.

She was so filled with the momentous moment that I felt like going on my knees in gratitude for those small blessed ordinary handrails of speech.

"Would a gin and tonic be all right?"

"I'm sure I can get you that."

She started to arrange her handbag, to take off her gloves.

Though she wore a hard-working smile, when I got back with the drinks she was quiet compared with her attack of an entrance. She had crossed her fine legs and was smoking.

"I hope it's all right," I said as I put her drink down.

"It's fine. It's just wonderful to be here. I don't know what's happening but I've hardly been able to think of anything else but you since the last night."

"It's nice to see you," I raised my glass.

"It's wonderful to be here and to see you. It's one of those days everything had to be done two or three times over at the bank. I just couldn't wait for five to come and the day to be over and to get out and to come here."

"You got home all right the last night?"

"Sure," she laughed. "I took off my shoes and carried them in and nobody heard me come in. Even my door on the landing was ajar. My aunt noticed that I yawned all through breakfast, that was all. I felt tired but I didn't feel any guilt or anything and everybody seemed happier than usual. The milkman who always has a joke with me in the morning, though I'm mostly running, caught the tail of the long red scarf and shook it and asked me if I was in love. But the day was sure hard to get through. After lunch I could hardly keep

52

my eyes open, and the letters just kept coming and coming. I went straight home and fell into bed and must have slept sixteen hours straight. I had the most wonderful dreams. You were in the best of them. And when I woke I didn't feel a shred of guilt. I just felt relaxed and wonderful. Don't you want to hear about any of the dreams you were in?"

"No."

"Why not?"

"I'm not much interested in dreams. I'm more interested in the day."

"Many say that you can learn a great deal about the day from dreams and the night."

"I think the best way to learn about the day is from the day," I had grown restless.

"Why don't you relax? You make me feel as if I was sitting in the dog's chair."

"How do you mean?"

"You know when you come into a kitchen and there's a dog that's used to sitting in a chair you happen to take by accident. All the time you're sitting there you feel him agitatedly circling the chair."

It was so sharp I slowed. "I can see you write," I said. "I'm sorry if I was restless. I'm afraid I was just feeling the need of another drink. What'll you have?"

"I'll pass," she placed her hand over her glass. "I can't drink at that pace. You sure can shift that stuff."

"It loosens you up. But don't worry. It'll slow, as soon as the first injection starts to work."

The tension had gone when I came back from the bar. She was working, farther off. People are usually more charming when they are farther off. Perhaps she'd realized her own danger while I was getting the drink—that she had pushed too close. Such foresight makes the longest hells.

I too had a reversal of feeling while I was away. We hardly knew one another and we were already hating. This evening was a gift we'd never hold again. We were a man and woman

53

travelling through it together. We'd never pass this way again. We might as well make some joy of it.

"Tell me about Amalgamated Waterways, this paper you write for," and she grew excited as she told. The magazine was small but had fantastic growth potential. There was no country in Europe that had so much water and space per head of population as ours—in Germany, for instance, you had to wait for someone to die in order to get boat space—and it was just beginning to be recognized as the great natural resource it is, like oil or coal. There was this great scheme, which the Troubles had postponed, to connect the waterways of the Shannon and the Erne by reopening the disused canals of Cavan and Leitrim which had once been connected through the lakes. The North and South would join in friendship. "An embrace of water," she said.

"Or a watery embrace."

"Seriously, it'd open hundreds of miles of water, from Limerick to Letterkenny, and it'd only cost a fraction of what the bombings and killings do, and stop the bombings and the killings. It's our editor's great cause, poor Walter's. You'd like Walter. He gets paid too little and works far too hard and he worries, how he worries, and never more than whenever we try to give him a raise. It's arranged that when we get a little bigger I'll give up this boring bank job and go to work full time as his assistant, and he worries about that too. We could afford it almost now but he won't agree. And everybody agrees the paper needs more zip. But you, how did you start?"

"I was a teacher. And then I got into this advertising agency. My work was to put out trade magazines for five or six of our accounts, which meant you had to write or rewrite them from cover to cover. I once wrote a whole number of *Our Boys*. It was dog's work and I gave it up. Now I just freelance. I didn't need all that money anyhow."

"You get a great deal of money in those agencies?"

"A good deal. If they had paid less I'd probably be still stuck there."

"I get hardly any money but there are perks and trips. One of them is that I can have a houseboat on the Shannon for completely free anytime outside the high season. Maybe we could go some weekend together before too long?"

"That sounds like fun."

"It's more than that. The boats aren't like old boats. They have hi-fi, central heating, fridges, push-button starters. They're like hotels out on water, and all that lovely quiet water. . . ."

The couples had started to come in, the lounge to grow noisy and smoky. The barmen seemed to know each couple, and there were smiles and nods and a few words before each first order. With the red and green peacocks on the walls and the blue eyes of the carpet it must have made them feel as if they were getting away from it all when they came here.

"What'll we do?" I asked. "Will we get another drink or will we leave?"

"I'd rather leave. I can't stand all this noise and smugness."

I could see that she thought she was well above this suburban herd, a dangerous thought for anybody in case they happened to wind up in it.

"What would you like to do? Would you like to come back to my place?" I asked lamely because of my uncertainty. It passed for shyness or diffidence.

"Why not? I'd like that," she said brightly and took my arm as we went out.

We took off our clothes in total silence. As I covertly watched her in this dumb show it struck me how terrible and beautiful was the bending of the back, the lifted knee, at once consenting and awkwardly pleading, before prostration, to be wrecked in nature's own renewal. I reached and took a condom from an open drawer and drew it on as silently as I could under cover of slipping out of underclothes. We lay together in waiting silence, and when I moved against her she asked tensely, "What are you wearing?" She must have felt the rubber against the skin or noticed me draw it on as I undressed.

"A condom. Why?"

55

"I just couldn't with that."

"Why?"

"I don't know. It's unnatural. It turns the whole thing into a kind of farce."

"I was just wearing it for you," I lied.

"How wearing it for me?"

"You have more to lose. What if you got pregnant?"

"I don't know. It'd seem more natural. It'd seem far less of a farce. At least something would be going on."

You can bet your life something would be going on, I thought, but said, "If you don't want it that way there's no way you have to have it that way," and pulled away the rubber and threw it to one side. Both of us heard the light plop on to floor.

Just like the nights of old, bollock to bollock naked, but I said nothing as she snuggled close in gratitude, her full woman's body voluptuous.

"I couldn't do it that way. It'd make it all feel just like mutton."

I thought of those little light pale bags in which cooked olives and herrings were sold.

"It's all right. It's gone now. Seriously," I was the more withdrawn now, "what would you do if you did get pregnant?"

"I don't know. I suppose I'd go somewhere with my poor baby if the man didn't marry me. The whole family'd be shocked," she laughed. "Outraged."

"If I got you pregnant I wouldn't marry you."

"Why do this, then?"

"It's a need—like food or drink."

"You could come to love me."

"I don't think so. I like you. I desire you. . . ."

"Even if I didn't love someone to begin with, and I was doing this, I know I'd come to love after a time. I'd have to," she said as if willing it.

"Maybe we're talking too much," without even touching I could feel the wetness between her legs.

56

"We're talking far too much love," she breathed.

"We don't have to do it all the way. We can have this deliciousness of skin and. . . ."

"Now you are talking too much, love. I want to feel you completely inside me. And don't worry. I'm as regular as clockwork and it's only two days off."

If it's raw meat you want, raw meat you'll get, I thought as she said, "Easy," and as I went through like any fish feeling the triumph of breasting the hard slimy top of the weir I needed that sense of triumph to dull anxiety. Maybe it could not go easily and proudly through, I tried to lull myself, if it was weighted and made clumsy with the condom.

The moment is always the same and always new, the instinct so strong it cancels memory. To lie still in the moment, in the very heart of flesh, the place of beginning and end, to snatch it out of time, to move still in all stillness of flesh, to taste that trembling moment again, to hold it, to know it, *and* to let it go, the small bird that you held, its heart hammering in the cup of the hands, flown into the air.

"Now. O my God," I heard her call as it flew.

"You are beautiful," I said as we lay in sweat, our hearts hammering down.

"Wait," she said as I stirred.

Death must sometimes come the same way, the tension leaving the body, in pain and not in this sweetness and pride, but a last time, the circle completed, never having to come back to catch the flying moment that was always the same, always on the wing.

"O boy," she said. "That is what I seem to have been needing for ages without knowing it. I don't feel any guilt or anything. I feel just wonderful."

"How come you sometimes have a touch of an American accent?" I asked tenderly, now that she was stretched out, relaxing above me.

"There is, of course, the movies. I must have spent half my life at the pictures. My two best friends are Americans, Janey and Betty. They work at the embassy and they're at *Waterways* too. They're both crazy about Ireland. And they're the only ones I've told about us, about the fairly big differences in our ages. . . ."

"What do they think?"

"They're all for it. They say no one pays any attention to that kind of difference in the States. In fact, they drove me to the Green Goose this evening. I wanted them to come in for a minute but they said they'd meet you another time."

"Would you like a drink?" I asked as the old fear of being enmeshed returned. "You can have almost anything."

"I'd love a glass of white wine, if that's possible."

I poured it in the light of the open door of the fridge and got a very large whiskey for myself.

"What are you drinking?" she asked.

"Whiskey."

"It's just wonderful to have all this time and ease," she said.

"Your good health," I drank.

"Do many people live in this house? I didn't realize it was as big as it is till I came in tonight."

"There are ten flats. It's an old house. It was converted about five years ago."

"What kind of people live here?"

"Much the same as I, mostly single. Once they marry they don't seem to stay long. Civil servants, school teachers, there's a girl who works on the radio, a solicitor, an accountant, that kind of person. I'm afraid I don't know much more about them."

"Aren't you ever curious?"

"Of course I am but I make sure to restrain myself. We meet on the stairs. Sometimes they run out of salt or sugar, mostly the girls, or they cut their hands washing up. It's all very polite."

"I'm afraid I wouldn't be long here till I'd know everybody. Do you ever wish you could go into another flat and sit and talk?"

"No. Because I'd be afraid they'd come into mine. And bore hell out of me. There are times when you can't stand even the best company in the world. Why I avoid getting involved with anybody here is that I know myself too well. This place suits me. If I got involved with someone and they turned out boring or bothersome. I'd not get out in time—because I can't stand the tension that sets up—and I'd wind up having to do something violent like leaving the house altogether."

"You sound a very unsocial person," she laughed, "but I don't think you're unsocial at all."

You're the sort of person who needs a woman, I thought I saw behind the words; you're the sort of person who's ripe for plucking. And I'm the one for the job. "I don't know what sort of person I am," I said and took her in my arms.

There was no need of caution any more. If the seed was going to its source it had already gone.

The night was set for drinking. Whether we would drink more or not, the day was already useless and hungover. Pour the bottle out.

And so we took our bodies till the sweet mystery of the wine turned to the glass of vinegar we flinched from lifting in the fuddled light. And we towelled our dank bodies and walked to the taxi rank at the bottom of Malahide Road.

"When will we meet again?" she nuzzled close to me and shivered in the cold light.

"In three days' time, say."

"All that length of time?"

"There's this aunt I have to go in to see. And the next evening I have to bring stuff into the paper. That's the two evenings in between gone."

"Come with me in the taxi, then."

"What's the use?" I was reluctant.

"I want you to," she pressed her lips on mine.

The house she lived in was in a tree-lined road, detached and prosperous, surrounded by gardens. She seemed to want

59

me to see it, even in this impoverished light, and I got out of the taxi and walked her to the gate.

"I'll see you in three days," I said.

"In three days," she raised her lips a last time. There were no lights on in the house.

She left off from fumbling in her handbag to wave to the taxi as it came out of a turn on the empty road. I waved back and saw her lift a key cautiously towards the lock. I watched to see if she'd take off her shoes but the taxi had taken me out of sight before the door opened.

"I'll get out anywhere here," I said to the driver soon after we had left the road. I needed to walk.

I ended the Majorcan holiday with a simple ringing of the changes Maloney had asked for : the Colonel with Mavis; Mavis and the bullfighter Carlos; the Colonel and Carlos' sixteen-year-old girl friend Juanita—all four of them in delicious, unending revel—cunt and tongue and tit and rod and sperm. At the end of the story they all take a taxi together to the airport, addresses are exchanged, promises made. I had finished so early in the day that I decided to walk the five miles across the city to the hospital but it was still an hour too early when I got there. I bought an evening paper, read it over a hot whiskey in the pub closest to the hospital and got the bottle of brandy there too. It was night when I came out, starlit, with frost. I paused at how beautiful the chrysanthemums were—rust, yellow, pink—under the naked bulb hanging from the canvas of the flower stall in the cold-steel light. I knew she'd hardly like the flowers but on impulse bought her a bunch because of their amazing beauty in the frost. On many frozen evenings such as this she and I used to go to Lenten Devotions, down the hill and to the left up Church Street, and stand at the back of the cold, near-empty church.

"God bless you," she said as I put the brandy down. "I wouldn't take it off you but I know you have plenty of money, but I'll never forget it," and I saw her eyes fasten on the chrysanthemums in disapproval. "What did you want to go bringing in those old flowers for?"

"I was just passing them and I thought they looked nice."

"They're a waste. And I'm not likely to get married again," she began to laugh, but painfully, catching at the laughs. "And I'd hardly be here if I wasn't trying to put off the other thing."

"Ah, but look, all the people around you have flowers."

"They're from the city," she said. "A good head of lettuce or a string of onions would give me more ·joy than all the flowers in the world."

I thought of her own garden beside the little creosoted wooden gate off where the railway siding used to be, blooming with good things for the table. "You look far better, and I don't think it's just in my eyes."

She did look better. Though I knew it was of little use. All sorts of clover and sweet grasses glowed here and there on even the steepest slopes. They were not meant to be clutched at.

"Maybe because they've stopped that old deep X-ray. It used to make me feel horrible. I don't trust any of those drugs and gadgets. But what can you do? When you're here you have to put up with whatever they want to do to you."

"Do you ever hear from Cyril or Michael?" I asked.

"No, it'd never occur to them that there was such a thing as a pen or paper. They'd not write," and she started to chuckle. "But there was someone asking for you. She has me persecuted about you. It's that blackheaded nurse that jumps around."

"Well, tell her I was asking for her. She's a fine looking girl."

"I will not. There's nothing more sets your teeth on edge when you're down as someone going around showing the joys of spring."

"Would you like a little brandy now?"

"No thanks. I can do without it for a while. The pain's been not so bad. I'll keep it till I need it."

61

Through the window above the bed I could see the clear sky of frost, pierced with stars, and the reflection of all the lights of the city beyond the bare trees, and beside them this woman's fierce desire to live, and in the long ward, all the little groups about, the same desire in each bed, small shining jewels in an infinite unfathomable band. Everywhere there was a joy that was part of weeping.

Suddenly I felt my eyes blind. I had been taken completely by surprise. There was the need, too, to give thanks and praise; and no one to turn to. So that she wouldn't see my disturbance, I pretended to fix the brandy bottle more carefully out of sight in the locker.

"I suppose I might as well be going now. Before they put me out."

"What hurry's on you? Ah, but wait, tell me the truth now, do you think will I ever get out of this old place?"

"Of course you'll get out but you'll have to have patience."

"I don't know. Sometimes I think I never will."

"There's the bell for the visitors," I said.

"You can still stay on a few minutes."

"It's great to see you better," I couldn't bear to stay.

"You'll be in? I don't know what I'd do without you."

"I'll be in the day after tomorrow," and I saw her relax and then ease to let me go as soon as she had the promise. And now that she was willing to let me go I was ashamed of my haste to be away, and wanted to stay.

The next day I put aside for what I liked doing best. I did nothing, the nothing of walking crowded streets in the heart of the city, looking at faces, going into chance bars to rest, eating lunch and dinner alone in cheap, crowded restaurants.

And without any desire for meaning, in the same way as I had been surprised at her bedside, I sometimes felt meaning in this crowded solitude. That all had a purpose, that it had to have, the people coming and going, the ships tied up along the North Wall, the changing delicate lights and ripples of the river, the cranes and building, lights of shops, and the sky

62

through a blue haze of smoke and frost. And then it slipped away, and I found myself walking with a light and eager step to nowhere among others, in a meaningless haze of goodwill and general benediction and shuffle, everything fragmented again.

And then came the quiet or the tiredness that said that if that was the way it was it too had to be accepted, and when night fell it was possible to go home with the easy conscience of a sport's reporter writing, "No play was possible today at Lords because of rain."

I tried to write a new story. I thought if I got another story done before Maloney started to ask for it I would give myself several free days, but I wasn't able to write. It must have been that I had got used to deadlines. I went early to Kavanagh's to meet her and had drunk two pints by the time she came.

"It's good to see you," she bent to kiss me as she started to unbutton her jacket.

"What'll you have?"

"I'll have a gin and tonic—to celebrate," she said mysteriously.

"To celebrate what?" I asked when I brought the drinks back from the bar.

"You see, silly, there was no reason to be worried. I told you I was regular as could be. It must have been all that exercise."

"I'm glad. I'll drink to that."

I must have been worried for I felt a weight lift, as money suddenly come upon that had been feared lost. The evening brightened. Having realized the fear in being set free, I resolved never to put it at risk again. And I thought of how many times this celebration must have taken place, people made light-hearted as we by the same tidings. For this time we had no bills of pleasure to pay. We were not caged in any nightmare of the future.

"We've never met any place except in these old pubs," she said suddenly. "Why don't we start going to different places?"

"What sort of different places?"

63

"There's the cinema," and she named a picture that was playing on the quays that had received much praise. "Or we could go to the Park next Saturday, to the races."

At the mention of the Park, I remembered the days at the races I'd often gone to with her I had loved, and I drew back as if I knew instinctively what she was seeking : if we could meet people that either she or I knew it would give our relationship some social significance, drag it out of these dark pubs for christening.

"No. I don't feel like going to any of those places. But why don't you go?" and I saw it fall like a blow. She made no attempt to conceal it.

"O boy! That sure puts me in my place," and there were tears in her eyes.

"I don't want to put you in your place."

"But you did. Don't you understand that those places don't have an interest for me in themselves but are places that I want to go to with you?"

"There's no future for you in that—for either of us. You'll only get hurt. That's the way you fall in love."

"That's all the music I need to hear. Maybe I'm hurt all I can be hurt already. I don't know why you have to be so twisted and awkward. Especially with the news I had I thought we'd just have a nice pleasant evening."

"There's plenty of places we can go together."

"Where?" she put her hand on my knee, smiling through her tears.

"We could go down the country," I said awkwardly. "And stay in some nice hotel for a weekend."

"I have a far better idea," she was laughing now. "And it won't cost a thing. I was going to mention it when all the silly fighting started. We can take a boat, one of the new cruisers, out on the Shannon for a weekend. They've been pushing us for weeks to do an article. In fact, Walter was saying that someone will have to do the article in the next few weeks. Why don't we do it the weekend after next? That'll give time to fix everything. Those cruisers are as comfortable as a hotel and far more fun. Why don't we?"

"All right. That's agreed, then."

"It'll be great fun. And I can do the article. Poor Walter will even be happy for a day or two," and in a glow of enthusiasm she started to describe the part of the river that we'd take.

"I suppose we won't bother going back to my place," I said when the pub closed.

"Why?" she said in alarm, having obviously taken it for granted that we would.

"I thought you mightn't want to because of the time of the month."

"No. That doesn't matter. We can talk there. And I can hold you, can't I?"

We went by a side lane which cut the distance back by half, along a row that was once fishermen's cottages, and then in the sparse lights by ragged elder bushes and rows of dumped cars. I took her jacket when we got to the flat, stirred up the almost dead fire, and put some wood on, and asked if she wanted anything to drink. I was waiting to see what she wanted to do. She said she'd prefer not to drink, just to take a glass of water, but for me to go ahead; and then suddenly, lifting the page in the typewriter, asked if she could read what I'd written.

"Sure. I have to warn you that it's anything but edifying, but it pays. It's pornography. No. What's in the typewriter is only doodling. You can read this story. It's set in Majorca. It's finished but I haven't given it in yet," and I handed her the story and a large glass of water. I poured myself a whiskey and sat in front on the fire. She sat on the bed, under the arc of the lamp, her glass on the marble.

"This isn't half hot," she said after half a page, in the same tone as she'd said "Boy, you don't move half fast" when I first tried to touch her in the room.

"You don't have to read it if you don't want to."

"I want to."

"That stuff might be hot for Dublin but it's old hat in por-

65

nography by now. The new pornography has polar bears, bum frigging, pythons, decapitators, sword swallowers."

"It sure seems hot enough to me."

"Do you really want to finish it?" She nodded. "I'll shut up, so, until you finish."

Warmed by the whiskey, watching the fire catch, I felt time suspended as she read. If God there was, he must enjoy himself hugely, feeling all his creatures absorbed in his creation; but this was even better. It was as if another god had visited your creation and had got totally involved in it, had fallen for it. Some gods somewhere must be shaking huge sides with laughter.

"That's something," she said when she finished.

"What did you think of old Grimshaw and Mavis?"

"O I don't know. I'm shocked. I suppose what shocked me most of all was to think you wrote it."

"But you know the stuff is around. That it's sold in shops. That people buy it."

"Yes, but somehow one doesn't think it has anything to do with oneself. It's for others. So it's quite shocking to come as close to it as this," she tapped the pages.

"Would you like a drink?"

"All right. I'll have the same as you. I somehow knew I needed an education but I never thought I'd run through one quite as fast as this."

I got her the drink, poured myself another, and stayed silent. It must have been the drink, for I felt the flat shake with an uncontrollable silent laughter, that I was both taking part in some farce and at the same time watching it from miles far off.

"What's so funny?" she asked sharply.

"Nothing. You and I. Mavis and the Colonel. The whole setup seems somehow such a huge farce."

"How do you mean?"

"Nothing much. Sometimes it seems that we're all being had, by ourselves as much as by others—by the whole setup."

66

"Writing that stuff is bound to have an effect on a person," she'd come and put arms around me. I drew up her blouse and brassière to feel her breasts, warm and full, the nipples erect.

"Did the stuff excite you at all?"

"Of course. That's what's disturbing about it."

"How disturbing?"

"It makes a farce of the whole thing, doesn't it. It's nothing got to do with anything. It just makes a farce of people, plays on them, gets them worked up."

"Like this?"

"This is natural," she'd put hands inside my shirt, and was running light fingers along my ribs and back. We kissed as I drew up her nipples till she caught her breath. "I just want to feel you. You smell so sweet. I just want to feel your skin, to lie beside you, even if it's only for a little while."

In bed she said, "Don't you know I love you? Don't you know I'm crazy about you? Don't you know I think about you all the time? I never fell before but when I did I sure fell hard."

"You shouldn't be telling me that."

"It's the truth. I love you."

"The truth's generally disastrous."

"I have so much love for you that I believe you will come to share some of it, no matter how hard you try to fight it."

"It doesn't work that way."

"If I believed that I don't know how I could go on."

"You'd go on. Everybody does. Or mostly everybody."

As much as from desire to stop the words as from real physical desire, I drew her towards me. Afterwards it was she who said, "That's far better than talking. It just makes sense in itself."

"It's not verbal."

I broke the long silence that followed, "Are you sure you want to go on this boat trip? I enjoy sleeping with you, being with you, but I don't love you. If you love me as you say you

67

do you can only get more hurt by going on. Since it'll have to be broken, it might be better for everybody if we just broke it off now."

"I don't know what you wanted to say that for. Unless it's just wanting to be brutal," and I could feel her cry.

"No, I don't want that," I rocked her. "I wanted the opposite. But are you sure you want that?"

"Does a drowning person want a life raft?"

"I don't think the situation is as bad as that, but sure, we can go on that boat trip. There's nothing else to stop it."

She kissed me, and there was a sense of rest. I knew it well. Two whole weeks were secured and rescued from all that threatened. A small heaven had been won. Within its secure boundaries love somehow might be set on its true course.

"What are you doing tomorrow evening?" she tried to ask with a casualness that only served to highlight her anxiety.

"I have to go to the hospital. It's a bore but she depends on me now, especially for the brandy. After all, it was she and my uncle who brought me up after my parents vamoosed. So it's no less than fair."

"How vamoosed?"

"Dying, I suppose, is a sort of vamoosing, isn't it? It's not playing the game."

"But it's natural," she said slowly. "It's making room for others."

The chrysanthemums had gone from the bedside when I next went to the hospital. Knowing her, she probably gave the flowers to someone she felt she owed a present to, possibly someone she disliked, maybe to the black-haired nurse. I thought she was watching me to see if I missed the flowers. "Mrs Mulcahy down the ward was saying how nice the flowers were so I gave them to her. You know I can't stand flowers," she said.

"How do you feel?" I put the brandy down.

68

"God and the brandy is all that's any use now. It's all I get any value out of. The pain's still there. I don't trust this place. I thought the pain was going but it's back as bad as ever."

"But you look far better."

"I don't feel as bad as when I was in the X-ray, but I don't feel right. There's a chance I may be let home. They're doing some tests. They'll tell me tomorrow."

"But that's great news. That contradicts everything you've been saying."

"Maybe they won't let me home after all," she said warily. "Or maybe they're just letting me home because there's nothing they can do."

"They'd not do that," I said and changed. "I see our black-haired friend is on duty."

Her swarthy, lovely form was moving between two beds at the far end of the ward.

"That one. She has me still persecuted. I think she must have arranged to be on duty because I had to tell her you were coming in. Whoever has his luck there will find he has more than the full of his arms."

"I must tell her what you think about her," I teased.

"You will not," she put her hand to her mouth as she attempted to laugh it away. "You can do anything you want. You're all right. But she can take it out on me here. You see she's moved now so that you'll have to pass her on your way out."

Outside her natural attractiveness, the very fact that she was probably available made her more attractive still. We seem repelled as much by the hopeless as by what is too ferociously thrust upon us. Between these two, longing and fearing, we are drawn on.

"I'll go then, so," I used the levity as an excuse to leave early without her opposition, "so that I'll not miss her."

"You'd not be able," she laughed.

"The next time I hope you'll have the good news."

"Will you be in tomorrow, then?"

"The day after. You'll hardly be gone home by then?"

"I might never be gone home. Except feet first," she put her hand again to her mouth as if to take away the words.

As I passed the nurse, she faced me. She was not pretty but more than pretty, handsome and lovely, in her perfect health and young strength. "My aunt says she may be going home soon."

"She probably will. She'll know for certain tomorrow."

"Thanks for looking after her so well."

"For nothing at all," she laughed directly.

"I hope I see you soon."

She didn't answer. The clear laughing look in her eyes warned me to ignore what she showed me at my own peril.

It was in Kavanagh's upstairs lounge that we met to arrange the boat trip on the Shannon. She was so energetic with happiness when she came that I could believe she was lit by some inner light, except I knew by this time that all her power came from outside. Walter was thrilled by the idea of the article. The people that owned the boats were falling over backwards to help. Her two friends, the American girls, thought it a wonderful idea and were really dying to meet me.

"Pornography and all?" I asked in more dismay than sarcasm.

"I thought they'd be shocked but it didn't phase them one bit. They were tickled pink."

I groaned inwardly at the sea of talk that must have been set rippling by our small dark meetings, and resolved to end it as soon as the boat trip ended. Out of guilt at my own withdrawal, my useless passivity, I made my own poor gesture toward the doomed charade.

"I'll be able to get a car," I said. "I'll drive you down to the boat."

"You'll drive *us* down."

"That's what I meant."

"Betty and Janey said they'd be glad to lend us their car for the weekend."

"No, I can borrow a car or van from the paper. I used to have a car of my own but I didn't have enough use for it."

"I'd have a car," she said, "if I could afford it. I think a car is a wonderful extension of your life. It's almost as good as a third arm."

"Will you have a last drink?" I asked towards closing time. "We'll not go back to my place tonight."

It was like pulling the trigger of a gun that had been following the movement of a bird settling in high branches, pulled as much out of the tiredness of following it among the branches as any desire of killing.

"Why?" she demanded.

It'd serve as a rehearsal for finishing it, I thought, a sounding out, though plain sense said that the only way to finish it was by finishing it now, and I flinched from that.

"There's a lot of trouble," I explained. "My aunt has taken a turn for the worse. My uncle is coming up. I'll have to shepherd him around. And I have all this work to do."

Maloney was fond of saying that every good lie must be flavoured with a little truth, as whiskey with water.

"He won't be up tonight, will he?"

"No, but there's things I have to do before he comes."

"When will we meet, then?" she didn't question it further.

"Say, Saturday night."

"All that length of time. It's almost time for the boat trip then."

"We'll have all that weekend on the boat and I just want to be free this whole week. Since you complain of these pubs, we'll do anything you want to do on Saturday," I said by way of appeasement.

She thought for a while and then said without hesitation, "I know what I'd like to do," she was suddenly aglow. "I'll come to your place and cook you a meal."

71

"My place is a mess as far as cooking goes. I'll take you out for a meal. Any place you want."

"No. I have this feeling you're not looking after yourself properly. I want to cook you a good meal. I'll get the food but I'll leave the wine to you."

I tried to protest but I saw that she had her mind made up. "What kind of wine will I get? Red or white?" I backed down.

"Red. Get red wine," it seemed she had the meal already half planned.

My aunt was sitting up in bed, combed and made-up when I brought her in the bottle of brandy the next evening. She looked excited and happy.

"I'm going home," she said, though it wasn't necessary to say it. "You'll not have to waste your money bringing in the old brandy any more but God bless you for it. I don't know what I'd have done without it."

"How are you going?"

"I rang last night. Your uncle is coming up for me tomorrow. He's taking the big car. He wants you to ring him tonight."

"Why isn't Cyril coming?" I asked her sharply.

"Poor Cyril is far too busy," she answered with equal sharpness, intolerant of the question.

My uncle was far the busier, but all the foolish sweetness of her late love was for Cyril and pardoned everything he did before turning it to praise. My uncle's hard-working, decent life counted for nothing by its side, his refusal to be anything but his own man just another woeful example of bad manners and general inconsiderateness. Facts were just left carelessly around by other people in order to trip you up. "He's certainly as busy as Cyril," I said carefully, but she flushed with anger.

"You never liked Cyril. Of course you'd take your uncle's side, what else could I expect?"

"Liking has nothing to do with it, just plain facts."

"It's no wonder poor Cyril always complained the both of you ganged up on him."

"I'm very fond of my uncle but that has nothing got to do with it."

"Oh has it not? If you were to strip off those city manners you'd find that both of you are the exact same breed. What passes for quiet is stubbornness and you're both thick as ditches."

"It's useful," I started to say, but then was appalled to find myself in the middle of a quarrel. These were the first unkind words we'd had all the time she'd been in the hospital, and she was going home tomorow. "I'll see you tomorrow and I'll ring him this evening," I changed, but she didn't answer. After a few steps I wanted to turn back to say that I was sorry, but by then I saw that she was crying.

"O, aye," my uncle said when I told him my aunt had asked me to telephone. "You know I'm going up tomorrow?"

"I know that."

"Well, I was wonderin' if you'd meet me somewhere out of the city. I don't like driving the big car in the city."

"I'll meet you at Maynooth, then. Would eleven be all right?"

"Eleven would be fine. Say, at the gates of the priests' factory," it was one of his few jokes. "Is everything all right?"

"Everything's fine. How are you keeping yourself?"

"Couldn't be better," he said. "And there'd be no use complaining anyhow if it wasn't."

I took the bus out to Maynooth the next morning, and was waiting for him at the seminary gates when the "big car" pulled up ten or fifteen minutes after eleven, a black V8, old and heavy enough to have come out of any of several gangster movies. Among other things, he kept it on the principle that, since driving was so careless in Ireland, someone was bound

73

to hit him sooner later and when that happened "The other fella wa'sn't going to come out looking for a light." Since he took it out so seldom, the fact that it swallowed petrol was a small price to pay for such insulated misanthropy. He left the engine running and moved over to let me take the wheel.

"It's a great ease for me that you're taking her in," he shuffled in his pocket and took out a box of small cigars. "There was a time I used to take trucks three times a week through to the docks but not any more with this traffic."

"She running beautifully," I said, and it was a pleasure to feel her roll, solid and stately.

"There's no plastic in this old bus. They made them to last in those days."

As we drew in towards the city, I saw people nudge and smile at us. I smiled back and was glad my uncle didn't notice. It would not have pleased him that the big car had now reached the status of an antique.

"Well, how is the patient?" he had to ask at long last.

"I'm afraid I ran into trouble with her last night."

"What sort of trouble?" he asked apprehensively.

"It was nothing. I got a bit annoyed when she said poor Cyril was too busy to come up for her and told you were far busier. It was just a puff. It'll be all over but you're as well to know about it."

"The only time poor Cyril gets busy these days is on the high stool," he chuckled. "But you couldn't tell that woman that. And you should hear the pity he has for himself, you'd think it was him that should be in the hospital, especially if there's a woman near to listen, and you know there's no use talking to a woman once her mind's made up. Trying to talk to a woman with her mind made up is like trying to turn back a pig in a wide meadow : they'll always go past you."

"I was sorry I got into it. It was no time for crossing her," I said.

"Is she not coming home cured, then?"

"I don't know. I doubt it."

74

"Why are they sending her out, so?"

"Maybe there's nothing more they can do for her," and I was glad not to have to watch his face.

"Will you go in for her?" he asked when I parked at the hospital. "I'd sooner sit out here in the car. And there's nothing much I can do in there anyhow." And when I looked towards him he had already looked away.

"I thought yous were never coming," she was all waiting, her cases by the armchair at the entrance to the ward.

"We're hardly late at all."

"Once you know you're going you can't wait to get away. Where's your uncle?"

"He's waiting out at the car."

"That's just like him. Let you haul out all the cases," she started to complain.

He was standing outside the V8, the boot up, the back door open.

"Will you look at him, standing there, like a railway porter," I saw now that she was just complaining out of happiness and relief to be entering again into the familiar. He hid his nervousness by busily stacking the cases in the boot, and then settling her among the rugs and pillows in the back, she making noises of protestation. "Well, it's great to see you better and going home," he let rumble out as the car rolled away from the hospital.

"Maybe I'm not well at all."

"Ah well, Mary, you never missed! You were always a great one for having both ends. Sure, you're even looking well," and though she grumbled on I saw that the tiny scold had reassured her.

At Maynooth I left them. "There'll be a bus back in any minute. I don't want you to wait."

"You'll be down soon?" my uncle said as we shook hands.

"Promise," she said as I kissed her. "And thanks for everything and God bless you."

"I promise. If you don't go now you'll soon find yourself

75

driving into the sun." I shut the door but she continued waving from the back window as the big car nosed out into the traffic.

I took the story in Friday evening to the Elbow Inn. Every Friday evening the people from the paper met there just after work. I took the story in instead of posting it because I wanted to borrow a car or van for the river trip.

Maloney had his back to the counter when I came in, pulling on a cigar. Around him there were three or four different conversations going but they all formed a single and distinct whole from the rest of the bar, and people were continually circulating between the points of conversation. There was a tradition of wit on those Fridays which resulted in a killing and artificial tedium. Though they put out pornographic papers it would be difficult to tell them from any bank or insurance party except that their dress was perhaps that bit more attractively careless. Some of the girls said "Hello, stranger" to me between the smiles and handshakes but it had as much significance as "yours sincerely". Maloney bought me a drink and I gave him the story.

"I don't suppose you'll like it," I said carelessly.

"If he doesn't like it he doesn't have to publish it," one of the girls who was with him laughed.

"Even if we didn't like it there's a special place for odd-ball stuff our regulars come in with from time to time," Maloney countered quickly, and started to slip through it. As he did I asked the girl where she intended to go on her summer holiday. Maloney interrupted tepid talk about the Aran Islands to say in his mock pompous voice, "It breaks no new ground but it's up to your usual high, traditional standard and of course there's the usual spunk, old boy. Where do you intend to exercise the Colonel and our good Mavis next?"

"I thought of a trip in a cruiser up the Shannon."

76

"Excellent idea. Spend your holiday discovering Ireland. Support home industry. I'm all for that, old boy."

"In fact, I've got an invite on one of those trips and I want to borrow a car for next weekend. It's all the paper will have to contribute to the field work."

"Very in-ter-est-ing. Do you have a Mavis to take along to your Colonel?"

"Sure," I tried to cut the joking short. "She's seventy-nine and after every time we do it we have to search between the sheets for her false teeth. What about the car?"

"Hi, John," he called across to a young bald-headed man in a blue duffle coat, "What cars are free next Friday?"

"There's a few, I'd take the black Beetle if I was him."

"The Black Beetle, then," I said and Maloney nodded gravely.

"What can I get you to drink before I go?" I offered, but it was refused, and I made the final arrangements for picking up the Volkswagen late afternoon of the next Friday.

There was a time I'd have hung on in the pub, afraid of missing something if I left, afraid of being mocked as soon as I left. But now I knew it didn't matter, and anyhow it could not be controlled. There was always a time when you'd have to leave.

I spent the Saturday she was to come to cook dinner cleaning the kitchen. Then I got the fire to light and went out and bought the red wine.

She came with a large cane basket. The way she returned my kiss left no doubt as to how she planned for the evening to end. There was fresh rain on her face, and as we kissed I had no chance of curbing my own desire. Suddenly I wanted nothing but to sleep with her.

"I'll show you the kitchen. Then I'll set the table and draw the wine and leave you to the cooking. I'd only get in your way. All that can be said about the kitchen is that it's elemental."

"It has all that I need. And it's even clean," she said.

"I tried to clean it but I'm afraid it's not all that clean."

"It's just lovely," she raised herself on her toes to be kissed again.

She unpacked the parcels from the basket: two steaks, a head of lettuce, mushrooms, three different kinds of cheeses, four apples.

"You see, I kept it simple."

"It looks delicious. There's fruit here as well. What'll you have?"

"I'll have a sherry."

After I poured a glass of sherry, I said, "I'll leave the bottle out. Is there anything else before I leave?"

"Yes. A kiss. And a radio. I like to play the radio while I cook."

I took the transistor in from the other room, and the kiss was so prolonged that I put my hands beneath her clothes, moving them freely. It was she who broke loose. "I suppose I better make a start," her face flushed. I wanted to say, "Why don't we before you start?" but left the room.

I set the table, poured out a large whiskey, threw some more wood on the fire and stood leaning against the mantel sipping the whiskey while noises of utensils and smells of cooking came through the radio music from the kitchen. The evening was on its way like a life. There was no use kicking against it now. It had to be plundered like a meal.

"Everything's ready," she called from the kitchen. The smell of the grilled steaks was delicious. "We'll just have the steaks with the mushrooms and we can have the salad at the same time," she handed me the salad bowl. "There's just one thing missing," she cried out. "No candles!"

"There are candles somewhere," I said and found an old packet among the liquor bottles. When she lit the candles and fixed them in their own wax in ashtrays round the room, she switched off the light. There was hardly need of candles because of the leaping fire which flashed on glass and metal and made the plates glow white.

When I praised the meat she said, "I got it from Janey and Betty's butcher. They told me he's expensive but that you can always be certain of him. When I mentioned their names he put down the piece he was going to give me and went back and searched among the hanging pieces in the cold room."

"So they too knew about the meal," I said and she felt it as a rebuke for she didn't answer. This was how quarrels usually began, and I stopped. When it had mattered to me I was never able to stop.

"Did you ever eat by candlelight before?" she asked. "It's such a lovely light."

"No," I lied instantly. "The candles are here since the last blackout."

"They certainly look it," everything was running easily again. The candles hadn't been used since She and I were here before going into the country, the last night we spent here together. The pain of that night still wavered in their flames, but wearily. It was over.

I helped her clear away the plates and we started to kiss after the cheese was brought out.

This time I said, "Why don't we give the meal a rest? Come back to it. . . ."

"Why not?"

Between the sheets she said, "I feel marvellous. I don't know what I was doing all those years, making the nine Fridays, going to the Sodality, out on the streets with the Legion of Mary, always in for nine when my uncle was saying the Rosary. I must have been crazy. Everybody must have been crazy. I was wasting my life and now I am doing what is natural. I don't feel dirty or sinful or anything. I just feel that I have a great deal of lost living to make up for."

"Sex is only a small part of living," I said warily.

79

"Yes, but what is it without it? I'm crazy about you," she raised herself so that her body shone above me before she bent to kiss. "I thought of nothing else all week. I wanted the week to run to Saturday night. I'd find my fingers reaching out, and I'd wonder what they were reaching for, and then I'd realize they were reaching for your skin."

I drew her towards me, "This time we can take all the time in the world," and when it was over, all the grossness of the food and wine seemed drained away and a peace that was almost purity seemed to settle on what a few moments before had been muscular and wild.

I put more wood on the fire when we rose and drew the cork of another bottle of wine. She lit the candles that had been blown out. They wavered on the half-filled wine glasses, on the Brie and Stilton and Cheddar and water biscuits on the wooden platter.

"This girl," she said with a pause that I knew to be the pain of jealousy, "this girl, the girl you were in love with, who was she?"

I looked at her, how vulnerable and open the face was. She was going to hurt herself by searching about in a life that no longer existed, that she had been unaware of when it *was* going on. Crazy as it was, she was determined to cause herself that pain.

"We met much like we met—like most of Ireland meets—at a dance. We went casually out for a year. At first she did most of the running, and when she tired I took up the pursuit. It's a usual enough pattern. The more I pushed myself on her the more tiresome I became to her, and that speeded up her withdrawal, which made her ten times as attractive. I felt I couldn't live without her. Which made me ten times as tiresome. I was ill, lovesick, mad. If she'd finished it then it might have been easier, but who knows. She kept the thing going, interested in my madness, which was after all about her, and we can all do with an awful lot of ourselves. I think it nearly turned into a farce in the end."

80

"I don't know how you can call it a farce. It sounds horrible. What's worst about it is that I wish I had her chance."

"Marriage to a madman is hardly a recipe for domestic bliss. Because of her interest in this madness about herself I think she nearly fell in love with me. If she'd done that then it'd have been the farce."

"Isn't that what you'd want? Isn't that what everybody wants, two people in love at the same time."

"It doesn't work that way. If she had fallen in love with me I think it would have soon cured me of my madness. No world can afford to have all its inmates mad at the same time."

"You seem to have it all figured out. If I didn't believe there wasn't some happiness I don't know how I'd be able to go on."

"You would," I said. "Anyhow it all got too much. She drew the line."

"I don't see what's funny about something as horrible as that. All the sex writing must twist and blind you to everything about love, make it just pure cynical."

"On the contrary. It clears it out of the way. You learn it has nothing to do with love or living. It's like sport. Except it's between the sheets instead of in the gym."

"Was she younger than you?" she was still biting into herself.

"She was, a few years. Why don't we go to bed?"

The pain made her look tired and older. "Let's clear up," she said. "I hate waking up to a dirty kitchen."

After we tidied up I fell into a drugged sleep and woke with the splitting headache of a hangover. Later in the morning she asked, "Since it's Sunday why don't we spend the day together?"

"I'd love to but I have to work," and I walked her part of the way to where she lived. It was one of those spring mornings, the sun thawing the white frost out of the front gardens, and people with prayerbooks were going and coming between the Masses.

81

"Look. We'll have the whole of next weekend together," I said as we parted. "What'll you do for the day?"

"I think I'll go to Mass like the other people," she said.

We drove in the stream of traffic out of the city the next weekend. It didn't build any speed till it got past Lucan, and even there we found ourselves continually shut in behind slow trucks and milk tankers.

"Ireland will soon be as jammed up as everywhere else. That's what's wonderful about the rivers and lakes. They're empty. Isn't it exciting to be spending the whole weekend away from people?"

"People are all right," I said morosely.

"There're towns and villages that we can put in at. That's what's wonderful about the Shannon. You have a choice. You can be with people or get away and there're pubs up lanes or a few fields from the river. There's one in particular that we must visit in a village past Carrick, the man is fat and lovely and he's always in good humour."

After Kinnegad the road emptied and we drove steadily and fast. Outside Longford a great walled estate with old woods stretched away to the left and children from a tinker encampment threw a stone that grazed the windscreen. In the distance, between rows of poplars, the steel strip of the Shannon started to flash.

"There it is—the Shannon River," she greeted excitedly. "They said they'd meet us in the first bar on the right. That's it. Over there. The Shannon Pot."

We had hardly time to look around the big lounge, a large pike preserved in a lighted glass case above the bar, the only sign of a connection with water, when a man in a well-cut worsted suit came up to us and enquired, "Would you be the people from the magazine?" When we told him we were he shook hands in the old courtly way, standing far back and bowing. "Mr Smith, the man who owns the boats, asked me

82

to apologize for him. He meant to be here himself but was called to England the day before yesterday on sudden business, but he said all the information was here in these brochures, and if there was anything else you needed to know for the article to just leave word and he'd phone it in as soon as ever he got back. I'm supposed to see," he smiled, "that you lack for nothing on the voyage. I'm known everywhere as Michael. And how was your journey down—good?"

"It was easy. We drove down," I said.

He then introduced us to the barman, a young man in shirtsleeves.

"What about something warm after the journey? The evening is fine but it's chill enough," and we all had hot whiskeys. We had hardly touched them when another round appeared without a word, and then another. We started to protest but Michael waved our protest aside as if it was an appreciated but thoroughly unnecessary form of politeness. "We better see the boat first," I had to say firmly, "then we can come back here."

"The boat's just across the road. There's nothing to it," he said and led us out.

The boat was across the road, a large white boat with several berths. It had a fridge, a gas stove, central heating and a hi-fi system. The Shannon, dark and swollen, raced past its sides. Night was starting to fall.

"There's nothing to these boats," he said and switched on the engine. It purred like a good car, the Fibreglass not vibrating at all once it was running. "And there's the gears— neutral, forward, neutral, reverse. There's the anchor. And that's the story. They're as simple as a child's toy. And still you'd grow horses' ears with some of the things people manage to do to them. They crash them into bridges, get stuck in mudbanks, hit navigation signs, foul the propeller up with nylons, fall overboard. I'll tell you something for nothing : anything that can be done your human being will do it. One thing you have to give to the Germans though is

83

that they leave the boats shining. They spend the whole of the last day scrubbing up. But do you think your Irishman would scrub up? Not to save his life. Your Irishman is a pig," he said. Only for the speech I'd not have noticed that he was by no means sober. "I've used this type of boat before, Michael," she interrupted the flow. "They're a lovely job. But—this shouldn't have been done. The fridge is full, there's wine, a bottle of whiskey. . . ."

"Mr Smith wanted everything to be right for yous. Mr Smith is a gentleman."

Outside the misted windows the Shannon raced. When I wiped the port window clear the gleam of the water was barely discernible in the last lights.

"What'll we do?" I asked. "Will we make a start or stay?"

"I'd hoped to make Carrick tonight," she said.

"I think it's too late. I think we should stay here tonight and leave at daybreak."

"It's the best thing ye can do," Michael chorused.

I unscrewed the cap from the whiskey bottle in the fridge and poured three whiskeys.

"We'll just have one drink here with Michael and then we'll go and get the things out of the car. What kind of man is Mr Smith?" I asked by way of conversation.

"A gentleman. The English are a great people to spend money. They're pure innocent. But your Irishman's a huar. The huar'd fleece you and boast about it to your face. Your Irishman is still in an emerging form of life." The whiskey was large enough to have lasted a half-hour but he finished it in two gulps. When I poured him another drink he finished it too. Then, in case he'd settle in the boat for the rest of the evening, I suggested we should go back and have a last drink in the pub.

"I'll stay," she said as we went to leave. "I'll check out the things on the boat, see what we need for the night, and I'll join you later."

84

"There's no beating an intelligent woman," Michael said as we climbed out of the boat.

"Do you live far from here?" I asked him over the whiskey and chaser I bought him in the bar.

"I've a few acres with some steers a mile or two out the road. There's an auld galvanized thing on the place, and it does for the summer, the hay and that, but in the winter I live on one or other of the boats. It's in the winter we do up the boats for the summer."

"Who looks after the cattle?"

"A neighbour. I let him graze a few of his own on it and that keeps him happy. Before the boats started up I used to work here and there at carpentry. The wife was easy-going. She always gave me my head," he joked since it was plain he had no wife at all.

It was with great difficulty he was prevented from buying her a large brandy when she joined us though she only wanted a soft drink. Afterwards he told us stories, all of them fluent. We only got away early by saying that in order to do the article we had to be on the move at first light. He caught both our hands at the wrist, murmuring, "Good people, good people. The best," and making us promise several times to see him as soon as we got back. He got unsteadily to his feet to wave, "God bless," as we went out. We got our things out of the car and went across to the boat.

"Well, that was a bit of local colour to start off with."

"He was nice enough," she said, "but he's spoiled with the tourists."

I was uneasy when she came into my arms in the boat. There was the pure pleasure of her body in the warmth, the sense of the race of water outside, the gentle resting movements of the boat, but I did not want to enter her.

"Why?" she protested.

"It's just too dangerous."

"According to the calendar I am back into the safe days."

"It's too risky."

85

I felt her stiffen and recoil as I came outside and when I tried to touch her she angrily drew away, "You may be skilful but it's not skilfulness I need. I would put a little warmth and naturalness and trust ahead of a thousand manuals but obviously that doesn't rate very high in your book," and she crossed to the other bunk. I could feel her anger in the close darkness but fought back the desire to appease it. I listened to the simple, swift flow of the water. All over the countryside dogs were barking, the barking starting up at different points, going silent, and then taken up again from a different point, like so many footnotes growing out of a simple text. Suddenly there was a loud banging of car doors, revving engines, horns, indistinct shouts in the night. The bars were closing. I must have been close to sleep for I did not notice her till she was kneeling by the bunk, her lips on mine.

"I'm sorry, love," she said. "Let's not do anything to spoil the trip."

I took her in my arms. "I should be the sorry one. I want to but I'm afraid. In fact, there's nothing I want more."

"Goodnight, love. I've set the alarm for five."

"Goodnight," I said. "I hope you sleep well. You have a hard day tomorrow getting the article together."

We got the boat away before it was quite light and the early morning mist didn't look like rising. In the white mist and cold of morning, the boat beating steadily up the centre of the still water, the dead wheaten reeds on either side, occasional cattle and horses and the ghostly shapes of tree trunks and half-branches along the banks, there was a feeling of a dream, souls crossing to some other world. But the grey stone of the bridge of Carrick came solidly towards us out of the mist around eight. We tied the boat up, had a breakfast of fried eggs and bacon and scalding tea in a café by the bridge that had just opened. Afterwards we separated. She went about her business of collecting material for the article. I walked for an hour about the town, bought news-papers, and went back to read them on the boat. Nobody came by until she got back.

"I'm sorry," she said as she climbed down into the boat.

"I was just reading the papers. Did you get everything you wanted?"

"Everything," she flipped through notes and showed them like a trophy. "The people were wonderful. In fact, if any-thing, they were just too co-operative," she jumped about like a girl. "We're still ahead of time. In not much more than an hour we'll be in that village I told you about."

The wind had risen, blowing the mist away. The fields along the banks were all flooded, the river defined only by its two narrow lines of dead reeds. After about two miles we came out into a large lake, the waves rocking the boat; but when I turned the power up the boat, big enough to be com-fortable on the sea, smashed through the waves. It was excit-ing to feel its chopping power. All this time she worked on her notes in the cabin. On the far side of the lake we joined the river again, passing between a black navigation sign and a red, the banks flooded for miles, the distance between the lines of reeds growing narrow. Soon, across the flooded fields the village came into view, goal posts upright in a football field, smoke rising from a few houses or shops scattered at random round a big bald ugly barn of a church.

"It's certainly not much to look at," I said when she came out of the cabin.

"But the fat man is lovely. That's his bar next to the church, with the smoke rising from the chimneys."

We tied up the boat at the small stone pier with four metal bollards that made an arm with the stone bridge, flooded fields and woods, another lake shining in the three eyes of its arches in the next distance. We walked to the bar, the village scattered round a single field, no two shops or houses together, all standing away from one another at angles and distances of irreconcilable disagreements.

"Probably half of them aren't talking," she laughed. "The fat man says he'd go mad with the boredom except for the boats."

Because of the talk of his fatness I did not find the man all that fat: he had limp thinning hair, a pleasant red face, and he wore a striped butcher's apron, the formality of any apron unusual in these villages. Two hatted men nodded drunkenly at the corner of the counter. The man knew her at once, seemed delighted to see her, saying only that she was early this year. He made up delicious ham sandwiches, offered us a choice of coffee or white wine, and refused money for either the coffee or sandwiches. While we ate he sat with us on a heavy ecclesiastical bench that must have come out of some old church. She had several questions to ask him about the river and the trade from the boats, and she wrote down most of his answers. When they'd finished she read back to him what he'd said. While they worked I tried to follow the whispers of the hatted pair at the counter who continually cast spying glances our way but all that came clear from the words and half-phrases was one hoarse whisper, "That's the answer. Get up early. And you'll win them all. You'll bate the whole effin' lot of them if you get up early."

All day I'd been seeing a far more attractive person than the woman I had known up till then. For the first time I was seeing her work, and she shone in the distance its discipline made.

We had shared nothing but pleasure, and no two people's pleasure can be the same at the same time for long, the screw turned tighter till it had to be forced on the wrong threads. If we'd shared some work instead of pleasure would it have made any difference? It didn't matter, it was ending now, and ending on an older note, one withdrawing before becoming enmeshed in the other, intolerant of all chains but those forged in its own pain.

"What are you thinking?" she asked as we went back down to the boat.

"I was thinking how well you work. That you make notes, write everything down. It's not that usual. You'd be surprised how many try to get by on that old amateurish *flair*."

"I'm grateful for that," she said gravely.

We hugged the black navigation signs after going through the bridge, a series of barrels between pans set on stone piers. We went faster when we came out into the lake, two small islands to the left, one wooded, the other of pale rocks ringed with reeds, and on the shore a great beech avenue waited for spring as it ran to ruined coach houses. The river was so narrow where it entered the lake that we'd to slow the boat down again to a crawl. The woods were to the left and we could see far into them where a red sun was slipping down between the trunks. The flooded fields were so close beyond the right bank of reeds that we had to move very slowly.

The man was waiting for us at the lock house. It was so long since a boat had gone through that I'd to help turn the wheels that operated the gates while she took the boat up through the lock. For a while it seemed the handle wouldn't turn but then it gave with a grinding of cog-wheels. When the boat had gone through the lock she joined the lock-keeper to ask him some things for her article, and I went back to the boat. With the water pouring like glass over the wall, then foaming out into the black water where it went still, a broken-down boat-house away in the shallows, the man and woman intent in conversation on the solid arm of the lock gate, and the trees and water held in frost as the light started to fail, the evening seemed so beautiful that it was hard to believe it was real. There had been so many interpretations of beauty as such an evening and scene that it had grown abstract and unreal.

When she joined me again in the boat she closed the note-book triumphantly. "That's it. All I have to do now is write it. I've at least twice as much as I need."

In ten minutes we were letting the anchor down in a half-moon of a bay, sheltered by old woods. "We must come

89

together sometime in the summer," she said. "In the summer the whole bay is choked with water-lilies."

She took lamb chops out of the fridge and I uncorked two bottles of red wine. "I feel we've earned this meal," she said as we kissed. Before she put the chops under the grill she gave herself a quick sponge bath at the other end of the boat and changed into a lovely, clinging brown wool dress. Except for the grey hair and heavy breasts, the naked back was so trim and taut that it might have been the back of a young girl.

"Do you not want to know who I was here with the last time?" she asked.

"Who?" I asked, thinking as I watched her move in perfect ease in half nakedness close to me how far we'd come in bodily intimacy in the few short weeks since the first dancehall night.

"Certainly no man. Those two American girls, Betty and Janey. But it's far better with a man, especially with you," she laughed.

I was ravenous even before the meat started grilling, and as soon as I'd eaten, with the early morning on the river, all the raw air of the day, and the red wine, I began to yawn.

"Sleepy?"

"I'm almost dead out."

"We'll leave the washing-up till tomorrow."

It seemed inevitable, it could not be put off now or avoided, and the feeling grew that it didn't matter. Nothing mattered but the tiredness and the desire.

"Are you sure it's all right?" I made a last fainthearted protest as she came naked into my arms, my body taut with desire.

The next day both of us were grateful for the boat. Getting it back down the river kept us separate and busy.

"What'll we do about Michael?" she asked in Carrick. "We hardly need another session."

"We'll have one drink with him and tell him we must get away."

When next we met she had given in the written article.

"Walter's delighted with it. It's going into the next issue." I read it in the upstairs lounge of the Green Goose, while she sipped nervously at her drink, and watched my face greedily. It read quickly, was full of useful things for anybody going on the river, and almost off-handedly caught something of the very withdrawnness of inland waters.

"It's no wonder Walter is pleased," I handed her back the typescript, and we went back to the flat that evening.

"I can't see you this weekend," I said close to morning, before she could press me for a meeting. "My aunt is out of hospital. I have to go down to see her."

"I might as well go down the country too," she said. "My sister has adopted a second child. I've been promising for a long time to go down to see her. I'd only spend the whole weekend moping if I stayed in Dublin. When will we meet when you get back?"

"Wednesday," I was determined to finish the whole affair. "We can meet in the Green Goose at eight on the Wednesday."

"I don't like the pub," she said.

"We can just meet there and go some place else if we want to after."

"How is the pain? You're looking far better than in the hospital," I lied uneasily to my aunt when I went down to see them that weekend.

"The pain's there. I don't know if it'll go. I just pray. And I take the brandy. It's all that does any good."

"I brought two bottles. They're two different brands."

"Thanks," she said. "Will you have a small drop with me?"

While we were drinking she went into the cold pantry where I remembered rabbits and game birds hanging before roasting, and I heard her drink on her own. She brought out a plate of lamb chops. After the secret drink she was relaxed and started to prepare me a meal. While I was eating, the hall door opened and she went still to listen. "It's Cyril," she whispered, and

91

started to tidy away the glasses. "Say nothing about the brandy. He's against taking the brandy for the pain. He says I should take the pills instead."

I listened to his feet come up the hallway. The loose brass knob of the door rattled as it opened. The handsome face had coarsened but the hairline was the same, oiled and parted in the centre. He'd been drinking.

"Well, if it's not our friend from the city, eating like a king," he said sarcastically.

"Cyril," she warned sharply but he ignored her.

The silver cups and medals of his footballing days shone on the dark sideboard, in the small coffin-like mirrors. I got up from the table.

"I didn't mean to disturb you," he said. "I meant for you to go on eating."

"You didn't disturb me," I said.

I saw her eyes plead : be easy with him, he doesn't know what he does, be easy with me.

"And did you find your aunt that loves you so dearly all right?"

"She seems improved."

"She seems improved. She's improved when she's half-crazed with brandy. Nobody will tell the truth. It's pills she should be taking not the brandy. They're far better than the brandy and a damned sight cheaper. You might see that I've even taken to a little drinking myself."

"I can see that," I said, and for a moment it looked as if he was about to hit me.

I thought I might see her cower by the stove, but instead she stood at her full height, all her thought for him. "Cyril's upset that it's taking me so long to get better, when we just have to be patient," she said as if she was straightening his tie.

"I have to go to see the boss," I said. "I'll be back in an hour."

"We'll see you in an hour, so," they both said, his aggression gone.

She followed me to the door, "Don't mind what he said. Cyril doesn't mean what he says. It just flashes out. And you'll not forget to come back?" she seized me by the arm.

"I'll be back," I said as we quickly kissed.

She mumbled something like. "God bless you," as I walked quickly towards the car.

The mill was four or five miles outside the town, towards the mountains. All the woods that had once surrounded the mill had been cut down. The new woods on the lower slopes of the mountains hadn't matured yet, so most of the timber had to be brought in. As I drew close to the mill I saw my uncle high on the back of a big truck, unloading pine trunks with a lift, the iron fingers jerking down to fasten about the trunks before swinging them free. As I drew closer I could feel the spring of years of sawdust beneath my feet and the sharp sweet smell of fresh resin. My uncle waved to me but continued unloading the truck. Away at the mill proper—a large crude shed of timber and galvanized iron—I saw Jim getting a trunk into position on the rollers. From one of the smaller sheds came the harsh, brutal clanging sound of a saw sharpening.

Having unloaded all the pine trunks and turned the engine off, my uncle stretched out his hand. "You're welcome," as slow and confident here as he was dwarfed in the city.

"Things are going well," I gestured toward the sheds and saws.

"Well, not too bad. The price of timber keeps going up, but that doesn't bother us. We just shove up our prices as well, we're not behind in that," he laughed. "Are you down for long?"

"Just for a few hours. I have to be back."

"And you've seen the patient?"

"I've just come from there. Cyril has a few over the top."

"I never see him any other way. I was thinking if things get much worse I might even move out to your place?"

"You don't have to ask me that. You can move any time you want."

"I know that," he said with feeling.

"Would you be able to manage?"

"The house is in perfect shape. I could move in tomorrow as far as the house goes."

"How'd you manage the cooking for yourself?"

"I'd not cook," he started to laugh. "There are restaurants in the town. What do you think I did when your aunt was in the hospital? I got all my meals in Caffrey's. Any fool can get a bit of breakfast for himself!"

"Why don't you move, then?"

"Well, I wouldn't like to just now," he said awkwardly. "Your aunt might think I was moving out on her. Are you going out to take a look at your own place at all?"

"I suppose I might as well. John Hart still has the grass?"

He nodded, "John Hart is all right. If you put it up for bidding you might get a few more pounds, but someone might come and eat the heart out of it. You'll be down soon again?" he had work to do.

"If I go to see the place I'll not have time to see her, and I promised her that I'd go back. But will you just tell her that I ran out of time—that I'll be down again very soon."

"I'll tell her," he nodded. "You might as well go over and have a few words with Jim before you go or we'd never hear the end of it. He's not been in the best of humour this weather either."

"Well, how are things in the big smoke?" Jim greeted.

"The same as usual," I said, and we talked that way.

"I suppose you'll want to be off," he was the first to change. "Your uncle will have been glad to see you. He's not been in the best of humour lately."

I drove straight out to the house. There were several signs of recent fires having been lit all through the house. New fire-bricks had been put in the grate of the Stanley cooker in the kitchen and the stone floor had been swept. Except for flaking paint on the wall it looked as if it had been prepared for some-one to move in.

94

I had so lost connection with the house and fields that I felt I was walking through a graveyard. For the first time I thought that except for my uncle I'd be glad to sell it.

I felt easier outside in the fields, the crowns of the lime trees, the glint of water through the moss-grown orchard, and the mountains beyond. In the fields down by the lake I met John Hart. He had a cattle cane and hat and collar and tie. He obviously did no other work except look after dry cattle now.

At the end of the formal pleasantries he started to complain of the lack of young people in the countryside.

"The only person I see regular around is your uncle, more than I used ever see him. Only last week I was passing the house, after cattle just like I am now, and I saw smoke and happened to look in. And there he was, sitting in the rocking chair, looking into the big fire. He never even noticed me at the window."

As I took leave of John Hart and what he told me, I thought how sure and well people act in their instinct. Sensing an approaching death, my uncle was already beating himself a path to a new door.

I went early to the Green Goose and waited for her beneath the red and green peacocks' eyes.

She looked harassed when she came, as if she hadn't been sleeping much.

"How did your weekend go?" I asked when I'd got drinks.

"It was awful. I suppose the worst was nothing had changed. My sister has her two children. She is happy. Now that she is, her husband's handicap will fall by two strokes. In the evening Father Paul came in from the Augustinians. He was so glad to see me. He joked about me getting married soon, that I must hurry, since he wanted to be the priest at the wedding. We drank too much sherry. And suddenly we both found ourselves crying in front of the fire. He asked me if I had someone I was interested in and I told him about you. I told him that you didn't love me," there were tears in her eyes.

"It sounds pretty grim."

"What right have you to say that?"

"No right. And I'm sorry. It's what I want to talk about."

"This is all I need tonight!"

"We only know each other a few weeks, and things are happening far too fast for me. I'm fond of you," I could hear the lie slithering on the surface of thin ice. "But I'm not in love with you. I want us to call a halt, for a time anyhow, to these regular meetings."

"I see you have it all worked out, just like one of your plots."

"I haven't it all worked out, but I want to give it a rest. We'll drop it for a month or so and see how we feel then. And for that time both of us are free."

"But I love you. . . ."

"If you love me, then surely you can do that much for a month."

"You're letting nothing through and you can really swing them."

"Swing what?"

"Reasons. Figures. You have it all figured out, haven't you? There's hardly need to even talk."

"I want to rest it for a month," I said doggedly.

"It'll be no different in a month."

"We'll see."

"I feel I have enough love for the both of us to begin with. It's that horrible stuff you're writing that has you all twisted and unnatural. I'd care so much for you. There's so many other decent natural things you could do."

"I suppose I could run a health food shop or a launch on the Shannon River," I said angrily.

"You don't understand. I love you. I only want the best for you."

96

"Well then, the best for me is that we agree not to see one another for a month."

"I don't suppose there's any use suggesting that we go back to your place and talk about it."

"No. There's no use. You know what that'll lead to, and we'll be only deeper and deeper in."

"There was a time when you were anxious enough for that," it was her turn to be angry.

"We both were. I'll get a taxi for you or I'll walk you home. Whichever you prefer."

"Walk me home," she said.

"I'm grateful, even flattered by your love. But you can't do the loving for the both of us," I said to her at the gate.

"O boy," she said bitterly. "I waited long enough to sure pick a winner," and I shook her hand and left before she began to cry.

I too had stood mutilated by another gate, believing that I could not live without my love; but we endure, as the first creature leaving water endured, having first tried to turn back from the empty land. Having drunk from the infernal glass we call love and knowing we have lived our death, we turn to love another way, in the ordered calm of each thing counted and loved for its impending loss. We learn to smile.

There was no smiling, nothing but apprehension when a telegram came several days later. *Please ring me*, and it gave her office number. The worst rose easily enough to mind, that maybe this time nothing as simple as a death was in question. A life might have started. I rang her from the kiosk at the bottom of the road. As the girl on the switchboard tried to get her I could hear the clatter of typewriters.

"I got your telegram," I said.

"Thank God you rang. I didn't know what to do."

"Is something wrong?"

After a long pause she breathed, "There sure is."

97

"Are there many people that can overhear you?"

"The whole office—thirty or forty."

"Is it that you're . . . late?"

"Right."

"How long?"

"Five days."

"I'll meet you after work, then. You get out at five?"

"I can leave just before."

"Meet me at five, then. At the Liffey Bookshop. Round the corner from O'Connell Street, facing the river."

"I know it," she said. "I'll be there at five."

I was fingering through the boxes of second-hand books displayed outside when she came, taking in nothing but the discoloured spines, once red and grey and blue and brown.

For once she said nothing, swallowing slightly. There were tear-stains on her face, and I feared she was about to start to cry again. "We'll cross to the river. That way we'll get out of the rush," I said, the pavement round us starting to swarm. We began to walk slowly away from the city, out towards Kingsbridge.

"It's so good to see you," she said. "I didn't know what to do. Yesterday evening I must have walked seventeen times by your place, but I was afraid to go in. I'm sorry," she wiped away tears with her handkerchief.

"There's no need to cry. I'm not running out on you. If you're pregnant, then we're in this together."

She leaned across and kissed me, "I knew you were a good person. Deep down I knew I could trust you. I didn't know what I'd do after that last evening. I couldn't get through to you at all. It was like speaking to a stranger. You seemed determined to let nothing past you. And then I was late. You can imagine what I felt then, and I've always been regular as clockwork. It was like one nightmare followed by another. I thought I was going crazy. I think I would have too, except deep down, somehow, I knew I could trust you."

"Anyhow I'm here. Is it all right if we walk out towards

Kingsbridge, just to get away from this crazy rush hour? We'll have to talk things out."

"Anywhere you want," she took my arm.

Her face had completely cleared, and she was smiling now through brimming eyes. It was as if she'd put all her money on red and the wheel had just stopped and red had won. Below the rounded granite of the wall, the Liffey lay at low tide, two ungainly swans paddling about among the noisy gulls on a mudbank beneath the trickle from an effluent. The small plane trees in their irons along the path were putting out the first leaves.

"We won't have a white wedding," she said. "White is to signify virginity, and I'm hardly a virgin. One person who'll be thrilled is Father Paul, the Augustinian I told you about who came in when I was down with my sister. He's known me since I was a little girl. When he left there were tears in his eyes, and he put his two hands on my shoulders, it seems now he must have sensed or known something, for he said I was made for loving and children. One day soon he'd have to see me married. He'll marry us. You'll like him, and I know he'll like you. I won't need to get any clothes. The plain blue costume will do. And that grey suit of yours will be fine, with the wine tie. We won't have more than half a dozen people each, and we'll go to a good restaurant, Bernardoes or Quo Vadis, not to an hotel. I suppose I'll have to have my sister and her husband, and poor Walter from the magazine, he'll be so surprised, and the two American girls, Betty and Janey. We won't have a Protestant family. I'm not so old that I can't have two or three more children yet."

A cold sweat broke out over me as I traced my own place in her words : the grey suit, the church, her friend the boozy priest, her doting face above me, "This is what I need," as I place the gold ring on mother's finger, and afterwards the prawns, the long-stemmed wine glasses, the toasts, each cliché echoing its own applause, the laughter, "We are no common crowd. . . ."

99

At each bus stop she released my arm as we walked on the concrete high above the filthy river and seized it again as soon we got past each queue. If I had got my love pregnant she would have walked beside me in this same misery, and I, released from suffering, would have no hint of it in my gross triumph. I, too, busy with my sudden reprieve, would be making similarly hurried arrangements for the funeral of her singleness.

At Kingsbridge we crossed from the river pavement and went into Phoenix Park. "No Protestant family", four long summers swelling by my side, and the lawnmower and conversations across the new back gardens.

"You'd get a job. There are several jobs you'd get. And you'd not have to write pornography any more. I can see it's affecting you for the worse in every way. And I'd get a whopping great gratuity from the bank after all these years that'll keep us till you get a job, even until the child is born. The only demand I'd make is that you give up Mavis—what's-her-name—Carmichael? Otherwise I'd be a compliant wife, an old-fashioned wife."

We sat on a green bench deep in the Park. It was beautiful. The daffodils and narcissi were out and the first small hearts of the leaves. In the far distance beyond the white railing men on horses were lining up before the start of a polo match.

"We have to talk," I said.

"I love you so much. All this I feel can have only happened for the best. I know we'll be very happy. I'll make you happy."

"The first thing we have to find out is—are you pregnant or not?" I had to say it brutally for it to get through.

"I've never missed before."

"That's no way to be certain. You'll have to take a test."

"What sort of test?"

"A urine test. We'll have to get a sample of your urine first thing in the morning, and have it analysed. They inject it into an animal and if it comes out positive then you're pregnant."

100

"You seem to know an awful lot about this. As if you've been through it all before."

"I haven't. You don't have to be through everything to know about it. It's just one of the side benefits of writing pornography, you have to know all the facts, even the ones you don't use."

"Won't we get married, even if I'm not pregnant?" she suddenly said.

"Are you crazy?" it was the first time I looked her full in the face. "I'm not running out. And I will marry you—if I have to, if there's no other way out. But the first thing you have to do is to take the test."

"O boy, O boy, I sure picked a winner."

I turned away and dug nails into my hands. If she said O boy once more I wasn't sure I'd be able to hold myself in check.

"We might as well go for a drink or something to eat," I said, and we both rose from the bench. The polo game was now on, the horses with their white-breeched riders racing backwards and forwards beyond the paling. A car with a school of motoring sign went slowly past, a young woman tensely upright at the wheel, the instructor slumped by her side.

"Stout and a sandwich would suit me better than a proper meal. What about you?" I didn't feel like eating at all.

"Anything. Anything you like. I know everything is all right now," she took my arm.

We walked further out, as far as the Angler's Rest, facing the Park Wall. They served beef and cheese sandwiches.

"Last Sunday was the worst day. I hadn't heard from you, and I hadn't yet got up enough courage to send you the telegram. I went out to Betty and Janey's place for lunch. Afterwards we sat around and read all the Sunday papers. There was this article in the *Observer*, about unmarried girls in England who'd got pregnant . . . did you see it?"

"No."

"Many of them were Irish, and there was this peach of an Irishman too, who got his English girl friend pregnant. When

101

she told him she was, do you know what he said—it's hardly believable—'You can keep your baggage here, then, in this heathen country. I'm heading back for the auld sod.' I must have turned beetroot. I felt Betty and Janey could see through me as I read. I left the flat as soon as I could. They wanted to drive me but I said I needed to walk. As soon as I got out of sight of the flat I turned and went down to the sea. I stood on the rocks and thought I'm one of those girls now. I couldn't believe it. I watched the waves come into the rocks. There was one big ship far out. And I wanted to walk out into the water, and farther and farther out until the waves would cover me."

"Anyhow, you sent the telegram and you're here."

"We might as well go back to your place. We have nothing to lose now," she said later, at the end of the evening in which nothing had been resolved, everything having grown, if anything, more blurred, fear and shame and dismay and revulsion following one another like the revolving lights that coloured the darkness for the slower dances in the ballroom where we'd first met.

"We'll not go back tonight. We might as well make certain whether you're pregnant or not. I'll find out about the test. And I'll meet you after work tomorrow evening, same as we met this evening."

She was probably right—there was nothing to lose now. I had been careless and stupid, and stupidity is the one thing you're certain to be punished for, we'd been told it often enough; and here I was being scrupulous in the eye of the disaster, when it was certainly far too late to make a difference.

"I could sure do with some loving tonight," the pleasure was now free that had been so dearly paid for.

"We'll leave it for tonight," I felt sick. "We'll make certain first."

"It's not very long since you were eager enough."

"There's nothing I'd like more," and except to be free altogether it was true, to take this strong woman's body and enter

102

into it in rage. Nature has many weathers for drawing us within her gates.

"Then what have we to lose?"

"We'll find out first," and she began to cry.

"Look," I rocked her. "We're in this together. I'm not running out on you or anything. We'll find out first. And then we'll see where we'll go."

"I'm sorry," she was smiling through her tears. "I'm happy now. I somehow know everything'll be all right now."

"We'll get a taxi."

Sleepless, as when I'd been in love, images came to plague me, and they would not leave me. What were once the images of loss became the images that enmesh and fester round a life.

There was a semi-detached house at the head of one of the roads around the Green Goose, shrubbery just beginning to appear above the front garden walls, two iron gates, concrete to the garage door. The roof was red-tiled and the walls were pebble-dashed. A lighted bell above the letter box went ding-dong. Behind the house, on either side of a thin concrete footpath, the long, competing back gardens ran to the glass-topped wall : a piece of lawn, some roses, a cabbage patch, rhubarb, cold frames for early lettuce, raspberry canes that needed cutting back, two apple trees that every year brought vandals. The narrow kitchen was up a step from the back garden, the formica-topped breakfast table, the radio, the clock, the whirring fridge. A carpeted room wasn't far away. There was a solid table and chairs for compulsory entertaining, some books on shelves, a drinks cabinet, a tiled fireplace, a TV set. Upstairs two cupids kept blissful watch above the double bed and waiting carry-cot. The curtains that hid the road were hung and frilled. Swelling by my side she'd yawn O boy before she'd kiss and drill. And proudly, stretching towards the line and beaming benediction on the whole setup, she'd hang out her brand-washed flags as good as any.

When I had cried I cannot live without you, I had cried

103

against the loss of a dream, and believed it was worse than death, since it could not find oblivion. I had thought no suffering could be worse. I was wrong.

I had gone in and suffered, when it was clear my love could not be returned, like the loss of my own life in the other. This now was worse. The Other would now happily lose her life in me and I would live the nightmare. It would be worse than loss. It would be a lived loss, and many must have been caught this way and made to live it.

I called up Peter White, a doctor, a friend from university. We had met fairly frequently for a few years after graduating, to go to pubs and the theatre and once to a rugby international against Scotland at Murrayfield. I had been at his wedding, and afterwards the meetings naturally dwindled, and then stopped. Calling him up out of the past was like calling up a ghost. There are more awkwardnesses than with a total stranger because of the dead barrier of memory.

He seemed pleased enough to hear from me. I suppose there is always excitement—even when it is unpleasant—when the pall of everyday is torn away.

"I'm afraid it does me no credit," I explained. "I'm looking for something. And I didn't know who else to turn to. . . ."

"What is it?"

"Well, it's not money!" I prevaricated.

"We could even manage a little of that," his easy ironical laugh brought easy idle evenings vividly back, mockingly now.

"I may well be in trouble, may well have got a woman pregnant."

"How did you manage that?"

"Are there two ways?" I countered defensively. "I hate asking you this, but how do you go about getting this test done —to know for certain."

"I can take care of that for you."

"But I don't want that."

"It's no trouble. I can get it done at the hospital," and he gave instructions for getting the urine sample and we arranged to meet late the next evening in O'Neill's of Suffolk Street when I'd bring him the sample. Often we conceal our motives from ourselves. I had rung him instead of ringing any anonymous doctor because I was now looking for allies.

Spring was late, and when it came it was more like early summer. Fairview Park was full of flowers and young men, their trousers tucked into socks, kicking footballs under the greening trees, using their cast-off clothes to mark the goals. I had played with them once. They were mostly apprentice barmen on their day off. Corporation workmen started to assemble scaffolding and ladders and then to paint the bandstand. As I went to meet her, the faintest tang of the spring tides was getting through the city dump and the car fumes. Because of the angle at which I saw the world, the good weather was getting on my nerves.

"It's very simple," I explained to her when we met that evening in the Green Goose. "You take the urine sample first thing in the morning. All you have to be careful of is that the container is sterilized."

"It's as simple as that?"

"As simple as that."

The edge had nothing to do with the simple test. It just focused on it because it was nearest, as edges do.

"Life is very simple for you, isn't it?"

"No, but some things in it are. It's bad enough without complicating the simple things."

"How complicated?" she challenged angrily.

"The test will tell me for certain whether you're pregnant or not. If you're not, then there's no trouble."

"There's a test for love and life as well?"

"There's generally no need. They're too obvious."

"So a test will tell me what I already know full well?"

"No. It's only fifty-fifty at the most you're pregnant," edge was meeting edge. "Stress can cause you to miss. Disturbance

105

can. The very idea that you might be pregnant can. Only the test will tell us for certain."

"Where did you learn all this?"

"The doctor. He's agreed to do it," I was blind now. "Ease up. I don't even have to be here. You wouldn't use contraceptives. You said you were sure it was safe. All you did was lie on your back and get pregnant."

"And you had nothing got to do with it?"

"Sure I had. I was stupid. And I'm paying for it now by being here."

We'd been drawn so much into the heat of the quarrel that it had been forgotten that a few early evening people were around us in the Goose. It was when she began to cry that I noticed they were all staring our way.

"If you don't stop you'll get us into trouble here. Why don't we go?"

"All right. We'll go," she said, and as we left I thought I heard a shout behind us from one of the tables, but I did not look back.

Out in the car park, the metal goose hanging still on its arm in the calm and lovely evening, I said, "I'm sorry. Would you like to go some other place? Would you like to go and eat a decent meal, with wine?"

"I'm sorry too," she was smiling when she dried her eyes. "What I'd like to do is go back to your place. We can talk in peace there."

"Are you sure you wouldn't prefer to go to a decent restaurant?"

"I'm certain," she said and took my arm. "And don't worry, love. I know everything is going to work out fine."

"How do you make out that?" I asked.

"Because," she said, "because both of us are good people."

Peter White was waiting for me at the bar and I handed him the sample as soon as we met, "Just to get it over with."

106

"I'll take care of it," he put it in his pocket. "It's no trouble. I'll have the result in two days' time. By the way, Mary sent her regards, and asked if you could come to dinner on Saturday. I should have the result for you by then."

"I'll be glad to but there's no need. Is there any way I can pay you?"

"No. I'm a sort of big wheel now, a consultant. I can get it done at the hospital. I'm only sorry that you should be in this fix." His clothes were careful, as I suppose they had always been, but expensive too.

"I'm sorry it's over this we should meet," I began, but his directness saved me embarrassment.

"What'll you do if she is pregnant?"

"Do you really think there's a fifty-fifty chance she's not?" I couldn't resist clutching at the straw.

"At least that, but then there's no problem. What'll you do if it turns out that she is?"

"I suppose I'll have to marry her."

"Why?"

"It's the last thing I want to do, but I can't very well ditch her."

"Where did you meet?"

"At a dance."

"Did you make her any promises?"

"None. We only met a little over a month ago. If she wanted to do it, fair enough, I wanted to too, that was all there was to it. She wouldn't allow contraceptives but she always said it was safe. It didn't turn out that way."

"Whether she knew it or not she wanted to get pregnant. Why would you marry her?"

"She wants me to. She says she loves me. And she's worked at this bank for twenty years. She gets so much of a marriage gratuity for every year she's worked, so it's quite large. She'd get that much money if I married her. She doesn't get a penny if she just has to resign."

107

"But have you any fondness for her? Has the marriage any chance of working out?"

"None. I'd only marry her till the child came. Then I'd leave."

"Why marry then?"

"That way it'd seem I was the bastard. She'd get protection. I'd take the rap. It's the only condition I'd marry on, that I'd be free to leave as soon as it was over."

"Then you must be a younger man than I think you are. You don't marry people on conditions. You either marry them or you don't marry them. What's wrong with the situation now, from her point of view, is that it's outside the law. By marrying her you put it inside and she's protected in all sorts of ways."

"What'd stop me from walking out?"

"You'd be walking out on a new wife, a child. You'd be walking out on the law. It'd be a far greater mess all round. She may agree to it now but will she agree to it then?"

"What's to happen to her?"

"I think you have to help her in every way you can, but that stops far short of marrying her."

"You think then I won't have to marry her?" it was like grasping for pure joy.

"Unless you want to get yourself into a far greater mess."

I was set free. The wild inner hope had been given solid sanction from outside. All things *are* relative. I could not have known such happiness if I had not lived for days with the nightmare. I was so happy that I was careless that my rich prize was won from her ruin.

"We'll have another drink."

"What do you do now? Are you still with that agency?" he asked.

"No. I gave that up. I write pornography."

"You write pornography?" his clean-cut features, boyish still beneath the straight black hair, mirrored all the shades between incredulity and amazement.

108

"That way I don't have to go into the agency. I don't get all that much money but I get paid enough."

"This is too rich. You're getting elderly girls pregnant and writing pornography. It's too much," his bellow of helpless laughter attracted attention all around the bar. "What is the pornography like?"

"It's heartless and it's mindless and it's a lie. I'm stuck with it and I'm sick of it, a cold anvil that has to be beaten," I began.

"Anyhow we'll see you for dinner Saturday, though we may well have to fumigate the place afterwards," he said as we parted.

"What did you do for the evening?" I asked her when we met.

"I just moped," she answered. "There was a time when everything was certain. I knew exactly where I was going, everything I was doing. Everything had a purpose then, but since I met you everything gets more and more mixed-up."

"I gave the doctor the sample. We should know for certain by Saturday."

"What'll we know for certain?"

"Whether you're pregnant or not."

"I know I am."

"If you're not," I said determinedly, "we'll go out and celebrate. We'll have the biggest, most expensive, drunkennest meal in Dublin," and, I thought silently, we'll get to hell out of one another's lives for ever.

"What'll we do then?"

"We'll both be free."

"And what if the test is positive?"

"There's no use thinking about that now. We'll know soon enough."

"I don't see what's wrong with getting married. I know we'd be happy."

What was her meat was my poison. The trouble with the

109

old clichés was that they were all true and turned up for their renewal.

"We'll have to face into that in two days' time."

"But will we be married?"

"If we have to," I said quickly. "I won't be able to see you tomorrow evening. I have to have dinner with this doctor and his wife tomorrow evening."

"I'll go to dinner with Betty and Janey then. They rang today to see if I'd have dinner at their place. I told them I'd wait till I saw you. I think they must know that something's wrong."

"Did you tell them anything?"

"No. I was going to but I didn't. Will we go back tonight?"

"We'll wait till Sunday. We'll know for certain what we've let ourselves in for."

"I can do with Sunday coming. I find my hands all the time stretching out for you. I could do with holding your body for the whole of a whole week."

I brought champagne and whiskey and a sheaf of yellow roses to the dinner.

"What did you want to bring all this for?" Peter White asked sharply in the hallway.

"I feel it's the least I could bring. Turning up on such an errand after all these years."

"To pay your way?" he said sarcastically.

"Something like that."

"Well, thanks, but it's too much. I'm afraid it has no influence on your news though. The test was positive."

I waited, empty, feeling it sink like a stone to the bottom of the emptiness, come up again like mud.

"I'm sorry," he said.

"That means she's pregnant?"

"The test has a two per cent margin of error, but if I were you I'd take it that she is pregnant."

"Somehow I never had much hope that it'd turn out any other way."

110

His wife came in. She had on a white apron with a recipe for *steak au poivre* in black print across the front. She seemed prettier than when they'd married. We shook hands and she praised the roses.

"Did you tell?" she asked Peter.

"The news is bad," I answered for him. "It's a mess."

"I'm sorry," she said. "It's going to be a problem."

"We'll have plenty of time to go into it at dinner. What'll we have to drink?"

She had a dry sherry. He and I had whiskey. A log fire blazed behind the wire screen over the white marble fireplace. Persian rugs were scattered about the polished wood of the floor. Three places were set at the head of the long table, silver candlesticks down its centre. The heavy velvet curtains drawn the whole length of one wall gave a feeling that all the unpleasantness of the world lay arctic wastes away outside.

"It's quite lovely," I said. "It speaks of comfort and money."

"Is it that vulgar?" he fenced.

"It's not vulgar at all. It's lovely, as money is. It gives me the feeling of luxury and protection."

"Peter is still defensive," she smiled. "He feels like that about everything in life, that he shouldn't have it, but I'm quite used to it."

She withdrew and came back ten minutes later with three bowls of mushroom soup, on which sprigs of parsley floated. When the bowls were gathered away she carried in a roast chicken on a platter.

"It was a lot of work," I said to her.

"A girl comes in. Kitty. I let her home early this evening."

"Don't laugh," Peter said, switching on an electric carving knife. "I feel ridiculous with this thing but it works."

"What do you think it's best to do?" I began as soon as we'd started to eat. I was anxious not to put it off for any longer. It was as if I knew that my fate in the sad business would be decided here most favourably. She looked towards him but

111

he kept his eyes on his plate. "You have to think of the woman and more especially the child," she said.

"I'm prepared to marry her if there's no other way out."

"That's not on," he said, "since you're only prepared to marry her and then leave her. You'd only be walking out on a far greater mess."

"Why would he leave her?"

"Because I couldn't stand living with her. I'd marry her only so that I'd be seen to take the blame for the whole business."

"But you must have been fond of her in order for what has happened to happen?"

"No. I wanted to sleep with her."

"To do that you must have given her something to go on?"

"I never told her that I loved her or promised her anything. I suppose it's the only saving feature now."

"For God's sake," he said. "You don't have to love someone or even to be fond of them to want to fuck with them!"

Her very silence was a rebuke as she rearranged her knife and fork.

"What does *she* want?" she pursued.

"She wants to marry me."

"Does she know that you don't love her?"

"She doesn't mind that. She says she has enough love for the both of us."

He groaned but she ignored it. "Why weren't contraceptives used?"

"She said they weren't natural, that they turned the whole thing into a farce. Every time she said it was safe according to the calendar. It didn't turn out that way."

"She was using the Boles Method, no doubt. There's a fool of a gynaecologist in the hospital, a staunch Catholic, and a great Boles man. In this last experiment more women got pregnant using the Boles Method than no method at all. The woman obviously wanted to get pregnant. I see it every day in the hospital. Time running out? Get pregnant, and it'll be

112

taken care of. Bored with life? Get pregnant, and it'll stir things up. Not getting enough attention? Get pregnant, and it'll bring an overdose of attention. Hit me now with the child in my arms," he laughed jeeringly.

"The girl or woman probably didn't get pregnant deliberately. She'll suffer for it now anyhow," his wife said.

"If you can tell where instinct ends and consciousness begins you'll make all our fortunes. Here. Hold on to your seat belts," he said as he set the carving knife whirring. "I'll carve you a second helping of instinct any day of the week," and he poured what was left of the Moselle.

"All this riding of hobby horses isn't getting us anywhere," she said calmly.

"Right," he said. "She can have an abortion."

"Not here," she reminded.

"London's only an hour away. There's a good clinic in Woodford. She can be back at work in three days. It's expensive. That's all."

"She'd never agree to it," I said.

"You can't force her to have an abortion," his wife said. "It's probably her last chance to have a child at her age. If she were to have an abortion it's very unlikely she'd be able to conceive again afterwards."

"Then, if she won't agree to the abortion, she can have the child and put it up for adoption."

"What if she didn't want to have it adopted once she had it?"

"You'd have to cross that bridge when you reach it. She'd be pleasing herself then, wouldn't she? She'd be on on her own after that point. But up to there, to my mind, you'll have to give her all the help you can."

"Dublin is too small a place for her to have the child, with her kind of family," I probed.

"It probably is. London would probably be the easiest place all round, but again that's for her to decide."

"Is marriage completely out?" she asked.

"If abortion is out for her, marriage is out for him," he said.

"It sounds horribly logical." I didn't care to see it so brutally.

"Life isn't simply a logical business," she said.

"No," he said. "It's not logical, but it'd be a damned sight worse without some attempt to make sense of it."

When we rose, she said that Kitty would clear the table in the morning. He and I had large brandies. She had nothing.

By the time I left I no longer felt the vulnerable single person that has to take on suffering and death. We upholster ourselves.

She looked at me when we met under Clery's clock on the Sunday. "It's bad news," I said. "The test was positive. It's almost certain that you're pregnant."

"Now we're really in it," she said without seeming to realize anything of the words, and stood silent, as if gathering the knowledge within her, the way I'd seen her stand as if to collect herself before getting into bed for the first time, the way I must have stood when I first heard the test was positive.

"The doctor and his wife were very good. They'll give us all the help they can. They said the first thing to consider is an abortion. They can arrange it, perfectly legally."

"Would you agree to that?" she asked indignantly.

"Of course I would but it's not my decision. You have to decide that."

"To take a small life, and have it killed. Of course we'd get off scot-free. But how could we live with ourselves again?"

"That wouldn't bother me. It's not my decision though."

"I couldn't do it. I couldn't live with myself if I did that."

"Well then, if an abortion is out marriage is even more out."

"Why?"

"I'd be only marrying you because you're pregnant."

"Those sort of marriages are often the happiest. I know at least three."

"This couldn't. I'd only marry to cover for you."

"You'd change when you saw the child."

"No. I wouldn't change. I'd leave as soon as you had the child. We talked about it. They said that if I was certain the marriage had no chance—and I am certain it hasn't—it'd only be a far bigger mess when it happened than if we never married."

"Of course, they're your friends," she said bitterly.

"In a sense, they are, but I think they'd have said the same to any couple. It comes down to whether the marriage has a chance or not. The child makes no difference."

"The child, of course, has no rights?"

"It will have, but that has nothing to do with it. The marriage is between you and me. If it's not going to work without the child it won't work with the child."

"Do these people know our ages?"

"They do and they think that's not important either, if everything else is all right."

"I know those sort of people. They live in their comfortable houses. They have planned families. They have everything figured out; and yet they die."

"We all die."

"You have everything figured out too."

"It may be bad enough with thinking but it'd be a damned sight worse just following your nose," I heard my own voice echo Peter White's.

"Stop it," she said. "Stop it or I'll scream."

We'd crossed the bridge, and turned down Burgh Quay. Rows of people waited for buses the other side of the quay but the river path was empty. Below us the Liffey at low tide lay oily and still in the warm evening. I stood beside the granite wall and waited. Her distress was so great that it hid her beauty, as it would ugliness, had she been ugly. For a wild

115

moment I wanted to say, "I was only testing you. Don't worry. We'll get married," but the moment went.

"O boy," she said without looking at me. "I sure picked a winner."

"What do you want?"

"Stop it. I'm not ready for that. Not yet."

"Will we go for a drink?"

We crossed to the Silver Swan. She went straight to the *Ladies*. I bought treble gins and brought them to the farthest corner of the bar. She seemed to be gone a long time but did not look any more composed when she came back. The lights of the Silver Swan were so blessedly low that it wasn't possible to tell whether she'd been crying or not. She let me pour the tonic up to the rim of the glass. We sat for a long time in that silence.

"Why couldn't we be married?" the calmness of the voice took me by surprise.

"I'd only marry you to cover up till the child was born. We'd be only getting deeper and deeper in. The marriage would have no chance of lasting. It's better to face up to that now rather than go through a sort of charade."

"You might change, especially when we'd have the child. I couldn't see you walking out on the child."

"No. I'd not change."

"How do you know you wouldn't? You're not giving anything a chance."

"You'll just have to take my word for it."

"If we get married, I'd at least get that gratuity out of the bank. I hate to think of them being able to hang on to all that money just because I walked out without getting married."

"The divorce or separation would soon eat up the gratuity and it'd be a far worse mess."

"You sound more like a lawyer than a person," I felt the calm go. "At least if we got married I'd have the child."

"You can have the child anyhow. No one can stop you. Since I am supposed to be a lawyer, why can't there be an abortion?"

116

"How would you get an abortion?" she challenged.

"It's very simple. You'd fly to London. There's a first-class clinic in Woodford. The doctor can arrange it. It's a simple, fairly painless operation. If you had to, or wanted to, you could be back at work in three days."

"And live with that for the rest of your life? Thanks. O thanks."

"You asked," the tension gnawed and went on gnawing.

"I asked? I asked for a lot of things."

It was as if silence was turned like a lock and the key forgotten about. We sat in that silence for what seemed like hours. Once I got up and went to the *Mens* and got two more gins at the counter on my way back, but that didn't disturb the silence. Sometimes the tension wandered off into a sensuous mindlessness but then would startlingly snap back.

"I suppose we'd be better back in the room," she said as if it was now her room too.

"I suppose we couldn't be any worse off there."

We walked in the warm spring evening. Three hours had passed since we had met. That the curtains in the room were drawn as always seemed to mock us, the light lit above the Chianti bottle on the marble.

"It's the same as ever," she said looking round.

"It's always the same," I said.

"Somehow it shouldn't be the same," she said.

"Would you like a drink?" and when she shook her head I asked, "Do you mind if I have one?" and when she didn't answer I poured myself a large whiskey and started to drink it quickly.

It was then that she came into my arms. "Kiss me. Comfort me. I'm going to need a lot of comforting."

As I rocked her I said, "We'll find some decent way out. You can depend on that. It'll not be as bad as it seems now."

"Why don't we go to bed," she said. "We've certainly earned it. We have nothing to lose now. Nothing."

When I turned out the light we both seemed to undress with

117

abstracted slowness. There was no feverish slipping of knots and buttons and buckle and hooks but rather a sad fumbling with them before reluctantly letting them fall loose.

I felt her sobbing before I touched her shoulders, and when she came into my arms she shook there in an uncontrolled fit of sobbing. "I'm sorry," she said. "I'm sorry but I can't help it."

"It's all right. No one will bother us here. Don't worry about it," and when she quietened we began to kiss, laughing nervously when I dried the tears with the corner of the sheet.

"That is what I need," she breathed. "That is what I need. It is not talk I need but loving." I was silent. "I don't know why this happened to us. We're both good people," she took up.

"It happened too soon, before we knew one another. We were unlucky."

"I'll have to resign," she said. "It's going to be a hard road. I hate to think of them getting away with all that money after all these years."

"Where do you think you'll want to go?"

"To London. I always wanted to go to London. Two years ago a man called Jonathan wanted me to go. He owns magazines. I nearly resigned and went to work for him on a *Waterways* magazine there. I little thought then that this'd be the way I'd be going," she began to cry.

"I can go with you," I said. "I could get some job there, or even keep writing the old stuff. I could stay with you till the child was born."

"What would we do then?"

"We'd get the child adopted."

"As simple as that. To go through all that and then just turn round and give the child away?"

"That way the child would have a secure home."

"Listen," she said. "There's going to be enough hard times in the days ahead. What I need now is loving not talking or thinking. I'm going to need a great deal of loving to face into

118

the days ahead. And you have no idea how much you're loved. And I know how hard these days have been for you as well," she said as she drew me back into her arms.

My aunt came for a checkup at this time. She came on the train. I met her on the platform but when I took her bag at the carriage door she was impatient. "They wanted to drive me up, when it's just for a few old tests. If you heeded them, they'd have you in a wheelchair before long. You'd never be able to start making your own way again."

"There's no use pushing it though," I was dismayed at how ill she looked, yet as she walked she seemed to walk ahead of me. She had on the lovely old brown tweed with fur at the throat that I remembered in happier days.

"You're just as bad as your uncle and Cyril," she scolded.

"I'm not that bad," I said. "How do you feel? You look great anyhow."

"All I feel is that it's very cold, as if this year may never take up," and it made me even more careful. It was a warm day for early summer.

"What would you like to do—go out to the hospital now or wait for a bit?"

"We'll be out in the hospital soon enough. It's long since we had a chat," and I took her across the road to the solid comfort of the North Star Hotel. She wanted brandy.

"Are you sure it won't interfere with the tests?" my voice had no authority in its policeman's role.

"Bad luck to the tests," she said. "They're only a matter of going through the rigmarole."

"And there's no chance they'll try to keep you in?"

"No. They said I'd be able to go home the day after to-morrow. I have to be home because of the garden." She began to tell about her garden. She'd got James Prior to rotavate it. It had been a wilderness of weeds, not having been broken for the two previous years. She'd sown beans and peas, lettuce,

119

carrots, parsnips, Early York cabbages, parsley, shallots, beet, even marrows. The netting wire had to be fixed because of the rabbits. The garden had been part of the old railway. Every fine afternoon she walked the half-mile down the disused line. Cyril collected her with the car on his way home from work.

"I feel I get well there, just rooting about among the plants. You never feel the time pass. And every day there's something new. Around dinner-time you find yourself getting anxious about the rain. And you forget about the pain, unless it's playing you up horrible bad. I hadn't my foot in the train this morning when it started."

"I was thinking that something good must have happened when I saw you get off the train, you looked so much better."

She wanted another brandy and she joked about the black-haired girl, asking if I had anybody now.

"Not really anybody," I said.

"I know what that means," she laughed.

"I may have to go to London," I said.

"What would you want to go to that old place for?"

"The crowd I work for want me to go."

"You don't have to go?"

"It'd be hard not to. They want me to go for a year or so."

"You don't have to go anywhere, if you don't want to. Isn't it almost time you came home? Your own place is lying there. And whose for the old mill—bad luck to it—except yourself?"

"I couldn't afford to go home, unless you give me some of those houses you have," I changed to tease. Over the years she'd acquired seven or eight houses in the town, and as she didn't believe in cash was always on the lookout for more. They were let out as flats and a few shops and were jealously guarded for her beloved Cyril. She coloured like a young girl.

"Bad luck to you, but haven't you more than enough—without thinking of my poor shacks."

"They'd come in very handy," I laughed. "Will you tell me this now, am I right or wrong, is there anybody who has enough?" I mimicked my uncle, "There's only the one class

120

of people that has enough, and there's no prizes for telling where they are—they're all in the graveyard."

"Bad luck to both of you," she laughed into the last of her brandy. "Ye might look different but the pair of yous are the same thick old blocks."

We took a taxi to the hospital and I left her there.

When I went in to see her the next evening all the tests had been taken and she was ready to go home.

"Did they tell you anything?" I asked.

"No. It'll take them a while. They're sending the results to the doctor."

When I looked at her racked flesh, the few wisps of hair left on the crown of her head, I saw that it was little more than pure spirit she was living on; and from several random words I gathered that the place in eternity she most hungered for was a half-mile down the abandoned railway among the growing things in the garden.

"You'll come down soon," she said. "And you'll try to get out of going to that old London if you can."

"I'll be down soon—whether I have to go or not," I promised.

On the pretext of my aunt's visit, I hadn't seen her for two whole days. The readiness with which she agreed to the break took me by surprise, but we were to meet in Wynn's Hotel late that night. I waited for an hour before she came. She was very carefully groomed, even glamorous, and in seeming high spirits.

"I'm sorry," she said. "I'm a bit dizzy from the last two days. I saw poor Walter at the magazine. And then I spent yesterday evening with Betty and Janey. I rang Jonathan in London from their place and he insisted on ringing me back tonight. We must have talked for an hour. He's flying in tomorrow. I'm meeting him at the Hibernian."

"Would you like something to drink? There's just about time for you to have one."

121

"I'd like a long drink. A lager," and when I called the waiter he pointedly checked the hotel clock with his watch.

"Who's Jonathan? Is he the one who wanted you to go to London two years ago?"

"He is English, with handlebars. He's very charming. Married to this crazy wife who's been in and out of hospitals for years. He's a director of a company which publishes several magazines and trade papers, including the British version of the *Waterways* magazine. Several times he's asked me to marry him. He's been in love with me for years. It was he who wanted me to give up the job in the bank two years back and go to London."

She too had gone out in search of allies. There was a sense of gangs forming, their pressure upon all guilt.

"Maybe you'll marry this Jonathan?"

"Are you crazy? If I couldn't marry him two years ago how could I marry him now? And he's too old. He's in his fifties."

"How was Walter?"

"Poor Walter was so upset. His wife was pregnant when they married. He asked me if you'd ever said you loved me. You'll have to thank me. I took your side. Walter was so indignant at first but I swung him round. In the end he agreed that you weren't behaving badly, all things considered."

"What about Janey and Betty?"

"They think you're crazy. 'That guy will regret not marrying you all the days of his life.'"

"Did you tell them the whole story?"

"Sure. They partly guessed it already. They still think you're crazy. Did you see your aunt?"

"She's going home tomorrow."

"How is she?"

"She's very poor. I think it can be only a matter of weeks. I think she is dying."

"One person going out of life," I winced as she said it, "and another person coming into life. I suppose that's the story."

"That's the story. What'll we do next?"

"Jonathan warned me not to make a move until I saw him tomorrow in the Hibernian but it seems simple enough. I'll have to give in my month's notice to the bank though it galls me to think of them getting away with that gratuity money. But nobody thinks giving up the bank is a big deal. They said I should have got out of it years ago but my aunt won't think that; she'll be horrified at giving up all that security and a pension at sixty-five," she laughed.

"What will you tell her?"

"I'll tell her I'm going to London to seek my fame and fortune. That it didn't look as if I'll be married now. And that I want to try a writing career. That the bank was a dead-end job. She knows that the magazine has been my real interest for years. She's always giving out about it."

"Is that what you intend to try in London?"

"Jonathan more or less said he could get me a job in one or other of the papers, that there was always something or other coming up. You know I almost gave up the bank to go two years ago but I got cold feet at the last minute."

"Will we go?" I asked as the porter cleared away the glasses.

"At least we've nothing to fear going back to your place now. We're not trying to get anything on the cheap and easy. We're facing up to everything," she took my arm.

It was strange how rapidly things were taking shape, almost independently of us. We'd give up our lives here, go to London, live there until the child was born. Our lives could hardly be the same again. For years they had stayed the same. Now they were being rushed into some new and frightening shape.

After perfunctory desire, the body that many must have yearned for lay nonexistent by my side. I was going to have months and months and months to get to know it.

"We could have played it safe and had our fun and been just plain selfish like many others," she said.

"We were stupid."

"I can't believe that. We weren't just calculating people. Mean and calculating is worse than being foolish."

"Nothing is worse than being stupid."

"Maybe we were foolish but we are good people and I know everything is going to work out."

"We were selfish and greedy *and* stupid," I could hear the quarrel starting.

"I can't believe that. There are several ways out for us even yet and we're not taking any easy way out," I could hear her resentment, but the last thing I wanted was a quarrel, and fought down my growing anger.

Unable to read or work, and unused to having evenings free, I rang Maloney the day she was to have dinner with Jonathan. "Would you like to come into the Elbow or would you prefer a teat-a-teat? Very rarely we get the opportunity these days, old boy."

"A tête-à-tête, then," I said.

"I have somebody to see but I'll cancel. Meet me in the bar of the Wicklow and we'll treat ourselves to a good dinner somewhere. We deserve a good dinner. A teat-a-teat is as good as a cheek to cheek," he refused to stay checked.

He had on a beautifully cut dark pinstripe, hand-tailored black shoes, plain tie, a wine kerchief falling nonchalantly from the breast pocket; but his true talent was that no matter what he wore he always managed to look equally ridiculous. He was in one of his very generous moods.

"Everything's on the company tonight," he said when I asked him what he wanted to drink. "We'll put everything on the card and forget about it. The fruits of lust. The individual is dead. And God is dead and everything is a fiddle," he crowed. "Did you bring any of old Grimshaw's spunk along to pave the way?"

"I haven't been able to write anything. I'm fed up with the stuff."

"We're all fed up, old boy, except we can't afford to be fed up. We must never show the flag. We must give ourselves and everybody around us a true enthusiasm for living. We must flog enthusiasm. It's the coming thing."

"I may have to go to London," I said.

"It's a very good city."

"I'm not joking. I may have to go there for a year or so."

"Are you trying to ransom me for more money or what? You can't write and now you must go to London. You're an artist, old boy. We'll miss your physical presence among us. But we'll be philosophical. One of the few advantages of the artist is that he can set up his business wherever he happens to be or, putting it more simply, he can live anywhere he writes. London should be fine. A stimulus. But why, why have you to go into exile since your whole life and work is an embodiment of the idea of exile?"

"I've got this woman pregnant. She won't have an abortion. She insists on going through with the whole thing. And I'll have to go to London with her," I spoke as quickly as I was able so that he couldn't break in.

"Most unprofessional, I am pained to have to say," he spoke with exaggerated slowness. "Art is not life because it is not nature. If you spring a leak anywhere the whole boat may go down. You better not go and take up the idea of getting Miss Mavis Carmichael pregnant or you may well find that you've got yourself out of a job. Where did this unfortunate accident occur?"

"On the Shannon, I think."

"Going in for mythological stuff as well? Compound everything. This won't do. This won't do at all. And now you're off to London, modern style, the illegitimate father present at the birth. Very good."

"There was a time I thought I'd have to marry the woman and stay here."

"And why didn't you, old boy? That's how I got married— but I was in love. My wife was going to ditch me but then found she was pregnant and married me; then on our wedding night she discovered it was a false alarm, that she wasn't pregnant at all. Afterwards we laboured and laboured in vain until she decided to go to the doctor. Whatever he did, what-

125

ever rearranging he did, I couldn't hang up my trousers on the foot of the bed after that but she was away. There are lessons no doubt in all these things for those who care to observe them. Well, why didn't you follow father's good example, even in the eye of rejection, to the altar?"

"It was luckily decided that it wasn't a very good idea. Since I was only willing to marry her in order to leave her."

We moved from the bar to the restaurant. The wine waiter had a crest of embroidered grapes on his jacket. Maloney gave him a severe inspection as he took the wine list, but it had much the same effect as that of a tailor appraising a potential customer for a new suit, and it ended with the waiter choosing the wines.

"There's no disaster in life that can't be turned to someone's advantage," he was irrepressible. "Martin Luther King, you may remember, had a dream. I just have a plan but we'll fill the inner man while I outline it."

We had avocado with prawns, lamb cutlets with spinach, and cheese. The waiter picked a Château Margaux and Maloney ordered a second bottle to go with the cheese before we finished the first. Afterwards he insisted on moving back to the bar for brandies.

"You may remember in the *Echo* days when Maureen Doherty ditched me and I wrote that poem," he began.

"How could I forget it?"

"I was undismayed. I've always been undismayed. Many women have ditched me but I knew sooner or later one of them would leave it too late and get caught jumping out of the house shouting Fire! It's exactly of course what happened. And then after one of those rows with that fool Kelly down at the *Echo* I was even a bigger bloody fool and handed in my notice. Kelly accepted it with alacrity and I went off to Paris to be a poet. That cured me. A black man said to me that Paris was the one place where there was no racial discrimination, that everybody got treated equally badly there. I lived in a garret, of course, off the rue Buci. There were three hundred and

126

sixty-nine steps up to it, the wood worn away in the centre of the steps. That's what you mean by centuries of feet. The bloody house was built by Henry the Fourth in 1603. The windows were in the roof, glass in blacksmith's frames. I stuffed the frames with newspaper to keep the draughts out. Very cold days were spent in cafés with a book and a beer and coffee, the waiters clearing the table and trying to rout you out of it every hour or so; but you could look out through the glass at the rain and people passing and the red flop of the canvas and the deer and partridges hung across in the game butchers—and—have visions. My most frequent vision was that of an enormous tray of roast beef and browned potatoes back in Ireland. In hot weather the garret was like a glasshouse. Couldn't live in it then either. I used to go and sit in the Luxembourg. How well I remember the trained pears in their plastic bags. I have so many heart-shaking memories. Life is a great teacher if you can extricate yourself for a few moments every few years or so from the middle of its great bog.

"It was in the Luxembourg I got my plan. I used to hate the Parisian brats, going for rides on the ponies round the fountain, the overalled little man coming behind with the litter cart on bicycle wheels, cleaning up the pony shit off the sacred gravel. Then they put up a notice. Only old people or people with children were to be allowed into the park. That finally pissed me off with Paris and poetry and I swore never to return except with my plan.

"I had almost given it up entirely but your lechery may have saved the day. This is it. I'll get a pram made in the shape of a coffin, miniature handles, crucifix, brown varnish, the lid at an angle of forty-five degrees to keep out the rain, a white handgrip for pushing, big wheels and small wheels.

"You'll go to London, and see the baby off the assembly line like any modern father. The three of us—why, the four of us—will go to Paris, put the baby into the morality play of a pram, and go for our evening stroll in the gardens. Isn't that a stroke of genius? Of course I'll pay for the party. Or

127

the firm will. At one go I'll be going back to Paris, putting my plan into action, and keeping my word. Isn't the whole idea a poem in itself, a mobile poem, a life poem, an action poem?" In his excitement he slapped me on the back.

"I thought your *Echo* days were done with."

"I have no talent for writing. You know that. My talent is for management. It'd drive them mad to be confronted with the logical end of the activity, all these fat smug Parisian pigeons standing around and sitting at cafés. They'll be incensed. They'll turn on us in a fury. We'll be in all the newspapers."

"Maybe they'd only smile? Or it could become the new fashion in prams."

"It'd be striking too near the roots for that. It'd be too close to reality for that. Reality is a great stick for beating the people. They can't stand it, we're told, but everybody appears very vague about what it is."

"It'd be closer to a farce, if you ask me, which is exactly what the woman would call it. She'd never agree to it."

"But I'd pay for it. We'd have a week in Paris as well. We'd eat in the Coupole. We'd go to the Closerie des Lilas. We'd blow it at Lipp's and the Vendôme."

"She'd never agree to it, you can be sure. That's how I got into this fucking position in the first place. She'd say it was turning the whole thing into a farce, that it wasn't natural, that it wasn't the way life should be. If she wouldn't agree to putting a nosebag on the old penis she'd hardly agree to putting the baby in the coffin." And he was quiet. He took a pickled onion from the counter, showed all his front teeth, cut it in two, ostentatiously chewed it, and then washed it down with a big swallow of brandy.

"Well, old boy, you're crusading off to London, then. You'll be in illegitimate attendance while another white hope of the human race comes squawking into the world. And in the meantime you'll forward me your artistic endeavours."

"If that's all right with you."

"Perfectly all right. Even Queen Victoria saw that the artist

128

could move at ease in all levels of society, and thereby endanger the whole social structure."

"It's very good of you."

"Forget it, old boy. If she could do nothing about it, neither I'm sure can I, though I'm a queen of sorts too. And since I can't have my Paris idea I want the Shannon written up, and written up well. I'll pay well over the odds for it. You'll need the money in London. I wouldn't mind spending a few months in London myself, watching over a future clown flashing out into the world," he said dreamily.

"You mean Mavis and the Colonel on the Shannon?"

"What else?" he almost roared. "Do you think my readers would want an account of two incompetent nincompoops like yourself and this fool of a woman? My readers want icing and sugar, not loaves of bread. And be careful not to let life in. Life for art is about as healthy as fresh air is for a deep-sea diver."

She was in a high state of excitement when we met the next evening, full of her dinner at the Hibernian with Jonathan. I couldn't resist feeling that she was having the time of her life.

"Jonathan was waiting for me in the foyer. In his pinstripe and flowing bow, silver hair, he looked extraordinarily distinguished, like an ambassador or something. The table had red roses. We had oysters, Dover sole, cheese, and we drank too much. Jonathan had an enormous cigar the waiter cut for him, with his brandy. And then, suddenly, both of us started to cry, in the middle of the full restaurant. 'It's such a pity, love, that it's not our child. We'd be married. We'd have a whole wonderful life together,' he said. 'Who'd think two years ago when I pressed you to come to London that we'd be sitting here like this. Life deals us strange cards.'

"He was wonderful. He's making everything so easy. His wife is in hospital again and he lives alone in this enormous

129

house in Kensington. And do you know what he's going to do? He's going to do up the whole basement part of the house as a separate flat, and I can live there till the child is born. He says, too, that there'll be no trouble getting me a job on one of the several magazines, that I needn't confine myself to *Waterways*, that if I can write about waterways I can write about theatres, London restaurants or parks. Once I get the hang of it it'll all be the same thing. It's like a dream come true."

"Where is he now?"

"He came to see me but he's using the visit to do some business as well. We're having a nightcap later in the hotel after he's seen his guests off. And I'm having lunch with him at the airport tomorrow just before he flies off. We're going to write the letter of resignation together."

"I can see little place for me in London in such a new setup," I ventured cautiously.

"That's what Jonathan says. He says that if we're not to be married that it doesn't make any sense being together, that we'd only get deeper and deeper involved with each other, that it'd make a separation worse."

I waited in silence, hardly daring to believe. What I'd longed for seemed to be falling like ripe fruit into my hands.

"Jonathan says that you'd be far more help to me by staying here. You could help me with money, with everything, all the help you can give now, if we're not to be married."

I felt like a badger must feel among blackthorns when someone inadvertently opens the teeth of the trap. I was afraid to go free in case by moving at all it might prove not true.

"You have a whole month to think about it. But what Jonathan says seems to make sense," I made the first cautious move, staring down in amazement at the bared teeth of the loose trap. I could go free.

"Jonathan and I wrote out the letter of resignation at the airport, in the upstairs lounge. We laughed a great deal over the words *beg* or *wish* or *desire* or *state*. And then he just dictated it straight and I took it down. Then we went and posted it. As it dropped I said, 'There goes my future. All those years with so much being contributed each year towards my marriage gratuity.' We were both too nervous for lunch, but Jonathan insisted on buying a bottle of champagne. It's strange how coincidences happen. It was his birthday. I had never known when his birthday was before. He's fifty-seven. 'To London Airport. I'll be waiting for you there. You may seem old to your young man but you look awfully young and pretty to me,' he said."

"You *are* beautiful and young."

"I sure picked a winner, didn't I?"

"We both had bad luck."

"How?"

"Everything happened too soon," I said. "We never had a chance. What did you do after you left the airport?"

"Well then, I caught myself rushing back to the bank. I'd got the morning off and then after sending in my resignation I was worried and rushing back. Are you crazy, I said to myself. You've worked for them for over twenty years, and you've got not a thing out of it, and now you're rushing back, when even if you were caught trying to burn the building it'd take at least a month to fire you. It was hard to get used to, so I turned back for home. I knew I'd find my aunt alone at home and I wanted to get the whole thing over with. It was only when I was near the house that I had second thoughts and I wished I had gone straight back to the bank from the airport.

"The kitchen door was open and she was in the garden, her rubber gloves on, at her roses. She asked me if I had a headache or something and I decided to bungle it through. 'No, Aunt Josephine, I took the day off. I've been offered a job on a magazine in London and I've resigned from the bank. Don't worry: I'm not going at once. It takes a month for the resignation to take effect and I'm sure I can withdraw it at any time before then.' You should have seen her face. 'Have you thought about the pension you'll lose?' were the first words when she found her voice. 'How will you manage all on your own in a place like London?' So the story is out—I'm going to London to seek fame and fortune."

Angrily she intercepted my glance towards her body. "No," she said. "The two per cent chance of error is gone. I practically didn't make it to the bathroom this morning. Early morning sickness."

"What do you want to do now?" I asked.

"I want to go back to your place," she said. "I know it may sound exciting, going to London—but I know, I know I'll hardly be in London before I start missing you. The fame and fortune is all a lie. It's going to be a hard summer and a longer autumn and winter. And I'll not have you. I'm going to need a lot of loving in the next month to get me through all that length of time without you."

"It seems I'm not going to London after all," I said to Maloney. We met in the bar of the Clarence. He had insisted that we start to meet regularly since I was soon going to be away for at least the most of nine months, and he had picked the Clarence as out of the way and suitably grey.

For the hot day he wore baggy flannels, an expensively ragged corduroy jacket, and his buttoned-down shirt was open enough to display a wealth of grey hair on the chest.

"A false alarm," he chortled. "Following in my own august footsteps."

"No such luck," I said.

"You're going to do a skunk, then?" he looked at me in admiration, and started to laugh, a secretive high-pitched laugh, "I always thought you were one of those priested types, a lot in the head but not much on the ground. That you'd do the decent, follow your conscience, even if it meant tearing your balls off, but apparently I was wrong," he shouted.

"No," I ignored what he'd said. "She knows this rich English-
132

man with a house in Kensington, a crazy wife, several companies. He's been an admirer of her for years. It's just poured out in the wash. He's already flown in from London and out again. They had dinner in the Hibernian, and he's taking charge of the whole business. She's going to live in the basement of his Kensington house and he's getting her a job writing for one of his magazines. Naturally he doesn't want me to go with her to London."

"Why didn't you tell me? This broad must be good looking. I thought she was just an ordinary turkey, a bit dim as to the facts of life."

"She's very good looking and this Englishman is old. I can hardly believe my luck. It's almost too good. I hope she marries him. If she'd marry him it'd take care of the whole mess in one beautiful stroke."

"I detect a disgusting note of self-congratulation," he changed. "And it won't do. It won't do at all. You've behaved stupidly, even by your own admission. You've got this woman into a frightful mess. In your conceit you refuse to marry her though she is a beauty, a far cry from your own appearance. And your bad behaviour and general situation is making us feel good. It's making us all feel very good."

"How?"

"How can you ask such a question? Your behaviour has dropped the moral averages to zero overnight. It makes some of our own reprehensible past acts practically beatific. We're disgusted with you."

"Anyhow you won't want the Shannon River thing written now."

"That's what you think. I want every word of it. And I want both history and myth respected. There are too many people up to their elbows in myth without the slightest respect for history."

"Why don't you let up?"

"Would you if you'd just lost a Paris trip and was barely consoled by looking forward to a few nice saunters round Soho

133

and found that even that was pulled out from under your feet because a friend wasn't being asked to pay his bills?"

"You're too much," I said.

"I know I am," he beamed suddenly. "I work very hard at it."

In four weeks she would go to London. Jonathan would meet her at the airport and take her to the basement flat in Kensington. In seven to eight months she would give birth to the child. It was still all that time off, time enough for something to change it back, time enough for it to never happen. Vague and fragile as that sense was, it was enough to blur the sharpness, keep it farther off.

"I'm going to need a lot of loving to get me through all that length of time in London," she said again. "And since you're always muddled as to where we'll meet," she laughed, "We'll decide the meeting places for the next four weeks tonight."

There was no point meeting in the middle of town, she'd have to be there to say her own farewells, the goodbyes being prepared for her at Amalgamated Waterways and the bank, and she wanted as much as possible to keep our lives separate from them. So on wet evenings or on evenings when there was a threat of rain we'd meet in Gaffney's bar. And if it was fine we'd meet half-way in Calderwood Avenue. She was in high energetic spirits that evening, insisting on counting the small almond and cherry trees in Calderwood. There were two hundred and forty-nine trees in the avenue. She wore a blue ribbon that was too young for her and took it off and tied it round the one hundredth and twenty-fifth tree.

"People will think we're crazy," she said as she took my arm to walk back to the room. One evening out of the four weeks we had to meet in Gaffney's but we saw the blue silk ribbon round the bole of the one hundredth and twenty-fifth almond tree so regularly that we did not notice it fade and grow ragged in the dust and sun.

There is not much difference between seeing someone every

evening who is to go to London in four weeks and going to hospital every evening to see someone who is dying, except that we can measure more accurately, and hence control it, a departure for London and imagine more easily what will happen when it's reached. And each evening as I went to meet her I did not think there was much difference (except in the quality of affection) from going in to see my aunt in the hospital and meeting at the ribboned almond tree, except my male body in its cloth covering replaced the brandy bottle in its brown parcel.

She was always on time. Walking towards her down the long avenue of cherries and almonds proved far worse than walking into my aunt's awareness down the hospital corridor during those first visits. As soon as she'd see me come her walk would change, as if a band had suddenly struck up, and she'd start to smile and wave. If I waved in answer, there'd follow an excruciating few minutes of waving, smiling, walking up to the beribboned tree.

"Right on the dot," she'd say as she kissed. I tried coming a few minutes late but as soon as she'd see me along the line of almonds she'd take off towards me waving, smiling, walking. "You're late," she'd say. "The ribbon is half-way, a symbol of equality." I started to come early, examining the parched grass around the roots of the almond tree as she came waving, smiling down the line.

"I guess that grass must be awfully interesting," she said as her high heels clicked close.

"I'm not much good at waving," I said.

"That is, I suppose, a tick-off for me. I can do nothing right."

"Why should it be? I'm just not good at it, that's all. It may well be what they call a character defect."

Once or twice we went to suburban cinemas but in good weather we cooled our thirst in pubs, walking sometimes afterwards some miles out to the sea in the lovely evenings; and always we went back to the room.

"I need all the loving I can get to see me through the months in London," it sounded as if she was working hard at getting a suntan against the winter. Her body was as sleek and beautiful as when we'd met. Morbidly I'd let my fingers trail along her stomach but there was no sign of swelling. The only pleasure was in staying outside oneself, watching the instinct that had constructed this prison suffer its own exhaustion within its walls and instead of bounding with refreshed curiosity to some new boundary of sense, having to take off its coat, and wield a painful pick. In this bright early summer weather it was always daylight when she left.

Sometimes we touched danger. "Jonathan rang today," she said, and when I didn't reply asked sharply, "Are you not curious what he had to say?"

"What did he say?"

"He said if his wife will agree to a divorce we might be married. Have you nothing to say to that?"

"I can't very well object to Jonathan marrying you."

"He says that if we got married he's willing to accept the child as his own, but that you'll have to sign over all your rights to the child. Will you do that? It means you can never lay eyes on the child again in your life," she continued angrily.

"I'll be glad to do that."

"Have you no curiosity about the child?"

"None."

"I don't know, there must be something wrong with you, something missing. I don't know whether you picked it up writing that pornography stuff or not but there's a lack of feeling that makes me feel sorry for you. Often I sincerely pity you."

"I can't do much about that," I avoided.

"O boy I sure picked a winner."

Another evening she asked, "Do you play tennis?"

"No, I've never played. Why?"

"I used to be a fairly good player. This is the first spring I haven't played though it must be five or six years since I was on the club team. Anyhow they heard I was going to London

136

and they're giving a dance and presentation. Would you like to come to the dance?"

"I think I better stay out of everything. It'd only mix things up, especially with Jonathan in it now."

"What has he got to do with you?"

"You said yourself you'd want the child to appear completely Jonathan's. And since that's the case I would like to keep out of it as much as possible. That makes sense, doesn't it?" and she was silent for a long time.

"Of course, since your rights mean nothing to you, it's no sacrifice for you to give them up," she said bitterly.

"I never pretended it was any other way," I answered.

These parties were the only nights I didn't see her, but even so they were no holiday. Hardly able to believe I was escaping so lightly, I felt I had the whole frail month in my hands, to be guided as delicately as possible towards the airport. From these functions she brought back trophies. A large clock with a scroll of names, an ornate silver tray, an ice bucket. Amalgamated Waterways gave her a cheque.

"There were speeches about my courage, how I was throwing mundane security over in order to seek fame and fortune. That I made them all seem small. If only they knew the truth," she said, and I did not answer. Even within the boundaries of the four weeks, I was aware of possibilities within myself for doing something wild and stupid. Troubled by my own confusions in meeting her at the idiotically beribboned almond tree, I started to take down books in the room, unconsciously searching for some general light, as I'd gone out for allies at the first news. It was an ungenerous attitude, but my position was hardly aristocratic. I eventually found a sentence which brought me to a sudden stop : "Everybody must feel that a man who hates any person hates that person the more for troubling him with expressions of love; or, at least, it adds to hatred the sting of disgust." I wrote it down, and kept it about my person like a scapular, as if the general expressions of the confused and covered feelings could licence and control them.

137

The last week we met at the almond tree at nine-thirty instead of eight. She was clearing out the room she'd lived in for more than twenty years and packing. She'd booked her ticket to London on an afternoon flight so that Jonathan could meet her. They'd arranged to go from the airport to the flat and then to his favourite restaurant for dinner.

"It's only fair that I pay for that ticket."

"I accept that," she said gravely. "In fact, I want you to collect it. It's booked in O'Connell Street but you can pick it up at any Aer Lingus place."

"Why have I to collect it? Why can't someone else do it, as long as I pay for it?"

"I don't know. I just want you to."

I didn't know either, unless the ticket was a sort of personal receipt she had to have for the whole bitter business.

"Did you get it yourself?" were the first words when I handed her the ticket, the words weighed with a significance out of all proportion.

"I got it my very self. The girl who wrote it out had blonde hair, blue eyes and a Mayo accent. She was very pretty."

"It's all right for you. You haven't to uproot yourself and go to London."

"I was prepared to, but I thought it was just a simple air ticket that's in question."

"Thanks," she said sharply, and thrust it in her handbag.

Between making love that night she cried, and I kept touching the verbal scapular that was part of my mind by now. As I walked her a last time down to the taxi rank at the end of Malahide Road she said, "I know that you've suffered as well as I have. We could have taken the easy way out of it and we didn't and I think we're both the better people for it."

"I don't know," I touched my scapular a last time.

"And you'll keep that promise. You'll come and see me in London."

"I'll come. That's if you want me."

138

"I'll want you," she kissed me passionately. "Whether I'll be able to afford you is the only thing in question."

When I had loved, it had been the uncertainty, the immanence of No that raised the love to fever, when teeth chattered and its own heat made the body cold : "I cannot live without her."

"I cannot live. . . ." If she'd said Yes, would not the fever have retired back into the flesh, to be absorbed in the dull blessed normal beat?

And was the note of No not higher and more clear because it was the ultimate note to all the days of love—for the good, the beautiful, the brave, the wise—no matter what brief pang of joy *their* Yes might bring?

If she had loved me that way—she who was now with child —had not that love been made desperate by my being its hopeless and still centre? Now she had the child. Was that not another Yes, a turning back within the normal beat?

I too had heard the hooves of the tribe galloping down on us. We had not kept within its laws.

I watched the clock. Her plane took off at three-forty. When the minute hand touched eight the plane taking her to London would sail heavily into the blue sky. It had flown. A cloud of dust on the road, the motor climbing the last half-mile, and then suddenly below, in a blue flash : the white houses, the masts of the tied-up fleet, the creamy haze of the sea.

As slowly as the hand had come to the eight, it as quickly raced to nine, ten. . . . It was four o'clock, and moving fast. I felt foolish in my excitement.

The whole city was restored to me, islanded in the idleness and ease of timeless Sunday mornings, church bells stroking the air and the drowning of it in wild medleys, the whole day given back to me because I had lost it.

When the red-bricked Georgian house had been converted into flats the entrance wasn't changed at all except to put in an aluminium panel of electric buttons. They'd left one laurel, the ragged lawn, three granite steps, the old roses pinned with rusted staples to the wall, a heavy black knocker; and the letters for all the flats spilled through the brass flap onto the hall floor each morning and early afternoon. There was a dull click after they'd all been pushed through. Whoever was first down put them on the half-circular glass table with iron legs under the St Brigid's cross. The nervous girl who worked on the radio was always the first one down in the morning. She must have watched for the postman from her window and left her room as soon as he'd come through the gate for she generally reached the door at the exact moment the letters were pushed through the brass flap. If he'd any delay in sorting the letters she used to have to wait in the hall, and I hated catching her apologetic, embarrassed smile whenever I'd found her waiting, the noises of the postman uncomfortably present on the other side of the door.

The letter-box became the focus of my precarious happiness, precarious because it was so fragile. When the afternoon post fell to the floor and there was no letter from London I felt released into another whole free day. When three days went by and there was still no letter I began to feel sometimes as if it had been a very vivid, bad dream. It might turn out, like the dream, not to be real, but I was still getting no work done. So I decided to secure my freedom for at least several more days by making the visit I had promised to my aunt and uncle and had been putting off for long.

I slept in my uncle's room. "I'll not get up for a while yet but why don't you put on the light," I said the first morning as I heard him fumble for the clothes he'd let drop on the floor going to bed.

"There's no need. It's just a matter of trousers and shirt," he refused.

Home on school holidays I used to sleep in this room. Early

140

in the morning I'd start to chatter with him, chattering like old starlings in the rafters my aunt had called it, and it must have been boring for him, but he'd never checked me, no more than he'd turn on the light now to find his clothes or draw the blind.

"I'll go out to the mill around quitting time," I said as I heard him pause before leaving the room.

"Whenever suits you. If I was you I wouldn't start getting up or anything for long yet. You might as well lie back and take it easy when you have the chance."

I heard steps in the hallway, the click of the lock, a car starting outside, the lock shut, my aunt's slippers shushing back up the hallway. Cyril was on his way to work. Each morning my uncle must have timed his getting up to avoid Cyril. (Say it again, say it over, people do not find it easy to face one another.) When I heard my uncle leave, I too rose. As I sleepily drew the blinds the empty tarred square met me with a shock, the row of old railwaymen's cottages beyond. There used to be a footpath to that station along the high cut-stone wall, two carriages and a van waiting to be towed to Dromod; beyond the darkness of the engine sheds, the long elephant's trunk of piping from the water tank, the maze of rails, and the three stunted fir trees. It was said they never grew because of the poison of the coal smoke though they had blackened cones that dropped between the sleepers and onto the carriage roofs. Now it was level and empty: a tarred square, the cottages, a filling station. I felt like Pirandello and his wife rolled into one, the beginning of all that's new, the continuance of everything old. What she saw, which wasn't there, seemed more real to him than what he saw, which had the disadvantage of being there. The dancehall where I had met my first love was gone. We were waltzing in the sky.

This room had not changed, and neither had the bathroom, full of the smell of oranges and pink Jaffa papers speared on a nail above the toilet roll. The stairs with the strips of bicycle tyre nailed to the edge of the steps hadn't changed, and the black-leaded Stanley—an antique now with its claw feet and running board—was used to fry rashers and egg and sausages. I ate them under the curtained spy window. My aunt used to be able to observe people in her first shop from behind that yellowed lace curtain, before she began to buy shops. Nothing had changed in the early morning except the smell of the brandy. The creamy blossoms of the elder half hid the coal shed still through the outer window out the back yard.

"I hope you don't think too hard of the brandy," to my dismay she brought the bottle out and sat with me at the breakfast table. By bringing it out so openly she was drawing me into the guilty maze.

"No, why should I?"

"It's a great relief to drink with someone in the open. Cyril and your uncle won't understand anything about it at all."

"Cyril drinks enough himself to understand," I said.

"He only drinks because he's upset. He feels I'm far too long sick now."

"He must have been upset the greater part of his life, so."

"Ah, you're all too hard on Cyril," she complained. "The world's hard enough."

"I didn't mean that," I said, "and I have nothing but praise for drink. It's like a change of country; only it'd be awful to become an old soak." What I said I believed, but there was no need to say so much. My instinct was to create room, to get out of the responsibility she had so suddenly thrust upon me. The blind instinct had run ahead of any seeing, of sympathy or fairness. I was learning to protect myself so fast now that I'd soon have a whole landscape of the moon to move around in.

"If you were like me," she laughed with a mixture of wry bitterness and pure amusement, "you'd not care what they called you, an old soak or a young soak, as long as you got relief. The country that I find myself in most of the time now, God forgive me, isn't fit for living in."

"Why don't you try the pills?"

142

"Ah, you've never taken those pills. They're not like natural pills. You can feel them spreading themselves around in you. They're killing you. That's what they're doing. After you take them you feel you're walking round in a big dead empty glove."

She poured me a glass. It was hateful in the morning, when the day was fresh, but I drank it. Later I found myself walking with her down the railway to the garden. Except for the beaten path, where the line had run, it was choked with enormous weeds, especially great pulpy thistles.

"The rails went to Scotland and the North," she said. "I heard they cut them up and sold them as posts for haysheds."

We went through a wooden gate made strong by the thin wire used to bind fruit crates, and down steps cut into the embankment. The garden was bordered by high banks on either side, covered with the same rank thistles of the railway, and below was an old hedge of whitethorn studded with several green oak and ash trees and one big sycamore. The clay was dark and loose, in neat drills : onions, carrots, parsnips, beet, peas and beans, the black and white miracle of the flower out, long green splashes of lettuce.

"It's a fine garden," I said. She'd already begun to weed.

"I do a bit every day. That way it never gets out of hand. There's no rush and push. And you can watch it for the bugs. Some of them would sweep you out of it in a day."

I weeded with her, hating the dry clay on fingers. The garden held no interest for me. I'd never watch it grow.

"That's all I ask," she drew up her back, and as I watched her I knew she'd be back in hospital before the fruits were gathered, and that it'd be the last garden she'd watch grow. "You think it'd not be much to ask. Just to get a bit better. Not to have to leave the garden—I hate to think of it running wild again—though Cyril complains it's nothing but trouble. To just go on. It doesn't seem much to ask. To let things stay as they are. To go on."

"But you will."

"Sometimes I don't know."

When I felt sure she wouldn't notice emotion in my voice I said, "There are some fine trees in the hedge."

"Yes," she said with spirit. "Your uncle made one great offer of help when I started the garden. He offered to cut down the trees."

"He would."

"I told him he'd be run if I caught him near them. But they must house a million midges. Some evenings they'd ate you alive."

She was tough. There was nothing but to salute that proud hardness with a perfect silence. She stood at the foot of the garden, under a far outriding branch of the oak, her ravished face and few wisps of hair turned away from the searching light, and she said in a voice matter-of-fact enough to be running through a tenant's contract, "I don't know. It's only after years that you get some shape on things, and then after all that you have to leave. It's comical. You want to go on and you can't."

"I think you'll be all right, that you'll get better, but there does come a time—for everybody, for us all," my own voice sounded so awkward and solemn that I felt bells should mock the still air.

"I know that," she said and we started to move slowly towards the gate. "But somehow deep down you can never feel it's going to happen to yourself. In your case somehow you feel the great exception will be made."

"If you can say that, there can't be too much wrong with you," I said.

When we went back to the house we finished the bottle of brandy. Then she said she was going to bed, before anybody could come back. She washed the glasses and put away the empty bottle before she climbed the stairs. And I drove out to the saw mill.

Neither Jim nor my uncle noticed me get out of the car and walk up to the mill. They were in the middle of a quarrel. I had watched these quarrels so often that it was like standing in front of a TV shop window and watching an old familiar movie. They stood with their backs to one another, beside two saws, both idling over; and each vigorous insult was addressed to a point high in the roof of the shed, the very farthest point from the person the insult was intended for. The intervals between the insults were lengthy. Each word seemed taken up, weighed and tested, and then the contemptuous answer would be fired furiously towards the farthest rafters. Their expressions did not change when they noticed my presence on the mound of sawdust. They dropped the quarrel with as much emotion as they might show when putting down a heavy, cumbersome tool they had grown tired using, and came towards me with outstretched hands, both smiling.

We three stood there, not talking, occasional words let drop into the silence like pebbles into still water, allowed to sink and bubble with neither more nor less attention than that given to the preceding and following silence; and when it seemed that an appropriate amount of such silence had been observed Jim walked away towards the big saw without a word.

"You seem to be using a fairly strong aftershave?" my uncle asked, having caught the smell of the brandy.

"It's brandy. I had a glass in the house with her. I don't like it very much this time of day."

"I know that," he said with an understanding patronage that irritated me. "But what'll happen to her, at the rate she's going? What'll be the end of it?"

"What'll be the end of any of us?" I was ashamed of my own sharpness when I saw him wince. Then he coughed, a cautious clearing cough, like sending exploratory noises out into the field before risking any compromising words. "You didn't run into Cyril at all?"

"No. How is he?"

"Worse. He's a pure dose. I'd move out long ago but it'd not be right with the way she is now."

Jim had started sawing. In the safety of the piercing scream, the sweet sudden scent of fresh resin, I asked, "What was yourself and Jim arguing about?"

"O that," he shook with laughter. "He took in some contract timber."

"What's that?"

"We don't do it any more except we know the people. A fella might have a few good trees he'd want sawed, to save him buying timber, and we used to give him a price. A lot of that stuff came from trees they used to plant round houses, beech mostly, and you'd never know what you'd run into, nails by the no time, handles of buckets, links of chains."

"They could be dangerous," I said.

"They'd go through you like fucking bullets except they're mostly rotten. They've been hammered in years ago and the wood has grown over them. I saw them ruin more saws than you can name," he was relaxed, holding forth.

"What's this got to do with the argument between Jim and yourself?"

"He took in a few big oaks for this fella that he knows. And I was going to use the big saws."

"Are the oaks all right?"

"Of course they are. But you have to make a stand sometime round here or you'd wind up taking orders. There's no giving of orders as it is."

"I can't see you taking orders," I said.

"You can never be too sure of that," he shook with the laughter of pure pleasure as he wiped his eyes with the back of the enormous scarred hands. "To make sure of that, you have to keep sitting upon the other fella every chance you get."

I hung about until they closed the mill, and after that it gradually grew plain that he was loathe to go into the house in case he'd meet Cyril or even possibly my aunt.

"What'll she say if we don't go in?" I asked.

"We'll ring her. We'll have our tea in the town. And we can ring her from there, from the restaurant. I'll say we have to go out to your place."

"You don't need to change or anything?"

"Not at all. Nobody cares round here. I'll just throw off these overalls."

He rung her from the restaurant. "She gave out," he reported afterwards. "But they're both there. Leave them that way. That way they're only an annoyance to themselves."

We had the usual restaurant meal, lamb chops, liver, bacon, fried tomatoes, and an egg, with a big pot of tea and plenty of brown or white bread. Afterwards we drove out to my place.

In all sorts of circuitous ways he detailed the several advantages I'd get from leaving the city and starting up the farm. "After all, the city is more a young man's place," he must have repeated several times. That, and teasing out the evening until he was certain that my aunt and Cyril were in bed, took care of the whole charming and childish evening.

I was happy there for five such days, islanded and cut off from the brass letter-box. Three letters waiting on the half-circular glass table with a London postmark were the first things I saw on entering the hallway. My island holiday was over.

Jonathan had met her at the airport. They had taken a taxi to his Kensington house. The flat was a little beauty, two rooms, a kitchen, bathroom, with all mod cons, including an automatic washing machine and drier, which would come in so useful later on. They had drinks upstairs in the lovely long reception room she had known from before. The windows were open. It was much warmer in London than in Dublin. In another few weeks, Jonathan said, they'd be able to sit out and have drinks on the lawn.

Then they took a taxi to Jonathan's favourite restaurant. The table was piled with flowers. And yet she felt depressed. She missed me dreadfully. Didn't I know how greatly I was loved, though I seemed to do my very best to avoid seeing it? But she was grateful to Jonathan. She did not know that such a genuinely selfless and good person existed in the world. If only Jonathan was me, and I was Jonathan . . . but she still believed that everything that happened was basically good, because both of us were good people. She still believed that, no matter how it seemed to other people.

She was already working on a magazine. The magazine's office was close to Covent Garden. She took a bus into the Strand and walked from there. The people all helped her and were very nice, but it was child's play compared to all the scrivening she'd done for practically nothing for poor Walter and *Waterways*. She ate such rich meals at the different restaurants with Jonathan in the evening that at lunch time she just walked around and had fruit she bought in Museum Street and a cup of coffee in a little Italian place next door to the fruit shop. The morning sickness had stopped but she was hungry all the time. I could guess what that meant. She was sure it was going to be a boy and exactly like me.

Next, she was cooking dinner for Jonathan and herself. That must remind me of something. They had avocado pear, sirloin, an endive salad, and a special dusty bottle of Burgundy Jonathan had brought up from the cellar for the occasion, several cheeses and an Armagnac to finish. Compared with what she'd been used to, her own basement kitchen was luxurious but Jonathan's kitchen made her feel more like an airline pilot than a plain cook. There were so many knobs and panels! Jonathan said she was a fine cook and Jonathan's wife had a fantastic library of cook books. Now she cooked for Jonathan and herself every evening he hadn't a meeting and they'd only go out to restaurants weekends. Jonathan had also got fantastic reports about her as a writer. Everybody on the magazine was pleased with her. Disaster was turning into a dream.

They were wise, the people on the magazine, I thought; she might become the owner's wife. There must be many who have cursed themselves for not seeing that some young secretary would one day be the wife. O most common apotheosis, the sexual : and the most common ruin : poison of the sweet mouth.

I replied gravely to these letters. There was an early heat

wave in Dublin, a stream of people passed out towards the sea in the evenings, many of them on old bicycles. My life was boring. I wasn't writing but soon I'd have to earn money. I'd been down the country. My aunt was growing worse, but fighting hard to live. If pure desire could make a person live, she would live, I wrote.

It was hot in London too, the place beginning to crowd with tourists. Jonathan hated the tourists. Even a simple stroll in Kensington Gardens on a Sunday morning turned into a tirade against the tourists. Jonathan was so funny when he got angry, with his shiny head and handlebar moustaches, so small when he shook. At times she couldn't resist pulling the moustaches. That morning they had a lovely quiet drink in a local but she didn't have alcohol any more. It didn't agree with her and anyhow it was bad for the baby. They didn't want to have a fully fledged one-week-old alcoholic on their hands.

What she couldn't get over was the number of men who'd asked her out, and one or two had even made passes. It was so sad. She wondered what they'd feel if they knew the truth. Jonathan said she looked amazing, and she did feel good, but in Dublin that sort of attention hadn't been paid to her for years. Was I not jealous at all?

She couldn't describe how grateful she was to Jonathan. She wouldn't have believed before this all happened that such a purely good person existed in the world. He'd suffered for years with his crazy wife and he'd never had what's called a normal happy life. The only snake in their Eden now was that Jonathan's wife might discharge herself from the institution and find her in the house. Since she'd come to the house she'd started to read the wife's leters. He'd asked her to. One of the forms the madness took was crazy, irrational jealousy. They could only hope and pray she'd not discharge herself.

My aunt was taken back to the hospital, this time by ambulance.

"Bad luck to it," she said when I went in to see her. "I'm here to cause you trouble once again. They talked me into giving this X-ray treatment a last try. Somehow I feel I'd be as well off in Lourdes."

"You can't talk that way. What'll happen to the garden?"

"Cyril said he'd look after it and he meant it but I also know he'll forget," she laughed. "What I did was give Peter McCabe, a brother of poor Sticks', some money. He'll look after it on the quiet."

"How is the saw mill?"

"Bad luck to the saw mill. You'd swear it was the centre of the universe. Nothing will happen to the same saw mill, and more's the pity. He couldn't even hide how pleased he was when he didn't have to drive me up."

"He's all right. I'm fond of him."

"Oh yes, he'll never be stuck for someone to stand up for him, the big haveril, as long as he has you, and if you don't watch out you'll wind up just like him, a selfish old bachelor."

I half expected her to go through motions of protest when I put down the bottle of brandy but instead she seized it like a lifeline, "God bless you. I knew you'd not forget it."

In London, all prayers were being more than answered. More and more belief in heaven grew. Even though she'd been foolish and had been left vulnerable there was someone who was looking after them up there, for she was no longer alone. Just when they were afraid Jonathan's wife would discharge herself, find her installed in the basement, and let all hell loose, what happened, but in a crazy fit, didn't she jump from the hospital window and kill herself. After all these years Jonathan was now free.

Jonathan was now pressing his proposal of marriage more fiercely and wanted to adopt the child as his own so that she and the child would inherit all that he owned. For this he demanded, and rightly demanded, that I should give up all rights, which would make us more strangers than if we'd never

150

met. If I changed my mind afterwards and attempted to approach either her or the child, I'd be arrested at once.

I could hardly believe my luck. Not only did my deep hope seem likely to be answered but to be given the force of the law to boot. At one stroke all the connection would be wiped out. It would be as if nothing had ever happened. We had held the body brute in our instinct, let the seed beat in the warm darkness, and were still free. I'd be glad to sign whatever was demanded. My own resolution stood and I felt that she'd be very foolish not to marry Jonathan. I was sorry for the poor part I had played in the sad business and wished her happiness.

I didn't hear anything for days and began to write "The Colonel and Mavis Take a Trip on the Shannon". I went in and out of the hospital with the bottle of brandy each evening like a man attending daily Mass. I started to see Maloney again.

"This woman, apparently, is to be married in London," I told him.

"This isn't right," he said. "You shouldn't get off like this. The averages should have come down instead of going up. And who is the ass who's about to bear your burden into Jerusalem?"

"He's the rich man I told you about who came from London to see her here. She's been living in the basement of his house in Kensington. He also owns newspapers."

"Nobody owns newspapers any more."

"Well, he's on boards, has shares. It may be magazines and newspapers. Already she has a job on a women's paper off the Strand."

"What's his name?"

"Jonathan."

"What's his proper name?"

"I don't know. That's all I've ever known him as."

"I could find out," he threatened.

"Why?"

"That sort of person is always useful to know. There may be a take-over. We may need to expand. You should start to cultivate him, old man, now that, if I may be so crude, you have a foot, a heartbeat, in the door."

"I don't know his name, you'll have to take my word for it. She's known him for years, probably through Amalgamated Waterways, but she's never volunteered much about him to me other than that his name is Jonathan, and I've never wanted to know more."

"Could it be Jonathan Martin?" he whistled. "He has a few small business things here. He looks like something between a walrus and a very small elephant but he certainly has the do-re-mi. If that's who's in question, she's doing more than well for herself. But why this rush of marrying? Because she's pregnant?"

"His wife has just jumped out of a window. That leaves him free after years."

"So that's it? I couldn't imagine a guy with that much power being let run round for long. He'd attract loads of broads, all mad about his moral and spiritual welfare of course. Anything that'd help them into an ocelot coat and a Rolls Royce."

"It's all due to God. God arranged for the woman to jump out the window at the right moment," I made the mistake of laughing.

"And God has arranged that you're going to write 'Mavis and the Colonel Take a Tip on the Shannon,'" he glowered when I started to laugh. "I hate cheap laughs at the Divine."

"I've started it. You'll have it in a few days."

"Good. Very good. All this, you realize, has far more interesting possibilities. But I'm a philosopher. I'm content with small morsels. A small morsel is my nugget of gold," he bared his teeth at me.

When I had no word for a long time I began to think they might be married. The last I'd heard was that she'd gone with Jonathan to his wife's cremation in Golders Green. She'd hated

152

it, the dreadful music, the coffin moving on silent gliss till it disappeared behind the flap, a poor man behind the flap, directing the coffin to the ovens. There was a floral wreath in the figure of eight on top of the coffin and they'd to hold it so that the flap didn't sweep it off.

It was the bone dust you took home after the bones were raked from the oven after it had been put in a drum they called a pulverizer. Our own custom of lowering the coffin with ropes into freshly dug graves was like a bunch of wild primroses compared to this ghoulish wreath of arum lilies. The organ especially turned the whole thing into a farce.

I wondered if they'd married in a church or a registry office, but mostly I marvelled at my luck. Other than never to have met, never to have slept together, for that fatal seed never to have swum, it could hardly have turned out better. But had they married? If they had they probably had gone on a glamorous honeymoon, a cruise perhaps. Circumstances being what they were, I could hardly expect a having-a-wonderful-time card, while each evening I went in with the brandy to the hospital, and wrote the story.

The Colonel collected Mavis outside the office and they drove in the stream of traffic out of the city. It didn't build any speed till it got past Lucan, but even then they found themselves continually shut in behind slow trucks and milk tankers.

"Ireland will soon be as jammed up as everywhere else. That's what's wonderful about the rivers and lakes. They're empty. Isn't it exciting to be spending a whole weekend away from people?" Mavis said tiredly.

"O people are all right, as long as they're well shaped," the Colonel leered. "And if they're not well shaped, by Jove, I still find them all right as long as they're willing, as long as they're not afraid. What's wonderful is being with you. To hell with the rivers and the lakes. It's the scene that's important, love, you and me, not the bloody setting."

"It's all right for you to say that. You don't work all week in a typing pool, with that bastard McKenzie blowing hot and cold."

"Why don't you take McKenzie into your rich, irresistible quim and drown him in blessedness."

"I've thought about it," Mavis yawned. "And it wouldn't work. There are some people so in love with their artificial limbs that they wouldn't throw them away if cured."

"Never mind psychology. Give us a hand. If someone is strangling you it's no use knowing that he wasn't loved by his mother."

The tiredness dropped away from Mavis, the whole week of the pool like old crumpled clothes left in the bathroom. She snuggled close to the Colonel, "They should have no gear-sticks in cars," unbuttoned his fly, drew out the already swelling tool, teasing it till it stretched rigidly towards the flickering needle on the dashboard.

He pulled his driving glove off, holding it in teeth before dropping it on top of the dashboard and let his hand trail up the long lovely stretching limbs, the warm firm smoothness of young flesh, drew the cloth down, let the finger stroke, slid the hand beneath the cheeks, closing it gently on the hair and soft skin, "I'm holding the whole world in my hand," he said. Shyly they caught one another's eyes in the driving mirror and smiled with the faintest vague plea of apology and drew tighter. "Being so feathered with those wonderful plucking fingers, holding the centre of the world in my hand, I start to find the grey arse of that milk tanker I've been trying to pass for the last ten minutes growing beautiful. It's never a change we need. What we need is to hold the familiar eternally in love's light."

"Never mind your psychology," she laughed. "And don't get carried away and drive up that milk tank. Metal is not to be confused with soft flesh. It's a harsh grave."

"Everything is riding high," he said, and seeing a clear stretch of road, he drew out, pressing remorselessly down

154

on the accelerator, the powerful engine taking up with a roar.

She leaned her head closer, so that the blonde tresses brushed the foreskin, and then she took the helmet in soft lips and started to caress and draw.

The tanker seemed to stand still, the long line of traffic, and swelling in her hands—cunning young hands—the sperm beat out towards the climbing needle behind the lighted glass, the whole glass milked over by the time the car pulled in ahead of the line of traffic, and the needle fell back to a steady seventy. After the sudden race of speed, the car seemed to stand still, rocked by a light wind and tide, while gently his ungloved hand stroked till rising above the gearstick, fingers gripping the top of the dashboard, her lips going low to touch the sperm on the glass, she came with a cry that seemed to catch at something passing through the air. She tidied up what had been undone, stretching back in delicious tiredness and warmth as the car rolled on at seventy. "I've been waiting all day for that," the Colonel said. "Getting it off on the road like that is like having a trout in the bag after the first cast. It's like being in the army while there's no war. You're doing your duty while just lazing about."

"I've a feeling it's going to be a wonderful, wonderful weekend. And it's already started."

After Longford, a great walled estate with old woods stretched away to the left and children from a tinker encampment threw a stone that grazed the windscreen. In the distance, between rows of poplars, the steel strip of the Shannon began to flash.

"There it is. And there's the bar on the left. The Shannon Pot."

"Charles said he'd have us met there if he couldn't be there himself."

The bar was empty. A large pike in a lighted glass case, its jaws open to display the rows of teeth, was the only hint

155

of a connection with water. A man in a well-cut worsted suit broke off his conversation with the barman and came towards them to enquire, "Would you be the people from Dublin?" and shook hands in the old courtly way. "Mr Smith asked me to give you his apologies. He was called away to England on a sudden bit of business. He hopes to get back before you leave, but if he doesn't he'll write. And he asked me to see that you lack for nothing."

"That's very kind of old Charles," the Colonel said. "What'll you have?"

"Mr Smith left orders that everything had to be on the house. You'll not be let buy a drink to save your life," he said truculently, and introduced them to the barman, a young man in shirtsleeves. They all decided on hot whiskeys with cloves and lemon. They'd hardly touched their glasses when another round appeared, and then another.

"We'd better see the boat," the Colonel had to protest.

"No hurry at all," Michael waved his arm. "The man that made time made plenty of it."

"We better see the boat," the Colonel insisted. "That is, while we're able to see anything at all."

"It's just across the road. There's nothing to it," he said with poor grace, but led them out.

It was a large white boat with several berths, a fridge, gas stove, central heating and a hi-fi system. The Shannon, dark and swollen, raced past its sides. Night was starting to fall.

"There's nothing to these boats," he said and switched on the engine. It purred like a good car, the Fibreglass not vibrating at all once it was running. "And there's the gears —neutral, forward, neutral, reverse. There's the anchor. And that's the story. They're as simple as a child's toy. And still you'd grow horses' ears with some of the things people manage to do to them. They crash them into bridges, get stuck in mudbanks, hit navigation signs, foul the propeller up with nylons, fall overboard. I'll tell you something for nothing : anything that can be done your human being will do it. One thing you have to give to the Germans though is that they leave the boats shining. They spend the whole of the last day scrubbing up. But do you think your Irishman would scrub up? Not to save his life. Your Irishman is a pig."

Because of his solid, handsome appearance, his saintly silver hair, it'd be difficult to tell that he was as drunk as he was except for the wild speech. When Mavis opened the fridge she gave a little cry. It was full of wine, smoked salmon, tinned caviar, steak, cheese. There were all kinds of spirits and liqueurs in a cabin beside it.

"It's very like old Charles not to do anything by half," the Colonel acknowledged.

"Mr Smith wanted everything to be right for yous. Mr Smith is a gentleman," Michael chorused.

When the Colonel wiped the misted port window clear, the gleam of the water was barely discernible in the last light.

"I don't suppose we'll make Carrick tonight," the Colonel said. "I was looking forward to a few tender loins tonight, including your dear own," the Colonel pinched. "But I suppose we'd better be sensible and inspect it in daylight instead."

"We'll have a drink," Michael said and proprietorially got whiskey and glasses out.

"No more than a taste," Mavis laughed as she withdrew a glass. "I just need the faintest aphrodisiac."

"Like Napoleon," the Colonel said. "Do you ever feel like an aphrodisiac, Michael?"

"To tell you the truth, I never sooner one drink more than another. Just whatever gives me the injection."

"You get on well with old Charles?" the Colonel asked as they drank. "He's a nice man."

"A gentleman. Mr Smith is a gentleman. No other way to put it. The English are a great people, pure innocent. But your Irishman's a huar. The huar'd fleece you and boast

157

about it to your face. Your Irishman is still in an emerging form of life."

"Did you grow up close to here?"

"A mile or two down the road, a few mangy acres. The galvanized shack is still standing. I still hang out there for the summer, the hay and that, it does for the summer. In the winter I live on one or other of the boats. It's in the winter we do up the boats."

"Do you do any farming?"

"Well, I wouldn't go as far as to call it that. I run a few steers on it."

"Who looks after them when you're on the boats?"

"A neighbour. I let him graze a few of his own on it that keeps him happy. That's been going on since my poor father and mother died, God rest them. Before the boats started I used to work here and there at carpentry. I never wanted to depend on the land. Depending on the land is a terrible hardship. I saw it all," and he filled his glass again to the brim, trying to press more on the Colonel and Mavis.

"No," Mavis stretched full length in the cabin. "I'm beginning to feel . . . If I drink any more I'll be out of commission," she laughed.

For a moment Michael seemed alarmed but with a swig of the whiskey his old jauntiness returned.

"Have you ever gone in for the girls, Michael?" the Colonel slapped him on the knee.

"Not in any serious way. I stick to this," he raised his glass triumphantly. "It's all right for the rich. But my generation, seeing the hardship our parents had to go through, decided to stay clear. Maybe we were as well off. Anyhow we hadn't the worry."

"No wonder the country is in such a poor state, but privately we're beginning not to be able to contain ourselves. But there's enough for everybody. You don't mind, Mavis? We don't want to sit down to meat—without offering our guest some."

"Not in the least. I was going to suggest it myself. He's strong, he's healthy, he's handsome. What more can a woman ask?" and she stretched her long lovely limbs, the thighs gleaming bare all the way into the darkness.

"I was beginning to fancy Michael myself. Rough sacking can give a great thrill after silk."

The Colonel started to unbutton the blouse slowly, letting the rich soft young breasts swing free; and he turned to Michael, "Forgive the liberty. Of course you'll be the first, old chap."

Finishing his whiskey, and rising in slow righteous anger, Michael said, "I'm getting out. You're nothing but a pair of fucking huars. I don't know which of ye is the worse, the young huar, or you, you old bald fool that should know better."

"Don't let him go," Mavis shouted at the insult. "We'll teach him."

Michael swung at the Colonel, who gripped him easily at the elbow, held him as he went down, where he struggled until the Colonel hit him, and he went still.

"In spite of all that drinking he's as strong as a horse, but you can't beat the old commando training."

"He's not hurt, is he?"

"He'll come through in a few minutes. I just gave him the one-two. He'll probably have a headache for a while."

"Tie him. Tie him and strip him. We'll give him an eyeful when he comes to."

They both undressed him, Mavis gripping the limp penis before letting it fall back. "O I'm glad he didn't join. It'd be worse than Lough Derg to have to fuck with him. He mustn't have washed since he last went to Bundoran and that must be twenty years before. To hell with him, but we'll still give him an eyeful."

They tied him with the sheets.

"Shall I bugger him? I rather like the dirt."

"Hold it. I'll take all of it after that. An old boy like that,

159

drinking all round the country, laughing at women, boasting he'd escaped—escaped from what?—wait till he comes to, we'll give him something to see."

Her fingers fluttered toward her true and trusty friend. The Colonel strained above her, bent to kiss her lips, touch the small thumbs of the breasts, and then went beneath the shaved armpits. They waited till they heard a stir. His eyes were open. "Let me out," Michael shouted, and they laughed as they watched his futile struggle on the floor. "See this." And they forgot him.

He lifted up her buttocks and drew down a pillow beneath, feasting on the soft raised mound, the pink of the inside lips under the hair. When she put her arms round his shoulders the stiff pink nipples were pulled up like thumbs, and he stooped and took them, turn and turn about in his teeth, and drew them up till she moaned. Slowly he opened the lips in the soft mound on the pillows, smeared them in their own juice, and slowly moved the helmet up and down in the shallows of the mound. As he pulled up the nipples in his teeth, moving slowly on the pillow between the thighs now thrown wide, she cried, "Harder, hurt me do anything you want with me, I'm crazy for it." She moaned as she felt him go deeper within her, swollen and sliding on the oil seeping out from the walls. "O Jesus," she cried as she felt it searching deeper within her, driving faster and faster. "Fuck me, fuck me, O Jesus," he felt her nails dig into his back as the hot seed spurted deliciously free, beating into her. And when they were quiet he said, "You must let me," and his bald head went between her thighs on the pillow, his rough tongue parting the lips to lap at the juices and then to tease the clitoris till she started to go crazy again.

"Wait," she said. "We've forgotten our friend on the floor. Is he snoring?"

"The blackguard," the Colonel shouted. "Did you ever see such an unholy erection?"

"It's huge."

160

Mavis took him in her soft hands while Michael turned away and moaned, "You're lucky we're kind," she said. "We could have left you like this forever," and she bent her hot body, drawing until he started to thrust towards her. "It's like milking an old bull." The spunk started to beat, and he cried as it fell, throb after throb, beating out, years of waste.

"We may have started something we can't stop. He may rampage the countryside now."

"What will we do with him?"

"I have something to give him," the Colonel put a pill in the whiskey and forced him to drink. They waited till he was snoring, untied him, dressed him, carried him out of the place, and placed him in the shelter of the boat-house, leaving the unfinished bottle of whiskey by his side.

"He'll wake in about half an hour. He'll be all right."

"What do you think he'll do when he wakes?"

"He'll do nothing. He'll think he was dreaming. Doesn't the whole country look as if it's wetdreaming its life away. He'll want to be no exception. He's a prime example of your true, conforming citizen."

I drove them up through the white mist over the river in the morning, half-remembered cattle and tree trunks and half branches on the ghostly banks. There were two flaxen-haired boys and a willow of a girl in from the country at the Bush Hotel. They took the girl up the river with them to the village, and left her with the fat man. "I could sleep for a month," the fat man said, he'd go back to Carrick that evening on a paper run. It had been easy, the old technique, morsel leading to juicy morsel, to lying down to several solid meals.

They went alone through the lake, the beauty of the glass wall of water touching Mavis. "It'd be nice to have a summer place on the hill up there overlooking the Weir."

"Yes, but you'd get tired. There's nothing more tiring than so-called beauty. It saps energy because it's an idea. You'd never know what you'd pick up off the boats. And we'd have

161

the insurance of ourselves if the fishing turned out to be poor," he put his arm round her shoulders as they went through the locks and kissed.

As I brought them naked into one another's arms a last time —"straight and affectionate"—the boat at anchor in the arms of the wooded bay, I felt sick enough to want to turn away from what I saw, to shout at them to stop. The old plays were not wrong: there are single moments of weakness when our whole life can be changed to nightmare, set in a sweet flutter so faint that we are uncertain if it touched us at all in passing; but already we had fallen. I remembered how grateful the two of us had been the next day for the boat after that cursed night. The business of having to take it back down the river had kept us from getting on each other's nerves. And now Maloney had his story.

I had a second drink while waiting for him to finish reading in the Elbow. He read it standing at the counter. He didn't touch his drink but stayed completely silent till he'd finished.

"It doesn't quite phosphoresce with your usual glow, but it's all right. We'll publish it. Anyhow the Shannon makes a change from Madagascar. You're a younger version of the Colonel of course?"

"Whatever you think."

"And your lady in London is a vintage Mavis? Did she pull you off against the dashboard of the company Beetle on your way down? I liked that. It was one of the better touches."

"No. She didn't. I wish she had. It would have been safer on the dashboard."

"Your yokel who introduced you to the boats sounds authentic. He couldn't have been invented. He's the very heart and soul in person of my dear friends, the plain people of Ireland. You'll please answer me that. Was he invented or drawn from life?"

"He can be found any day round Roosky."

"Thanks. I could tell. He was treated a bit harshly, but I'm glad to see our pair were kind. In Merriman's effort it was

162

done with less kindness but very much more gusto. Anyhow we're not in that untranslatable league. The boat was real?"

"Yes. It was a boat like that, and the morning was misty."

"The willow of a girl at the Bush is much more down our readers' usual line. Except they'll be disappointed you didn't follow up the fat man on his paper run. Licked lips must have gone dry. But the accident or miracle of life did take place while the boat was stationary. As you put it, in the arms of the bay?"

"Yes. That's your pound of flesh. That's where I think it happened. Now why don't you let go?"

"Because I find it very in-ter-est-ing. I can see how you've fallen between two schools. You should have written it as plain biography, with copious, boring footnotes. That way no one would doubt you. No one has the faintest idea as to why we exist but everybody is mad for every sort of info about other existences. That way they can enjoy their own—safely. You can't beat life for that sort of thing. They get someone else to do their living and their dying for them, there's no way they have to do it for themselves. And the first thing you have to convince them of is that it *happened*. Then you can tell them anything. Contrary to the sceptical view, your human being is mad to believe, to be convinced, especially that everything is going to turn out well in the end."

"O for God's sake, I didn't write the bloody thing to furnish a text for a lecture."

"You need a lecture. You've got off scot-free. This big sugar-daddy is taking on your growing burden. You've sullied the Shannon and you're still out there laughing, back at square one, ready to start all over again. You need a lecture all right. You need several lectures," he concluded.

The sense of getting off free was short-lived, dispelled by a short, plain note the next morning. No honeymoon had taken place.

163

"I am not going to be married, which—going by the tone of your last letter—can, I know, be little relief to you. I could not bring myself to marry Jonathan. Since I couldn't, it was only proper that I move from his house and give up the job on the magazine, which, I found, wasn't really a job at all, but something he created for me.

"I have found a cheap flat in North London and I'll have no difficulty finding another job, nothing glamorous, some obscure place that will see out the remaining time. I have money and you are not to worry in any way. I'll write you a long account as soon as I am completely settled. Jonathan's conduct in all this was exemplary. He put no pressure of any kind on me other than to marry him but once I knew I couldn't bring myself to do it I couldn't go on staying in his house or keep the job.

"You can imagine what a few weeks these have been and you'll never know how greatly loved you are. I don't know, but when it came to the crunch I just couldn't imagine holding Jonathan in my arms after your dear lovely self, and the idea just became increasingly funny. But, boy, I didn't feel like laughing at all when he turned up with this other woman. I knew it was crazy but I just felt hopping mad."

I was dismayed and furious and downhearted.

"You'll be glad to learn I don't need lectures now. This woman isn't marrying," I informed Maloney.

"I'm delighted," he crowed.

"Why?"

"It lets you off too easily of course. Too soft an umbrella. If she'd married him, you'd have been two-nil up on the night. Now it's even-steven. You're right out there in the firing line once more. I thought the game was closed. Now it's an on-going thing again. It's interesting. It's getting very interesting."

I bought a round of drinks. He wasn't able to contain his curiosity for long. "Why did this lady throw up the chance of fortune and respectability? Or did she just dally with it in her lap too long?"

"I don't see what's so funny about it," I said, and he went into convulsions.

"Give us some water to dilute this," he said to the barman when he'd recovered.

"Why?" he pressed. "Why didn't she marry her tycoon? She might have done us all a good turn."

"It's a sore point. Apparently she was so taken with my physique that the idea of doing it with this Englishman wasn't entertainable. It was just funny."

"A good definition of the funny, if I may say so. Tension set off by the realization of the difference between what should be possible and what is in fact impossible. The idea of seeing one take place in the other."

I stayed silent. There was no stopping him now.

"Our national poet was shrewder in sexual and other matters than most people give him credit for. 'Isn't it amazing,' he once intoned, 'the survival of the virginity of the soul in spite of sexual intercourse.' This bird may have opened up her oyster to you, but she's no Moll Flanders. Like our friend Yeats she's more of a spiritualist. She believes in the continuing virginity of the individual, in spite of all the evidence around to the contrary. Yes," he said, "I'll have another look at our Shannon story. Knowing that real people are involved gives the spice of pornography a very satisfying solidity. It might even phosphoresce a little more this time."

In a long letter she described how the idyll with Jonathan ended.

They'd been very happy for some days after the cremation. She'd cooked dinner most evenings upstairs and they'd stayed at home, sometimes going for a short stroll in the area before separating for the night.

" 'We're going out tonight,' he'd warned me mysteriously

165

that morning, and it was to his favourite restaurant we went, the red roses as usual on the table. He was in wonderful spirits, joking with the waiters, and he ordered champagne.

" 'No, my dear. It's not my birthday and I was never one for beating round the bush. As you know I've been in love with you for years but it took your sad business to bring us together. You always said you couldn't marry me while my wife was alive because of your Catholic faith. The other business— Gwen's death—has left me free after all these years. If you haven't already guessed it, I'm asking you to marry me.'

" 'When?'

" 'Now if possible. Perhaps not right now or even tomorrow but very soon, soon as we can get a licence.'

" 'We'll have to wait.'

" 'No, dear. We don't have to go through the church cere- mony now if that doesn't suit you but we'll wait for the child as man and wife, living together. The child will be brought up as if it were our child.'

" 'I'll have to think about this.'

" 'You have a few days, a week, no more than a week. I hope though you'll make up your mind before the week. You see, my love, I'm fifty-eight. I have no illusions and even less time. At most I have twelve years, ten, eight, maybe even less. Foolish or not, I want to spend those years as a happy, normal married man. I don't expect to be given happiness but I'm prepared to work at it. And I know we can make a success, with luck maybe a great success.' I was right up against it. I was very fond of Jonathan, but somehow I never thought of sleeping with him, of waking up with those funny handlebars every morning. And what clinched it, if it needed clinching, was that I could no more give up hope of seeing you again than giving up my own life, which I'd have had to do, if I'd married Jonathan.

"He was very nice when I told him that I couldn't, and then the very next Sunday he brought a tall Englishwoman, closer to his age than mine, and I saw he was behaving exactly

166

towards her as he used to me; and there was no doubt but that she intended to marry him.

"I moved out at once. The place I found is in a tradesmen's terrace, a house close to a football ground, and I've the upstairs, two rooms, a small kitchen.

"I've got a job, much like the job I had in the bank, if anything less glamorous, a firm that hires out scaffolding and ladders to small builders, and it's only ten minutes on the bus, a half-hour's walk from the flat.

"And now, after all this, I want to see you, to see you in London, to feast my eyes on you, my love, come soon."

I wrote that I was sorry she didn't take Jonathan's offer but that was her business. My mind hadn't changed and wouldn't change, so that in practical terms she had to leave me out of all considerations of her life, except to lend her what help I could throughout the pregnancy. I'd go to London to see her but only to see if I could be of any help and to keep a promise. It sounded a priggish letter when I read it through but I sent it.

My aunt had grown dependent on the brandy, and I gave her warnings that I'd be away in London for some days. I was worried about what would happen if she couldn't get her daily portion of oblivion.

"Will you be all right?" I asked for the umpteenth time when I went in to see her the evening before I was to leave for London, and when she was as vague as ever I pressed, "You know you don't have to worry about me. I know you only take the brandy for the pain. If you need some, how will you manage while I'm away?"

For a moment she bridled at the question but then she said, "God bless you for asking. There's a man comes round the ward in the morning with newspapers and fruit and that. If I want it, he gets it for me," and with that she drew a big wad of notes from beneath her pillow and handed them to me.

"What's that for?" I asked in amazement.

"You're going to London, aren't you? You'll need money in London."

"But I've enough money."

"I know but all that brandy you've brought me in for so long doesn't grow on the bushes. I just want you to know I know that. Take it. If you don't need it, spend it for me."

I took it, and little thought I'd see my aunt again before I got back from London.

I got the bus into O'Connell Street from the hospital. There, I went to the Elbow to see if I'd meet up with Maloney. He wasn't there nor was there anybody from the paper. I had a slow pint of beer at the counter and then went back into O'Connell Street to mix with the jostling crowds in the summer evening.

The next day I'd take the boat to London to see her. A crowd of girls, their little flounces of laughter brushing out to the sharp clatter of high heels, got out of a taxi and went in through the swing doors towards the dancehall where we'd met. I started to follow them, not singling any out, just following their singing excitement. I fell in behind them in the queue, not caring to follow their speech too precisely, some words falling about pilots in Dublin Airport, knowing it would drag them down to some uncommon commonplace. I bought a ticket after they had left the window, one girl paying for the whole bevy. The pale red *House Full* placard was on its easel but faced to the wall. The ex-boxer in evening dress tore the ticket in two at the head of the stairs, searching our faces as he handed us one half of the ticket back, sticking the half he kept on a piece of wire, his handsome battered face expressionless.

I got a beer and sat at one of the tables, watching trousered and nyloned legs swish past the four steps. When it was no longer possible to see the dance floor I finished the beer and pushed my way through, the men crowding together at the top of the steps.

168

There was an interval between dances. The women were away to the left, standing between the tables off the floor, some sitting farther back. One whole corner was crowded, spilling on to the floor, blazing with skin and colourful cloth and glittering bits of metal and glass, the best stand in the market. She'd blazed there a few months before and I'd walked towards her and asked her to dance. Now she was in London. All that waste, too wasteful to each, a pall of sadness.

A waltz was called. I'd to move farther in off the floor, to the strip of carpet along the entrances, as the men around me crossed to the women. Soon I found myself standing alone on the floor. I stood there in the fascination of watching bodies, a miracle of shape in a profusion of different shapes and colours and still all the same shape, and all in the tawdriness and splendour of the self and many; I stood there as one might stand watching light on water, but it was more amazing.

The dance ended. Some of the dancers paired off. Others returned to their single places. Another dance was called, a slow foxtrot, a ladies' choice, and suddenly a dark swarthy girl was standing in front of me and said, "Cheer up!"

I followed her onto the floor saying, "I didn't think I looked that miserable; in fact I was having a good time," when I suddenly saw that the girl I was about to dance with was the black-haired nurse from the hospital.

"You looked as if you were thinking," she said. "Everybody looks miserable when they are thinking. Did you not see me?"

"No. I only recognized you just now."

"You see, you weren't paying attention. If you were paying attention you'd have seen me. Well, here we are at last."

"I wanted to ask you out."

"Well, why didn't you?"

"It's not easy, with people there. I was in the hospital this evening. I've been in most evenings in the last weeks. And I haven't seen you."

"I work another ward now."

She danced with easy freedom, ripe and slack, but soon the

169

floor was so crowded that we had to stand, just moving our bodies to the music. Whenever our eyes met she laughed. She had on a blue dress of shiny material and her shoulders were bare. I could feel her thighs against mine as we moved to the music and the bones between the thighs. Her whole body was soft and free, open.

"Will you come for a drink with me?"

"You don't have to invite me for a drink because I used to nurse your aunt."

"I know that."

"Or because I asked you to dance," she laughed.

"Not for that either," I said and our lips met, she sealing the acceptance by closing her eyes and moving her lips over and back on mine. I put both arms round her and drew her closer. I stumbled as we moved off the floor but her arm held me. Arm in arm we went down to the bar and the waiter got us a window table.

"Here's to your health," the toast held a twisted echo of another not so long ago evening. A taunt, a warning.

"And to yours," she touched my glass.

Below, in the orange light of the street, the small dark figures hurried. The cars streamed past. Beyond was the bridge and the faint black glitter of the Liffey.

She'd grown up on a farm outside Monasterevin, an only girl with eight brothers. She'd never been treated differently from the boys, being let drive the tractor, work the milking machines, fight and kick football with them in the river meadow, two uprights crossed with fishing twine.

"Maybe that's why my aunt thinks you're a bit of a wildcap."

"Does she think of me that way?" she was taken aback by the careless springing of this picture of herself in another's eyes.

"Just a remark I happened to remember. Apparently, one day you danced in the ward."

"Maybe it is because of having grown up with boys that I'm such a poor hypocrite. I can't stand women who are lady-

170

like and fragile, never sniffing at a fact of life, while they'd carve you up in small pieces without batting an eyelid."

"I don't know, hypocrisy has its place. You can only do without it at your peril."

"Well to hell with it, then," she laughed.

We danced body to body in the dark huddle of bodies, enmeshed in their own blood heat and moving slowly to the dull beat across the crammed floor. My hands went over the shimmer of the dress, sleek as a second skin. Now and again we kissed. In a sudden jolt against her the roused seed started to pulse. I looked at her face to see if she showed any signs of noticing but the eyes were closed against my shoulder, the body moving slowly to the music in its own drugged sleep.

"Will I be able to leave you home?"

"All the buses to the hospital will have gone already."

"We'll get a taxi."

"It's nice to have money." she smiled. "I'm just qualified one year now."

"That must leave you not much more than twenty."

"No. I had to repeat a couple of the exams. I'm twenty-three."

"It seems very young to me. I'm thirty."

"Thirty is a good age for a man."

She had on a herring-bone coat with a grey fur collar when she came from the cloakroom. She took my hand as we went down the stairs. There were several taxis drawn up for the people coming out of the dancehall, and we got into the fifth or sixth. The night was warm and there was a full moon above O'Connell Street.

"St Mark's Hospital," I said and she added, "The nurses' home, in past the hospital. At the back."

"Picked up a fare outside the Metropole," he said into the crackle of his radio. "Going to the nurses' home of St Mark's Hospital."

"Will you be on all night?" I asked the driver when he put the receiver down.

171

"I don't come off till five," he said.

She leaned towards me and I slipped my hand across her shoulder and began to fondle her breasts. The cool night air came in the taxi's open window.

"Do you think will my aunt live long?" even as I said the words they sounded incongruous, and I felt her go tense.

"She'll hardly get better now. Hardly anybody in there gets better. They get respites. That's all. The ward she's in is terminal though she doesn't know that."

"I'm sorry for asking. It slipped out."

"I don't mind. That's the depressing part of a cancer hospital. No one really gets better in our hospital. Even the wards not classed terminal are. You begin to feel it's your fault. I'll look for another place as soon as I have my year done."

"That hospital is one place to avoid at all cost. Two of my pals went in there. They're both dead," the driver showed us he'd been listening.

"I suppose all hospitals are places to stay out of," I said to break the uneasy silence.

"If you're well," he said. "But you're more than glad of them once you're sick enough."

The taxi turned in the hospital gates, went past her window, the moonlight pale on the concrete framing the dark squares of glass. The wheel had many sections. She had reached that turn where she'd to lie beneath the window, stupefied by brandy and pain, dulling the sounds of the whole wheel of her life staggering to a stop. I was going past that same window in a taxi, a young woman by my side, my hand on her warm breast. I shivered as I thought how one day my wheel would turn into her section, and I would lie beneath that window while a man and woman as we were now went past into the young excitement of a life that might seem without end in this light of the moon.

An old sweet scent rushed through the taxi window as soon as we passed beyond the hospital, so familiar that I started, and yet I could not place or find its name, it so surrounded the

172

summers of my life, lay everywhere round my feet; not wood-bine, not mint, not wild rose. . . .

"They were cutting it today. I was on night duty last night and was trying to get to sleep but couldn't with the mower rattling past the window," she gave the name. Of course, it was hay.

"It'd remind you of the country," the driver added as he turned in a half circle in front of a big building set in trees, and stopped.

It was new-cut meadow turning to hay, and when we got out on the tarmac, long fallen rows stretched and turned palely everywhere between the white hospital and home.

"Don't be so quiet," she tousled my hair as we went in.

I followed her through a hall and down a corridor. The first room she went into sounded empty but as soon as she pressed the light switch a dishevelled couple sat bolt upright on a sofa to face our eyes. I could feel her low chuckle as she said, "Sorry," and put the room again into darkness. The same thing happened at the second door she tried. The third room was empty, a large room with coffee tables strewn with news-papers and magazines, several armchairs and sofas and a big television set.

"We'll leave the light on," she said. "That way we run less risk of being bothered."

We sat on a tasselled grey sofa facing the blank TV set, our backs partly turned to the door. When we started to kiss and play she put no restraint on my hands, and when I put fingers beneath the elastic she raised her back for me to draw it down, moved her knees sideways, and her feet were already out of her shoes. There was a rug on the arm of the sofa that she reached for and spread over us.

We heard doors of other rooms being tried from time to time, the sound of the light switch go on and off. The same footsteps would pause outside our door but did not come in. Only once was the door opened a foot or so and as quickly closed.

"Have you brothers and sisters?" she asked.

173

"No."

"Would you like to be married?" her directness took me by surprise.

"I suppose I would but I don't know. Would you?" I was surprised and unsure what she meant.

"Of course I would. To have my own husband and child and house and garden and saucepans and pets. All that."

"Why are you so sure?"

"It's far more fun, isn't it?"

"What if you found yourself married to a boring man?"

"I wouldn't marry a boring man. And I don't find all that many men are boring. Usually the very attractive ones are married, but that's a different thing. It's women I find who are mostly boring and small and spiteful."

"What would you do if you found yourself pregnant?" I asked tensely.

"You mean if I weren't married?"

"Yes."

"I'd want to get married."

"And if the man was already married or wouldn't marry you for some reason."

"I'd throw myself in the Liffey," she drew herself up in unfeigned alarm. "What are you laughing at?"

"You wouldn't. You're too young and healthy. And beautifully normal. Anyhow the man would be sure to marry you. I'd want to marry you."

Suddenly she pinned my shoulders to the sofa and we started to roll. She was unusually swift and strong, "I give up," I laughed, and then she loosed herself again to my hands. Afterwards she said suddenly, "Would you like to see your aunt?"

"Why?"

"The nurse on night duty on the ward is a friend. It might be fun to walk across the meadow to see her."

"But what would my aunt say if she saw me there?"

"She'll not see you. The lights'll all be off. You've come often

174

enough in to see her in the day but I'm sure you never thought you'd be in to see her in the middle of the night with a wild nurse," she drew me by the hand.

A heavy summer's dew lay on the fallen swards and our shoes left bright tracks across the meadow. The grey of day was beginning to be mixed with the moonlight, but the sweet fragrance of the new hay was everywhere. She searched among a bunch of keys after we'd crossed the meadow and opened a door down concrete steps between bare tubular steel railings, "It's the back way," she whispered, "where the laundry and that comes out."

We climbed bare concrete stairs and went through swing doors. Suddenly we were in a long hall with beds on either side. I asked her if it was the ward and she nodded. I hadn't recognized it, always having come to it from the other side. The ward was in darkness, except for the lines of moonlight, and the blue light beside the night nurse sitting behind the glass at the other end. My heart was beating as I counted the beds from the other end to discover where my aunt was lying. As I drew near to that bed I stopped and caught her.

"She may see us."

"No. Even if she were awake she'd think it was a change of nurses."

"I'm not going any further." I could feel my heart pounding. "You go on to your friend. I'll just stay here."

In the dim light, I stood and listened to the far roar of the night traffic through the city. I thought I heard a moan or few words of prayer in the night but could not be certain because of my pounding heart. All were women in this ward and they all had cancer. It was like being in the middle of a maternity ward in the night, and all those women were waiting to give birth, to their own death. I counted the beds again to the right of the door. Her bed must be the bed two beds away. I searched for the heap of bed clothes. I thought I saw them move. People have a second sense? What if she sensed me there? The two girls were smiling in the blue light behind the glass and

175

beckoning me forward. They were like what, like roses, I did not know, among pain, ignorant of all pain, like girls, like blue roses. They sank into chairs, laughing as I shook my head. When they started to call me again, still laughing, I turned away, and did not turn back till I heard them come towards me. I felt like kissing the other girl instead of shaking her hand, kissing them both, laughing and crying. Almost not knowing what I was doing, I followed her out into the night, and there was the sharp sound of the lock turning.

"Bridie was delighted to see us. It broke up the night for her. Often you'd long for an emergency at night though it'd mean more work. The night goes quicker then. You should have come into the office. The office is soundproof and Bridie wanted to meet you."

"I was afraid."

"You never thought you'd be coming in to see your aunt in the middle of the night, did you?" she laughed roguishly and I seized her in a long kiss, her body almost completely naked beneath the dress. When I released her she picked up two big fistfuls of hay and putting them up to her face pretended to be advancing slowly on me from behind a barrier of hay. When she was very close, with a sudden movement, she piled the hay all over my hair and face, and started to run. I clawed the hay free and as soon as I caught her we both went down into the wet grass. I could single out stale sweat now and perfume and ammonia smells mixed with scent of the new hay. When we rolled over and lay still on the ground it was amazing to see the moon so large and still, becalmed above the trees and out in the depths of the sky. We rose without a word and went in.

She went straight ahead after going through the door of the home, this time down a narrow straight corridor. She opened a door very quietly, and we were more in a cell than a room, white walls, a radiator, a narrow bed, a dressing table and wardrobe, and on the wall above the head of the bed a plain black crucifix.

176

"This is my room," she whispered and put her fingers to her lips. "The walls are paper thin."

There were photos of football teams on the dressing table and she lifted them, pointing out several players, "My brothers." More than half the players in one of the photos seemed to be her brothers. I lifted another photo, that of a handsome grey-haired man and herself, both in evening dress.

"He's very handsome. Is he your father?"

"No," she laughed. "He's the married man."

"Let me stay a half-hour. Let me hold you in my arms."

"The walls are worse than paper."

"I'll be quieter than if you were here on your own."

"But it's practically morning."

"I don't care. I promise to go in half an hour," and with a smile and almost resignedly she turned off the light.

The curtain wasn't drawn and I held her when she'd slipped out of her clothes to caress and worship her body in the soft yellow light. She was soft and amazingly beautiful, yet rugged as a young animal. I followed her as quietly as I'd promised into the narrow bed, and hardly daring to breathe held her in my arms.

This body was the shelter of the self. Like all walls and shelters it would age and break and let the enemy in. But holding it now was like holding glory, and having held it once was to hold it—no matter how broken and conquered—in glory still, and with the more terrible tenderness.

"We met on a poor night," I whispered.

"Why?"

"I have to go to London in the morning," and when she looked at me as if I was lying, "I know it sounds like an excuse but it's true. You can even ask my aunt if you don't believe me."

"How long will you be?"

"A week or so. I can't be certain. I'll ring you when I get back."

177

She took my mouth in a long kiss, sealing her whole body to mine.

"I suppose it's not safe?" I said.

"It's never safe."

"There's no use risking spoiling it, then."

"The next time I'll have precautions," and she went below the sheets, the peace that flooded out a perfect calm, the even moonlight only a thin tattered shadow.

"You don't resent I'm not a virgin?" she whispered as we kissed after phoning a taxi.

"I'm too old for that. Why should I? Why should you be idle while waiting for my white horse that might never gallop even close."

"I'm glad," she kissed me again. "You'd be surprised how many resent it."

"Their box of tools are the only ones fitted for the job, is that it?" and she caught me beneath the arm with her nails as she laughed.

As soon as the taxi arrived, men suddenly appeared from all directions, wanting to know if they could share my taxi into town. I told them they'd have to ask the taxi man.

"This is more like a brothel than a nurses' home," I said as I bade her goodbye.

"I know," she held my face a moment in her hands. "Don't say it too loud. There have been complaints."

Three men shared the taxi into town. One was very extrovert and sat in the front seat beside the driver.

"You're new," he said. "Welcome to the club."

"Thanks."

He picked up no hint of sarcasm as he went on to give his name, offered his hand as if he wore a bishop's ring, and said he was the sauce chef in the Shelbourne.

"What's your name and what do you do?" he asked as if I were lagging with my information.

I told him my name and that I was working in the advertising business.

178

"Doing what?"

"Writing ads."

That appeared to satisfy him and he introduced me to the other two men. One was a plumber. The other worked as a clerk in the Customs House.

"Do you know the name of the nurse you were with?" he asked.

"I don't think so, and by the way you're leaving out somebody," I said.

"Who?" he bridled.

"The driver. You never introduced me to the driver."

"O that doesn't matter," the driver said, the car going very fast through the empty early morning streets. "My name is Paddy Murphy. I'm a Knight of the Realm," he said. "And you, you're going to Cabra West?" he said to the sauce chef as if he knew him from a previous run.

It was too late to go to bed by the time I got back to the flat. I washed, had several cups of coffee, packed and got the train to the boat.

I'd get into London between five and six. I hadn't to see her till lunch of the next day though I was supposed to ring if I got in earlier. I'd have the whole evening to rest and walk round streets.

I stood at the rail, feeling the warm wind on my face as the boat chugged out of the bay. Passing Howth in the distance, and wondering by this time whether or not to go to the bar, I felt a silken cloth in my pocket. When I pulled it out and saw what it was I hid it quickly in my fist. I looked around. No one was close or watching. It was as white as any of the gulls following the boat. The whole tender strange night was gathered round the softness of the texture. Keeping it would be like trying to hoard the night.

I opened my hand and the breeze took it. Two gulls dived towards it as it flew past the stern, where a fresh breeze lifted it again, and suddenly it was swallowed up in the raucous crowd of gulls following the boat.

179

As she was on the Northern Line we arranged to meet outside the ticket gate of Leicester Square Station. She saw me while she was still on the escalator, and started to wave. The wave seemed less certain of itself than when she used to come towards me down the cherry and almond avenue. Instead of waving to that drumming inner music—I'm walking and everything is beautiful—it seemed to hesitate : It's all a bit confusing but boy I sure am keeping on trying. She was dressed in a tweed costume and she wore a pale blouse.

"You sure are one sight for sore eyes," she kissed and kissed me again, her eyes brimming, a blast of dead air driven up from below by an incoming train.

"Would you like to have a drink? Or would you like to go and have lunch now?"

"Wait. Wait a minute. I need to get used to you. You don't know how much I've missed you. I need to drink you in for some several quiet minutes."

"We have all day. We can go round the corner to a pub."

"I'd rather go and eat," she said. "I'm sorry. I felt hungry all of a sudden coming in on the tube. There's the two of us now. I'm sorry," she said again as she took my arm. "You can't imagine how much I've been looking forward to seeing you."

"You look very well," I said though I thought she looked nervous and tired.

"I don't know. I find it hard to sleep. Last night I couldn't sleep but that was the excitement."

"Does the place you work at close on a Saturday?" I asked as we walked into Soho.

"The yard is open till twelve, but the office is shut. Wild horses wouldn't drag me to work while you're in town anyhow, and I've arranged to take as many days off next week as I need. Will you be able to stay the whole week?"

"No. I may even have to go back tomorrow morning. I'm expecting a message. My aunt is dying. I was going to put off coming but I didn't want to change it."

180

"Thank God you didn't change it. But you may be able to stay the week?"

"It's unlikely. If there's no message for me, I'll have to ring them. It's unlikely I'll be able to stay longer than a day or two."

"Where are you expecting the message?"

"At the hotel."

"You should have given my place."

"I didn't like to. Anyhow it's done now."

After pausing at the placards outside of a few expensive restaurants we picked a modestly priced Italian place in Old Compton Street. It had glass-topped tables, and a black and white blowup of the Bay of Naples along the whole length of one wall.

"I got spoiled with Jonathan," she said as she looked through the menu. "We went out to all those expensive restaurants. And never looked at the price of anything. I'll have minestrone."

"You certainly can have anything you want on this menu. I wouldn't worry about prices today."

"I want minestrone, and after that I'll have the veal and spinach. You don't know what a pleasure it is to be sitting opposite you."

"What happened between Jonathan and yourself?"

"O boy," she said. "O boy, that's a story."

The waiter brought the minestrone and a carafe of red wine. I finished a glass of red wine while she ate the minestrone. I wasn't hungry enough to begin with anything. I blamed it on the travelling. I asked the waiter to suggest something light, and he advised lamb cooked with rosemary. I drank a second glass of wine while waiting for the lamb to come while she told me about the magazine and Jonathan's friends.

"It was a real eye-opener. Just because I was close to Jonathan I could influence what happened to movies and books and plays, give space to actors. I sure didn't think the world was run that way."

181

"What other way did you expect?" I was finding it difficult to curb my irritability in the face of the stream of words. "Who runs anything but people? Since God gave the Ten Commandments he's stayed out of it."

"I soon learned that. I thought things were run on lines of good and bad, according to some vague law or other. Virtue was rewarded, vice was punished. My eyes were certainly opened. I sure had some catching up to do," and she went on to tell me incidents which I found hard to follow not knowing the people involved.

"But Jonathan himself was all right, wasn't he?"

"I'm still fond of him. And basically he's a good person. He got a raw deal I suppose. But when the chips were down he turned out to be very much the businessman too, ruthless and self-centred."

"Isn't everybody?"

"I can't believe that. I couldn't go on if I believed that."

"But he had a point, didn't he? He wanted to marry you. You wouldn't marry him."

"Well, he never showed that side of himself. He was always the gallant knight," she said heatedly. "Roses and meals and wine and tears. And suddenly it was either-or. And it wasn't a fair position."

"But you seemed happy when you wrote to me about the wife's suicide, the time you were afraid she'd come home and cause trouble if she found you in the basement."

"He became a different person after that. He even made a pass at me. I had to use all my strength to resist him. And he said he was staying the whole night in the basement, so it would be as easy to sleep with him as not since I couldn't make up my own sweet mind. And he said horrible things about you."

"This all happened after the suicide?"

"A few days. O boy, will I ever forget that funeral service out in Golders Green. Apparently she used to gamble a lot. And she owned a racehorse once. And eight was her lucky number. This enormous floral wreath in the figure of eight—it must have cost the earth—went through the flap with the coffin. She'd put it in the will. They'd to hold it so that the flap didn't sweep it off."

"But why *didn't* you marry him? The child would be secure. You were fond of him."

"You weren't very concerned about the child."

"That's true, but I didn't claim to be, though that's no virtue. You said we should have been married because of the child, that the child was more important than either of us. What then was so different in this case? According to that logic shouldn't you have married Jonathan for the child's sake?"

"You sound more like a lawyer than a person," there were bitter tears in her eyes. "Everything was different. You were the child's father. The child was conceived in love, on my part anyhow. Jonathan was old, older even than his years. It was a last clutching at life. For the advantages I might get, I'd have to give him my life. You may be fond of an old person but when they try to be young, you find you can't help despising them. And I'd have to make love to Jonathan, like you and I used to make love, and no matter what you say there was nothing sinful or mean or ugly about our lovemaking. It was pure and healthy and natural. How could I make love to an old man, with the memory of that, and at the same time the child of those memories growing within me. Even if I married Jonathan I'd have to give up all hope of ever seeing you again, and there was no way I was ever going to do that."

"You sounded quite determined about it when you wrote to me."

"No, love. I was hoping it'd have the opposite effect on you. I suppose none of this has the slightest effect on you?"

"Of course it has. It's an awful mess to have got into in the first place. If you'd married Jonathan it would have cleared it up, only from my point of view, granted. Now it's just a mess again."

"I can't take that. I know it'll work out all right. I know that nothing but good will come of it. Because both of us are good people. We didn't try to dodge anything. You wouldn't be here if you weren't a good person."

"Tell me more."

"Do you still write that stuff?"

"It's all I get paid for."

"But you have some money from your family."

"Not enough to live on," I said abruptly, closing the conversation. "What are you going to do now?"

"I'll keep this job till the child comes. It's very boring but it makes no demands and it pays quite well. One good thing that this upheaval taught me is how valueless our prized security is. I can get a far more exciting job here with my skills than that boring job back at the bank. I'd never have had the courage to find that out except for what happened."

"What are you going to do with the child?"

"That's the six marker."

"Marriage is now out," the way she reacted I saw she hadn't by any means given it up. "It's out."

"That may change with the child. It'll be your child. People long for children."

"It won't change with the child," I said brutally. "It won't change."

"You can never tell those things."

"You'll have to take my word for it. It's out. Completely out. And there are only two other ways left now."

"What?"

"Adoption. Give the child to two parents looking for a child. That way it'll be as if the child were born into a normal home."

"It's all right for you to say that. That way your little mistake will have been farmed out, got rid of. You hadn't to leave Dublin. You don't have to carry the child around in your body all these months, cry over it, worry over it. And then after all that just hand it over to somebody else as if it were a postal parcel. And then spend the rest of your life wondering : where is it now, what's happening to it, is it happy...."

184

"Well, the alternative is simple. You keep the child. And once you do that you're on your own. You'll never see me again."

"I don't know how you can say that."

"I'm fed up listening to you prate about the child's good. The child must come first, but apparently only when it happens to coincide with your own wishes. Two parents can bring up a child better than one. There's nothing special about our seed."

"Stop it, stop it," she said.

"All right. I'll pay. And we can have a brandy in the pub."

"I need a brandy. And to think I wasn't able to sleep last night with looking forward to this lunch."

There was a bar a few doors down from the view of the Bay of Naples with its several sailboats and we had the drinks standing at a counter girdled by a thin brass rail. She took a brandy but I changed to a pint of bitter. As I came out of the *Mens* I was able to look at her for the first time. There were still no apparent signs of her pregnancy. She was a strong handsome woman, younger looking than her thirty-eight years. Years of regular hours and church-going had worked wonders of preservation on natural good looks.

"Do you know what I want you to do? I want you to come with me to Jonathan's place. No, we don't have to go in or anything, in fact we couldn't," she was in extreme good spirits again when I joined her. "But I just want you to see it. We can get the bus. We can just walk past the gate. It's no more than twelve minutes away on the bus."

"But why?"

"I just want you to see it. It won't take long."

"Whatever you say," I was anxious to avoid the tension of the restaurant at any cost. It had been the same argument as we had had several times in Dublin and we'd never reached anywhere except the same impasse, and never would. "I'm in your hands for the rest of the day," I said.

We left the pub like any pair of lovers in the centre of London for the day, and I caught her hand as we raced to get to the stop on Shaftesbury Avenue before a six bus which was stopping at traffic lights.

We got off a few stops after Harrods and walked. There was a feeling of decorum and quiet about the roads, of ordered, sheltered lives. The houses were rich and white, with balconies and black railings, and they all had basements.

"It's only three doors away," she'd grown very nervous. "If there are signs of anybody in the house we'll just walk straight past."

There was a magnolia tree on the bare front lawn, an elegant grey door, and the basement was down steps. It didn't look as if there was anybody in the house.

"They must be in the country for the week-end," she said. "When I left, the lawn was white with magnolia blossom. They must have vacuumed them up."

"Who's they?" I asked.

"Jonathan and his wife. Did I not tell you he's married? The woman is a widow, has money too. It's she who has the cottage in the country. Clutching at a late life."

"Come on. You never know, there might be somebody in the house."

"I'd love to just get one look into the basement."

"No. I'm moving on if you are. It's not right," I was afraid someone might open the door and enquire what we wanted or—worse—invite us in.

"I suppose it was just foolish of me to want to see if the basement has been changed."

"Why did you want to see the house at all?"

"I don't know. I just wanted you to see it. Often I used to wish it was just us two who were in the house. But I was very grateful for that basement when I came to London first. What do you think of it?"

"I think it's a fine house," I said.

I had a beer in the small local at the corner of the road, where she and Jonathan used to have a drink on Sunday mornings after walking in the gardens. Then we took the underground to Finsbury Park. Her flat was just seven bus stops from the station.

Cars were parked bumper to bumper on both sides of the road we turned into, the long rows of glass glittering each time the sun shone out of hurrying white clouds.

"There must be a home game," she said. "We're just a few minutes away from the Spurs ground. Both my landlords are fanatic Spurs followers," and as if to support what she'd said a huge roar went up close by, followed by a deafening rhythmic pounding of feet on hollow boards, broken by a huge groan that led off into sharp definitive clapping. The whole little terrace was grey, the brick dark from smoke or soot, tradesmen's houses of the nineteenth century, each house with a name plaque between the two upper windows in the shape of a cough lozenge. "Ivanhoe" was the barely legible name I made out as she searched for her key. A black and a grey cat met us in the narrow hallway.

"We have the house to ourselves. My landlords are on the Costa Brava. I'm looking after the cats for them. You should have heard all the feeding instructions I got before they left. The cats are their children," she stroked the cats in the hallway but they did not follow us up the stairs. I listened to the baying of the crowd: indignation, polite appreciation, anxiety, relief, abuse, anger, smug satisfaction.

"I'm hardly ever here on a Saturday. I do my shopping and laundry round this time every Saturday."

The flat looked as if it had been furnished from several junk rooms. There was a gas cooker, a gas fire, a circular table, armchairs of different shapes and colours, a corduroy sofa, a narrow bed against the wall. There was lino on the floors but what nearly broke my heart was the bowl of tulips, the fresh cheese biscuits, the unopened bottle of whiskey and the bottles of red and white wine, and even packs of stout.

"You have gone to far too much trouble," I said into her shining eyes. "How did you come on this place?"

"I saw it in the paper. And the two men liked me. They

187

thought I had a bit of class. Though they're men they're really married. George is all shoulders, masculine, deep voice. And Terry is the dreamy, flitty one, very so-so. They must have taken a whole case of suntan lotion to the Costa Brava. They'd make you die. 'I'm going to come back with a really sexy tan,' Terry said. 'And I'll hold George's hand when we go out to shop'!"

"Do they know you're pregnant?"

"No."

"Do you think you will have any trouble when they find out?"

"No. I don't think so. They're very nice. The house couldn't be more quiet. And it's cheap. I even save money now. Except they might want to adopt the baby, when they find out I'm pregnant, that's the only trouble I can foresee. It's the one thing in their line that poor Terry can't do."

She'd poured me a large glass of whiskey and sipped at a little white wine herself, sitting cross-legged on the floor.

"Does your family know anything yet?"

"No. And I don't intend to tell them. If they did find out, they'd hold their big middle-class conference. A course of action would be decided on. And they'd arrive *en masse* to take over the show. I'd be whisked home or into a convent or something. Boy, would they be thrown. Nothing like this ever happened in the family before."

"You won't tell them, then?"

"Not until it's over, if even then. As far as they're concerned I'm on an artistic jag, seeking fame and fortune in the environs of Fleet Street."

Her eyes shining, brimming with tears but smiling through them, she moved towards me over lino, a child rolling an orange across the floor. She leaned her face against my knees and when I put my arms round her I felt the sobbing.

"It means so much to me you're here," she said. I stroked her hair and rocked her quietly, glad of the burning whiskey numbing a confusion of feeling. Smiling apprehensively up at

188

me through tears as if afraid of my reaction, she started to undo buttons, and then she took my penis in her mouth. Excited, I let my hands run beneath her blouse, teasing and globing the full breasts.

"We might as well go to bed," I said as an enormous roar that sounded as if a home goal had just been scored rolled through the shabby room.

"You see, you can only notice for certain without clothes," she said, but in the narrow bed she pushed me away, crying out angrily that I was using her to induce a miscarriage, "That is what you want anyhow."

"If you think that, come on top," I pulled her on top of me. "You can control everything. The bed is too narrow."

"I'm sorry. I'm just nervous."

A sudden swelling roar from the crowd reached a pitch when it seemed it must sweep to triumph, but with a groan it fell back, scattered in neat handclapping. My hands went over her shoulders, her back, her buttocks, her sweating : and I willed all sense down to living in her wetness like in a wound.

When it was over, feet stamping impatiently from the ground on the hollow boards, she said, "Sometimes I lie in this bed and just cry and think how did I ever get myself into this. And other times I'm just so happy that I don't want to go to sleep. I think of the young life growing within me. I think how amazing it is. I'm giving another person the gift of life, of the sky and the sea and summer and the crowded streets of cities, everything that Man or God has made. And I can't get over what a miracle of a gift it is to be able to give to anybody, what a gift it is to give, not only a whole garden in the evening but everything, can you imagine it, everything, just everything?" She raised herself above me on one arm so that her breasts and fine shoulders shone. What sounded like a final roar went up from the crowd, and then a general round of applause for what could have been teams leaving the field, broken by the odd coltish boo. "How can you deny that it's wonderful?"

189

"Nobody can. No more than they can quarrel with the sea or the morning."

"What's wrong with you, then?"

"Nothing. I happen to think the opposite is true as well. It's horrible as well as wonderful."

"But that doesn't matter. There's nothing to be done about it."

"It's still the truth. I'd find it depressing if a place couldn't be found for it on the committee."

"Who knows the truth?"

"Nobody. The cowardly fall short of it, bravura tries to go beyond it, but they are recognizable limits and balances. We mightn't be able to live with it but we can't block it out either."

"O boy, here we go again."

"And it certainly doesn't seem to be getting anywhere."

"And I love you. I often cried out for you. Now I'm being selfish. I want to eat and drink you."

I thought nobody could tell anybody that, and I listened to the loud street. Footsteps were hurrying past. Feverish discussions or arguments, tired and contented voices went past. Car doors banged. Motors started. And then the clip-clop of a police horse came slowly down the street.

"What are you listening to, love?"

"A horse. It must be a police horse."

"They're always around on match Saturdays. That's the crowd going home. They always make that much of a racket. You'd hardly get moving in the streets around here now and the buses are all packed. Especially when they've lost, they'd trample you down."

The horse went past. Soon afterwards several horses trotted past the windows.

"There're going back to the barracks," she said. "This is the way they go back every Saturday. All this useless information comes from the masculine landlord, George," she said. "I'm sorry. I was nervous the last time. Come on top of me."

190

"We can lie sideways."

"No. Come on top of me. I want to feel you." I waited while she searched, and when I felt her panting reach for a thread just out of reach, and fall back with a catch of the breath, I let it be over. I poured whiskey and grew more and more restless, disturbed by the preparations for my coming, the flowers, the cheese biscuits, the alcohol, and God knows what else was hidden out of sight. They shone all the more disturbingly out because of the poorness of the room, the hopelessness of the whole venture, like primroses in a jam jar on a grave of someone who had worn the ragged jacket of the earth for all his days before donning the final uniform of king and beggar.

"What time do the pubs open?"

"I don't know. I was thinking I'd start to make us something to eat a little later," it was exactly what I feared.

"I think they must be open now," I seemed to remember that they were always open just a little time after the matches ended and then the classified evening papers would come in. "I'd love a pint of English bitter. And it'd be fun to check on the result of the match. My guess is that the home team must have won."

As I said it, I realized it was uncomfortably close to the note of, "I've just missed the crossed treble by a whisker," that tolled the passing of her virginity, but all she said was, "I'll be dressed in a few minutes."

"Take as long as you like. The sun is out. We can walk."

I drank another whiskey as I waited.

"Kiss me," she said when she appeared.

"I hope you don't mind the whiskey."

"Maybe we can come back and eat later?"

"Sure. Or we can eat out."

"If we weren't coming back I'd feed the cats now."

"Feed the cats, then. That way you don't have to worry about it. We have more choices that way."

As I listened to her feeding the cats downstairs, I poured

another whiskey, mentally taking leave of the room, all the preparations for my coming pointing the frail accusing fingers at me of all rejected poor endeavour. If I could possibly avoid it, I promised, I'd never set foot in that room again.

A brief sun was out and we walked to the pub, an enormous coaching inn close to the station. Its solid lovely structure had been battered by several puzzling decorational assaults and there was a bandstand at the back. I brought the pint of bitter, an orange and two evening papers to the table beside the bandstand.

"Spurs won. Two to one. They got the winning goal in the last quarter. That last great roar that went up must have been for the winner."

She smiled a nervous smile that seemed to say that she was happy because I seemed happy. We swapped the thin sheets. I got another pint of bitter from the bar but she had enough orange. She took a packet of crisps. We had exhausted the papers by that. A pretty woman somewhere in her thirties came round wiping the tables, and hearing our accents spoke to us.

"What part do you come from? Are you on holiday or living here?" She was from Dublin and worked weekends in the bar when a group played.

I offered her a drink. She had a lager and lime and sat with us. Though she was paid from six o'clock it was often eight before she had any work, and she was blinded with work from then till closing time. The best part of the night was when they sat behind the counter with a nightcap after the washing and cleaning was done, she told us.

She had a story. For all her prettiness her mouth was thin and bitter and she kept tugging nervously at the finger that would have worn a wedding ring.

She'd a clerk-typist's position in Guinness's Brewery in Dublin. She emphasized it as a position rather than a job. In those days if you got into Guinness's you were secure for life. It was harder to get into than into the civil service or a bank, and she'd already got her first promotion when she met this

192

man, an Englishman, an engineer, who was over installing some new plant in the brewery. She married him, left her job, came with him to London, where they had two children, two boys, and then, after seven years, discovered that the man she thought of as her husband all those years had been married to another woman, who he was seeing all that time, when *she* thought he was away on jobs. She still got angry when the lies she'd swallowed hook, line and sinker came back to her. She'd left him, of course, at once. It all poured out one night he'd had too much to drink. No, she didn't think she'd ever marry again, once burned ten times shy. She'd a good job now in the Westminster Bank, and the weekends she worked in the pub made that little difference of presents and extra luxuries for her two boys.

I was delighted with the story and bought her two more lagers and lime, encouraging her to elaborate, as Maloney's words came back to me, "It makes us all feel good. It makes us all feel very good." Compared to the despicable wretch this woman had the misfortune to meet up with, my own questionable conduct appeared positively exemplary. She only left us when the musicians came in and began to take the wraps off their instruments.

"I suppose we should go before the crowd starts to come in," the pub was already filling.

"That's if you can bear to miss another slice of that woman's life," the angry answer came.

"She seemed to want to talk."

"You encouraged her, went on buying her drinks, when we had only this amount of precious time for ourselves." It was precisely that same precious time that I had been anxious to avoid.

"Her story was sort of interesting, it was kind of a version of ours, but far worse. She seemed decent enough and I was thinking that if you were feeling low or anything you could drop in. She's Irish. Having gone through that herself, she'd know what you are going through here in London." A sudden flushed stare from behind two rows of bottles along the counter mirrors told me I was already well on the way to being fuddled as we left the bar.

"That's all I'd need if I was low," she said with angry contempt. "Go into that bar and listen to her story. That's what'd cheer me up. Boy, isn't that just the holy grail I've been looking for all this time. Come in and listen to a tale of woe that'll cancel your own woe out."

"I'm sorry," I said. "I didn't mean any harm. I meant it all for the best. What would you like to do now?"

"Why don't we go back to the flat? I'll cook us dinner there. There's plenty of wine and drink."

"I don't want you cooking. I want to take you out for dinner tonight. It'd be fun. It's Saturday night too."

"All right. We'll go out to dinner then," she smiled and we kissed. "I need to clear my ears after that woman's story. I guess that was just about all I needed."

"Will we go back into town and eat in Soho?"

"Everywhere'll be crowded tonight. I'd rather stay round here. There's a little French place round the corner, run by a fat Breton, who's cook and waiter and everything. I was there once. It's a bit on the expensive side though."

"That doesn't matter."

It could have been a hairdresser's window, except for the lobster pot and a piece of torn netting with rectangular cork floats and lead sinks. Inside, four of the eight or ten tables were full. The man was very fat, in a chef's hat and apron, arms bared, and he was sweating profusely. I was still not hungry and ordered a steak tartare as an excuse to drink. I then pressed her to eat as much as she was able. There was much laughter as the chef helped her to order. When she did, he brought us a carafe of wine, and we drank as we watched him cook. I ordered a second carafe when he brought our dishes.

As soon as I got out of the restaurant I staggered but covered up by thanking her profusely, "It was a wonderful meal and wonderful place. You have a real nose for restaurants."

194

I was drunk, but with the drunk's cunning of very limited, mostly negative ambitions : one, not to go back to the flat; two, not to have any serious discussion, which was easily achieved at this stage; three, to make trebly certain of avoiding serious discussions if there was any further need to be certain by going on drinking.

"I'm dying for a pint of bitter. Why don't we go back into that pub? It's the nearest and we don't have to see that woman. The pub is enormous and she works the tables at the far end. We can just have a drink near the door. It must be almost closing time."

The place was packed. Heads crowded together above the counter. A horn shrilled above frantic drums. There were glasses everywhere, cigarette smoke, flushed faces, the dark warm wood, grapes on the stained ceiling; but there were far too many faces to think of even catching a glimpse of the blonde Dublin woman among the dancers and tables around the band-stand in the distant crush and smoke. There was a table near the door where we could rest our glasses while we stood. The bitter tasted warm. There was no possibility of speech except in carefully thought-out monosyllabic shouts. The yellow bitter in its thin pint glass with the imperial stamp looked beautiful. I smiled and raised my glass and shouted, "Good health." Across the counter between rings of smoke I watched a girl weave her bare arms in a dance, cracking her fingers above her head, the black dress so tightly sewn that her breasts looked crushed. As in a light dream on the edge of waking, faces floated close out of the smoke, seemed to smile, and drift far back only to draw near again.

"You seem to be having a wonderful time," she shouted in my ear.

"I am," I shouted back. "And you?" Before her wan smile could take on meaning, it drifted off into the noise and smoke and came back changed.

The summer air, the clean streetlights, their unreal clarity shook me when I stepped outside, and the harsh words, "You're drunk."

"I'm tipsy. How can a man know he's drunk and still be drunk, know he's a fool and still be a fool, be a thief. I must be drunk."

"You're tipsy, then. You're far too tipsy to go back to the hotel. You can sleep the night in the flat. The short walk back there would even do you good."

"I can't," I hiccuped, leaning against the outside wall of the pub, the car park and the forecourt crowded. Limited Plan Number One (not to go back to the flat) came floating silently to my aid, waving its delicate legs like a deep-sea diver approaching a submerged wreck.

"You wouldn't have to sleep with me. I'll sleep on the floor," she said.

"I'd want to sleep with you. And it's me that should sleep on the floor, but I can't. I have to go to the hotel."

"You can go in the morning."

"No, I'm as well to go now. I'm well able to. I have to see if any message has come for me."

"I'll come with you, so," she took me by the arm.

"I'll be able to manage," but she ignored it.

I stumbled on the stairs, but I was conscious enough on the journey to be grateful for the grace of complete avoidance of everything that my condition conferred, and at the hotel the note was waiting that I had arranged to be there. I gave her the note to read in the lobby. I had to go back the next day. It was not so urgent, I said, that I'd have to take a plane. I could go on the nightboat and train. That way we could have most of the day together. We kissed and I saw her to the door after she said she'd call for me at eleven the next morning. I got my key off the porter and I saw him take his eyes from whatever he was reading to watch my feet attempt the first few steps of the stairs.

I was awake but hardly daring to move with pain when she burst into the room the next morning. By the way she looked around I knew she'd been hurting herself with the fear that I might have some girl with me in the room.

"Is it eleven yet?"

"No. I'm early but when the man in the hall said you were in the room I thought I might as well come up rather than walk around till eleven."

"That made sense. I feel horrible."

"I don't know what you wanted to go and drink so much for. Do you want me to go out and get you something for your head?"

"No. I might as well suffer it out now since I was so stupid. I'll get up."

Downstairs I paid for the room, and the man took in my bag behind the desk. The sun was out in Bloomsbury, the walls whitened with its light, and it hurt like hell. I was forced to laugh at the pain. We bought newspapers at the corner of Tottenham Court Road, crossed Oxford Street, and found an empty bench in Soho Square, and started to leaf in silence through the pages. Down in the bushes on the Greek Street side of the square a parliament of winos seemed to be in session. From time to time coins were collected on the grass, and one of their number left to return some minutes later with a quart of cider, which was passed around. To spin out this day like an invalid till the late train left Euston suited me well. When a person is both tired and ill they make few social mistakes. They make nothing.

"How do you feel now, love?" she leaned towards me after we'd been two hours or so on the bench and we kissed.

"Things are looking up. And you?"

"I feel a bit tired," and she broke a long silence, "What are you thinking, love?"

"I was trying to figure out why those winos get all het up from time to time. And talk and jump about and wave. And they all just seem to sit down again."

"Maybe that's when something important comes up."

"But what?"

"The price of cider? Who knows!"

After one o'clock we drifted down into a small pub that had flowers and bowls of nuts and a bald landlord leaned a shirt-sleeved arm on the counter. We had two drinks, stayed till it closed at two, and went back to the Italian restaurant we'd been to the day before. We teased out slow hours there with red wine and light dishes.

"It's going to be a long, long winter. I should be in hospital by Christmas. The child is going to be a Christmas child. The worst will be the autumn. Some of my cousins will be in London for conferences. I'll have to see them and it won't be easy to hide my condition."

"You can pretend you have to be out of town on some trumped-up business or other."

"Not all the time. Tom, the engineer, the boy I used play with, has written with his dates already. He'll be here in late October and staying at the Strand Palace. Boy, if I was out of town for that he'd not be long smelling a rat. He'd soon put two and three together."

In the slow drip of her anxiety there was the temptation: let us get married, let us face out this horrible mess together, but a mere glimpse of the way she'd rise and warm to it was enough to kill it unspoken.

"You should have married Jonathan."

"I should have done a lot of things and didn't. There's no use going over that now. I just couldn't bring myself to do it."

"Was Jonathan much hurt when you wouldn't?"

"I suppose he was. I think he was in love with me for years. For years he'd been trying to get me to give up the job in the bank and come to London. We used often to talk about that, the irony of how it happened when it did happen, getting pregnant. I suppose his vanity was hurt too, but what was shocking was how businesslike he was about it. I saw him for the first time in his true colours then," she said bitterly. "For all the champagne and tears and roses, people to him were just

198

ciphers. He was brutal and domineering as well as sentimental but above all everything had a price."

"Strange, out of all the ups and downs how starkly simple everything is now."

"How?" she said sharply.

"You'll have the child at Christmas. You'll either keep it or adopt it."

"It might be even simpler than that. I'm not that young for it to be all that simple, having a first child."

I wanted to say, it's not true that the old have shorter lives than the young. Many did not even get as far as us, no one has any rights in that line; but we had been in these waters before. They were choppy and disagreeable and led nowhere. It was almost five when we stepped out of the restaurant onto Old Compton Street.

"The train goes soon after eight. Will we break up here? I just have time to get my bag out of the hotel and make my way to Euston."

"I'll see you off," she said. "Otherwise I'd just go back to the house and mope and cry. All I'd think of is that the train is leaving in such and such a time and every five minutes I'd check the clock."

We sat in the late sun for half an hour in Soho Square. Some of the winos we had watched that morning were asleep, but others were still moving the bottle. One of the women dressed in a blue military overcoat seemed particularly angry. She muttered to herself and then took fits of shaking some of the men sleeping on the grass awake, talking to them in rapid bursts. All of them seemed to listen carefully to whatever she said and then to fall back to sleep.

After that we picked up the bag at the hotel and walked to Euston. We had an hour to wait and sat in the station bar.

"Can I give you money? I have plenty of money."

"No. I'm even saving money. When I have to stop work I may need some and I'll ask you then."

"Whenever you want, but maybe you should take some now, just in case."

"No. But I'm grateful. Will you come to London soon?"

"I don't know. It doesn't seem to do much good, does it, it's outside the main problem now. You remember how in the beginning when both of us thought to come to London together, and live here till the child was born, it was decided that it wasn't a good idea. And visiting seems to me even worse. It stirs things up, leaves everything exactly the same, so it's worse than nothing. But I'll come if you need me."

"It's going to be a hard time, but somehow deep down I know it'll be all right."

We kissed at the barrier and when I turned round before getting into the carriage she was still at the barrier. I waved and she started to wave back wildly.

It won't be all right. Nothing will be all right. And it'll end badly, I said to myself but had to admit that it was a very poor way of thinking. The train was set for Ireland. I started thinking of my mother to the carriage roll. There are women in whom the maternal instinct is so obdurate that they will break wrists and ankles in order to stay needed.

My mother, too, may have been such, if the old calendars were anything to go by : but then you could assert almost anything from those ranks of crossed out days, including, certainly, an impatience to get life over with.

The calendars were in a large bundle of papers, tied with yellowed twine. I got them when I was given formal possession of my parents' estate in the room above Delehunty's office, my aunt in another of the green leather armchairs with the row of brass studs, Delehunty's easy beefsteak face across the roll-top desk, behind him an ancient Bible on the wooden mantel above the fireplace.

They were very ordinary calendars, with scenic views such as shops give out at Christmas. Encrusted around many of the dates were faded notes in some private shorthand that I found impossible to decipher and every date was covered with the same large bold X. Seven years were crossed out this way. The X's stopped on the nineteenth of May, ten days before her death, around the time I'd been taken from the farmhouse to my aunt's place in the town. I sensed that God, having veiled the earth in darkness and seen all nature to restoring sleep, could hardly have closed down each day with much greater sense of personal control than the march of my mother's X's across the years seemed to proclaim. Maybe I had been lucky in my mother's death. Before she could get those X's properly to work on me she'd been taken away. And was I now acting out the same circle in reverse—leaving her in London with her growing burden?

I had been lucky in my aunt and uncle. They'd let me grow easy, and I'd escaped the misfortune of being the centre of anybody's "interest" till I crossed the dance floor, the cursed circle coming round again, that madness of passion that I had focused on "my love" now focused on me, her cry strengthened with the child's cry, the happy gods secure as ever in their laughter.

If they let me grow easy, I was letting her die as easily.

I did not go into the hospital till I was four days back in Dublin, since I'd said I'd be a week away.

I wrote more Mavis and the Colonel stories for Maloney. I did not go out at all, ignored day and night and conventional meal times, using alcohol and hot baths in place of exercise when I felt I needed to sleep. "A good bottle of port every day equals a four-mile walk," a British general had said. I used a well-tried formula I always used when I had catching-up to do, not unlike a cooking recipe: a description of Venice out of a guidebook, like a sprinkling of dried parsley; at Eastbourne the four leaves of the hotel door revolved on their own hinges while outside the brass band thumped and groaned "Bank Holiday", as the Colonel once again went up his Queen. It all went to cast a thin veil of a logical process over the main purchase, the shaft and clutch, the oiled walls opening to take the fat white spunk, closing with a painful catch of ecstasy as once again it surged straight home. I did not read any of the stories till I had all I wanted done. I had to read them with my own blood, sometimes changing the order of the words until they seemed to sing or cough or groan, supplying the personal salt without which suspicion could not be lulled. O rock the cradle with your own dark hands till sleep would come or lust would rise.

And out of this counterfeited rocking of lust sometimes the silken piece of white cloth became a texture again to my fingers before I had let the breeze take it out among the cloud of gulls, and I wanted to take her again in my arms in the cold of a room beneath the black crucifix. When it came to ringing her or not, I did not want to be born again. I had no doubt that I had enough of "life" for some time more.

This became a real problem only when I'd finished and worked through the reading of all the stories and wanted to go to the hospital again. What if I should meet her in the ward? I was back now and I had not rung her as I'd promised.

I bought two bottles of brandy and took the bus to the hospital. It was an incredible evening, a clear sky, and in the hospital grounds all was greenness. The new-cut grass we'd walked over a week before was now in bales, standing on their ends and leaning together in abstract groups of five in the clean field between the hospital and the home on the edge of the farther trees.

I walked mechanically in, went up in the lift, trying to keep the ghostly, wonderful, horrible birth and death of night out of mind, the sea breeze that took it like a whisper from my fingers, and let it die there among the gulls. I wouldn't meet her. If I met her I could always lie.

Getting out of the lift and walking towards my aunt became in spite of every effort the guilt of stealing towards her by the facing way of the meadow in moonlight and the garbage stairs, up the corridor from where I was walking towards, the blue night-light on, and the solid green swing doors at the farthest end were the palest green. What had I learned from that clandestine night? The nothing that we always learn when we sink to learn something of ourselves or life from a poor other —our own shameful shallowness. We can no more learn from another than we can do their death for them or have them do ours. We have to go inland, in the solitude that is both pain and joy, and there make our own truth, and even if that proves nothing too, we have still that hard joy of having gone the hard and only way there is to go, we have not backed away or staggered to one side, but gone on and on and on even when there was nothing, knowing there was nothing on any other way. We had gone too deep inland to think that a different physique or climate would change anything. We were outside change because we were change. All the doctrines that we had learned by heart and could not understand and fretted over became laughingly clear. To find we had to lose : the road away became the road back. And what company we met with on the road, we who no longer sought company, at what fires and walls did we sit. Our wits were sharpened. All the time we had to change our ways. We listened to everything with attention, to others singing of their failures and their luck, for we now had our road. All, all were travelling. Nobody would arrive. The adventure would never be over even when we were over. It would go on and on, even as it had gone on before it had been passed on to us.

And the dark-haired girl, and the woman with child in London, the dying woman I was standing beside, propped upright on the pillow, lapsed into light and worried sleep, what of them? The answer was in the vulgarity of the question. What of yourself?

The sound of putting the bottles down on the locker top woke her.

"God bless you," she rubbed her eyes. "I must have dozed off. It's great to see you. I thought you might be in yesterday, but then I wasn't sure when you'd get back from London."

203

"I got back yesterday."

"That black-haired one was in, to ask about you."

"Did she say anything?"

"No. She's too clever for that, but I can see she's after you, bad luck to her."

"Why?" that I was grateful for her tact of silence only increased the unease I felt.

"Because I know what women do, because I know she's after you."

"Everybody it seems must be after somebody. Look at yourself and Cyril."

"Cyril's all right. I had a letter from him," she laughed. "Knowing him, putting the few words together, must have been worse than turning a potato pit. Though he said nothing, I can see himself and your uncle are managing poorly. The next thing you'll find is that they've been fighting. I'll have to go home."

There were a few tests more, she told me, and no matter what the results were she was going home at the weekend. I promised that I'd come in in two days time. I was too afraid to linger and yet I found myself leaving with regret, walking slowly out past the reception desk, looking across the clean field towards the home—for what could be nothing but sight of her dark hair.

Maloney was alone when I handed him the stories at the Elbow. He wore dark glasses and the face looked heavy from alcohol or tiredness behind the darkness.

"That clears me, brings me up to date. There's nothing experimental, just the usual," he took the manuscripts and put them in his pocket without a word.

"No buffaloes? no rhinoceros? no tower of ivory? no fool's gold?" he yawned.

"No. Nothing but the usual."

"A pity. 'We are nothing if not advanced,' Miss Florence Farr, the future Lady Brandon, said as far back as 1894. It should have caught on by now, don't you think? The usual

204

appears to me as a diehard form of backsliding. Have you ever noticed that a person is perfectly tuned socially when tired to death?" he yawned as he changed.

"Sure. There's less of you, so you're easier for people to stand, more occupied staying alive than expressing yourself. Others don't impinge on you as much then either. For your own safety you have to follow what's going on, and because of your tiredness you make only the barest gestures. It works like a charm. You create room for people. You control everything, controlling nothing. You never make a mistake because you both exist and don't exist. It's quite perfect."

"That sounds as if I should have said it."

"What has you so tired?"

"Drink and girls or girls and drink. And youth ending. I could not get girls when I needed girls. Now I can get them when I'm no longer able for them. There must be a moral. You can't thrash the tide back with mere sticks, not even with the pure spirit. And you've been to London?"

"That's right."

"And you've visited your responsibilities?"

"That's right."

"And you've comforted them in the traditional manner?" he attacked.

"It happened but I didn't want it to happen."

"Of course you didn't but it still felt good, the finger in the butter dish, the heart doing its duty with the penis still in the right place."

"What are you to do when someone crawls across a carpet to you on her hands and knees?" he had rattled me.

"Give her a sermon. Put your arms round her like a brother, and put them no lower than any proper brother. Tell her that you've both entertained Satan in the past, but now you're both going to banish Satan together and join the Lord. Then take her to church. That's what churches are for."

"Well you've got your stories," I changed for the last time.

"What's she going to do?" he ignored what I'd said as he too rose.

"She's going to have the baby in London."

"What is she going to do then?"

"She'll either keep it or have it adopted."

"What do you think she'll do?"

"Keep it."

"What'll you do?"

"I'm out of it."

"That's what you may think, but keep praying, and staying out. Tomorrow I'll be a reformed character," he tapped the manuscript. "I'll read this and clear all cheques."

"Thanks," I said. "Good luck."

"God bless," he smiled, which exasperated me too late, for he'd disappeared when I turned around.

I had now visited my aunt so often and so regularly in the hospital that the visits had come to resemble those she was so well used to among relatives on Sundays in the country. Cars pull up outside. Apologies and cautious smiles ease themselves out of front seats. A child slams a back door. Having first discerned who has landed from the cover of the back of the living-room, smiles of surprise and delight are wreathed into shape on the doorstep of the porch. Little runs and thrills and pats and chortles go to answer one another, till all hesitant discordant notes are lost in the sweet medley of hypocrisy. Tea is made. After tea, with folded arms, outside on a good day, the men discuss their present plans for rebuilding Troy with suitably measured gestures. The visit ends as it began, relief breaking through the trills of thanks and promises and small playful scolds, "And now, be sure and don't let it be as long until you come again. We'll think bad of you. Now it's your turn to visit us next time, you've been just promising for far too long." And then each family settles down to a solid hour of criticism of the other, the boring visit ended. It is the way we define and reassert ourselves, rejecting those foreign bodies as we sharpen and restore our sense of self.

That my visits were growing similarly tedious to my aunt I could tell by her elaborate greeting. As I left, I could tell by her eyes that there was much about my person and presence that earned her disfavour. She too was a crowd. I, too, would get scorched as soon as I left.

But when she said, "I'm going out of this old place tomorrow," both of us could settle down to enjoy the visit, to renew pleasure that had gone stale because of the relief that it was ending. If we found it growing tedious we had only to glance beyond it towards our approaching freedom. We could be patient and virtuous because limits had been set.

My own ease in this luxury was soon cut short by noticing that the dark-haired girl was on duty at the far end of the ward. She was propping a woman's back with pillows when I noticed her.

All my attention was now focused completely on her for what remained of the visit, each move she made between the beds, and to cover my agitation I tried to summon false energy to keep a line of prattle going with my aunt; but all my attention was on the dark hair above the uniform and I was constantly losing track of what I was meaning to say. My aunt did not even trouble to hide her amusement, and the source of my confusion was drawing closer, six beds away, five, four.

"I'll be in to see you early tomorrow," I said to my aunt, casting all dignity aside, trusting to instant flight, forgetting my aunt was going home first thing tmorrow morning, and she burst out laughing as I seized her hand before making my escape. "O my God," she wiped tears away with her knuckles, laughter obviously cancelling any pain she may have been feeling. "Bad luck to these women. I thought I'd never live to see the day."

My last glimpse as I left was dark hair, bent over a young girl's pillow two beds away as I started to walk up the long corridor, the lift an awful long way off, so many steps for the rigid mechanical doll-step of a walk, all I could muster. I had not gone far when the clear words rang out behind me, full of rage and hurt, "You never come in to see us now. You just come in to see Auntie."

Appalled, I tried to continue walking.

"You never come in to see us now. You just come in to see Auntie."

It was a long way to walk, to keep walking, she standing there behind me, my aunt's laughter probably intercepted by this sudden violence, wondering with some trepidation how it would turn out. And then the natural fear, not to look back, to keep walking to the lift, to escape, to leave rage and mockery behind like a fired gun, suddenly went so far in flight that it stopped : this is absurd, this is ridiculous, if you don't face it now it'll rankle forever; and I turned and walked towards where she stood, her hands on her hips, rigid.

"I'm sorry. I'll explain it. Can I meet you?"

"I suppose that's possible, if you'd want that."

"I do. When are you off work?"

"At eight."

"I'll ring you at eight-thirty at the home."

"If you want that," she was close to tears.

"I do. I'll ring. I hope we'll be able to meet."

The cool was all the more cool since it was just barely being held, a shiver of a cord could break it, but it carried me back to my aunt's bed.

"I'm sorry," I said. "I was upset. I forgot you were going home tomorrow, but I'll be down within a week."

"O you're a sly one," she said laughing, for the whole muffled comedy was now so extreme that it didn't matter what words were said. "O my God, bad luck to you anyway. I never thought I'd live to see the day. You're a crowned pair. Bad luck to both of yez."

When I got out of the hospital I felt myself trembling, feeling the whole naked humiliation of life that we mostly manage to keep at bay with all those weapons that can only be praised.

I rang at the exact time I said I would and she must have been waiting by the phones in the hallway for she picked it up on the second ring.

"Will you meet me?"

"For what?"

"Nothing. Just to meet. I can hardly blame you after today if you don't want to."

"You know you don't have to meet me?"

"I know that. I'm asking if you'll meet me."

"When?"

"Tonight. In an hour's time in O'Connell Street?"

"Where?"

"Under Clery's clock at nine-thirty," and she put the phone down without affirming whether she'd be there or not.

I would have waited until half-nine or so if she hadn't come but she came into the space beneath the clock at ten past.

She wore a grey herring-bone suit with a plastic brooch on the collar, a brown butterfly. She was not, I suppose, what is generally called beautiful, but she looked beautiful to me, young and healthy and strong, the face open and uncomplicated beneath its crown of shining black hair, a young woman rooted in her only life.

"I'm sorry about today," I said.

"I'm sorry too. I was ashamed I shouted after you," she said but there was no plea as there was in my apology, just a plain admission.

"Would you like to come for a drink or go somewhere else?"

"I'd like to go to the pictures," she said.

We went to the Carleton, where *The World of Harold Lloyd* was showing. She sat stiffly by my side in the back seats, staring studiously at the screen, and not until the turkey got loose in the bus did she begin to laugh. When I risked my arm around her, she stiffened again, and I withdrew it. I had found an aggressive and unpleasant note in my own laughter, laughing in defiance of her silence rather than at anything on the screen. Once I was silent her laughter seemed to grow.

209

"Did you like it?" I asked as we went out into the unreality of the night street.

"It was great fun," she said.

She said she didn't want a drink or coffee because if we did we'd miss the bus, and the difference of the few minutes wasn't worth the taxi fare. When I asked if I could come with her on the bus she answered, "If you want to."

We walked in silence from the bus into the hospital grounds, past the hospital. The silence didn't change when we went into the same lighted room with the TV set and couches and armchairs and sat on the same couch where she'd let me take away the white piece of cloth that had gone out among the gulls. When I moved towards her I felt both her hands against my chest.

"That's all that you're after, isn't it?"

"No. It's not all but it's certainly part of it. Will you come out with me again?" I rose.

"Maybe you'd be better off just coming in to see Auntie?"

"That's not fair," I said. "Anyhow my aunt is going home tomorrow. What about next week? Next Tuesday? Will you let me take you out to a meal? I want to tell you something."

"Why can't you tell it now?"

"I don't want to. It'd take too long."

Though it lingered on the lips the kiss she allowed me was too wary to hint at any future, remember any past.

She looked lovely when I met her outside the Trocadero on Tuesday and I told her so. There is no better climate than separateness for loveliness to grow.

There was so much pretty confusion and smiling and choosing what to eat that the waiter helped her choose.

"What do you think of the place?"

"It's expensive," she said.

"Not compared with some other places," I tried to think of what places she must have eaten in with the older man in the photograph. I thought of soda bread and tea and a hotel beside the river in Ballina.

210

"It is to me," she said. "What were you to tell me?"

"We'll wait until we get the wine." When the wine came I said, "Do you remember that night when we met at the dance and I asked you what you'd do if you got pregnant?" and she blushed. "I didn't believe you when you said you'd throw yourself in the Liffey," I continued.

"I would take pills or something. I couldn't face into my family that way. I couldn't."

"You'd think that till it happened. I was going to tell you that night and I didn't. I've got someone pregnant."

"Are you going to marry her?" she coloured even more than before.

"No."

"And what's she going to do?"

"She's going to have the child. In London. In a few months."

"What'll she do then?"

"Keep the child or have it adopted."

"What are you going to do?"

"Nothing. I thought it better to tell you. That's why I didn't ring you. There was trouble enough without dragging you in."

"Why didn't you marry her?"

"I thought that's what I'd have to do when it happened first. But then it grew clear that I'd only marry her to leave her. When that was certain there didn't seem much point."

"But why?"

"I couldn't stand her."

"But you slept with her?" she seemed genuinely shocked.

"She was good looking. That's not living with someone, setting up house with them, marrying them."

"But you must have told her something."

"I told her that I wanted to sleep with her and that that was as much as ever it would be. It saved me in a way, but I don't find much credit in that either. If someone wants to sleep with you, you have very little to lose by being straight, even brutally straight. They'll trick it out in some way to

211

make it acceptable. And I had nothing to lose. I didn't care whether she slept with me or not."

"It sounds very hard," she said.

"It's what I wanted to tell you," I ended. "That's why I didn't ring you up when I got back from London. The night we met at that dance was a wonderful night for me. But I'm not free, at least not until after this child comes into the world. I didn't think there was any point trying to inveigle you into my mess. That's why I didn't ring, why I bolted when I discovered you in the ward."

"What'll happen to the child?"

"I don't know. I hope she'll have it adopted but I doubt if she will."

"What'll you do if she keeps it?"

"I'll be even more out of it then. I wanted her to have an abortion."

"I don't blame her for not having that."

"Anyhow you know the whole story now. And it's no pretty story."

She was silent for a long time, hardly picking at the chicken on her plate. I had seen women pause in much the same way on the edge of the first lovemaking, as if weighing the land before trusting to or turning back from the water; and if they trust to it, that water too must soon become the land.

"You've seen this woman in London?"

"That's why I went."

"What happened?"

"Nothing. What she wants I can't give her. What I want she can't give me."

"What do you want?"

"That it might never have happened."

"But it has happened."

"Well then as close to that as I can get."

"What is that?"

"I don't know. I don't want to know. I suppose it's called to extricate oneself as best one can."

212

"What does she want?"

"She wants the child. She wants me. She wants everything."

"What'll she get?"

"I suppose she'll get the child."

"And you? What'll you get?"

"As little as possible I hope. Now, would you have jumped in the Liffey if it had happened to you?"

"I wouldn't have let it happen," she said with such determination that I had to smile.

"Well, now that you've been warned will you come out with me again?"

"I'll have to think about it," she said.

The next time we met she came sheathed in a green wool dress and I took her to meet Maloney. I suppose I took her to see Maloney to show her that it was not just that one thing I was after. I was showing her into that part of my life that was made up of other people. Maloney was very charming.

"What are you, a beautiful healthy apple, doing in this den, with this degenerate," he moved his arm floridly around the Elbow after kissing her hand. "You'll get eaten by people with bad teeth."

"Better to be eaten than to go bad," she smiled as she risked speech. It would also have been a risk to remain silent, but she couldn't have known that.

"Very good," he pretended to stand back to inspect her. "V-e-r-y good. Better to be eaten than to go bad. Maybe just a little bit too good. Now tell me, what's your opinion of the emancipated woman? I am most anxious to have a straight-from-the-shoulder-no-holds-barred opinion of the emancipated woman."

"I don't know what an emancipated woman is. Maybe I am an emancipated woman."

"Quite right, my dear. I was beginning to fear for you for a minute, only a minute, remember. Not to know is to be

213

happy. Who'd want to leave that child's country to struggle with space and time and the seven-league boots of human rights. I'll tell you. Only a fool would want to leave that country."

"A person generally doesn't have a choice," I put in. "It just happens to them."

"Shut up," he said. "You've eaten the apple. And now you're addressing yourself to this beautiful fresh girl. Don't believe a word he tells you. He works for me. I never believe a word he tells me. He's a wastrel and a corrupter with a priest's face."

When we left she said, "He's a nice man. But he's tired."

"Why do you think he's tired?"

"He tries very hard, doesn't he? It's as if he's always racing to keep up with some idea of himself that he never quite catches."

"That's almost too clever," I said. "He started with the idea that he was a poet. That nearly finishes everybody off. He'd have been intolerable if he'd ever become whatever idea it was. He's just barely tolerable as he is."

She came with me to the room.

"What do you think of it?" I had so fallen under the influence of her charm that I was looking to see everything through her eyes.

"It needs cleaning and the letting in of some light, but it's not my room. It must suit you," and then she continued in a musing voice. "It's here that it happened?"

"No."

"But you must have slept with her—and maybe others—here?"

"Every room has its story. Many stories."

I felt a rush of desire, as much to cancel all those acts and that one suffocating consequence as desire for her fresh body.

214

"It's strange," she said as we kissed, "I suppose I should feel the opposite but I feel excited."

"I suppose we should leave it."

"We should. What are you laughing at?"

"A foolish phrase. A phrase that talks about the continuing virginity of the soul in spite of sexual intercourse. Our virginity seems well restored in spite of that first night when we walked across the meadow to see my aunt."

"Have you heard anything about her?" she asked.

"No. I was supposed to go down but I didn't. I suppose she can hardly last out much longer?"

"I was looking at her chart. I shouldn't be telling you this. In fact I could get into trouble for just reading it. But one night I took it out. The amazing thing is that she's still alive. With her history she should have been dead about six months ago."

"She has this fierce will to live. I don't understand it."

"Life is very sweet."

"I suppose it depends on how you're situated in it. It can be sweet," these were the sort of conversations that made me wince but I still fell into.

"Just to see the day and the sky and the night seems to me amazing. I can't imagine anybody wanting to let that go."

"But aren't some of the people you nurse tired of it?"

"Some but not very many."

It was very cold when we went outside but a bus came almost at once, and we separated. The summer had already gone. I shivered involuntarily, I who loved winters, because of what this winter might bring.

A steady stream of letters now flowed from London, and any doubts or hesitations about my ungenerous reluctance to partake in this festival of goodness and renewal that the letters proclaimed was completely quenched by the undoubting tone of the same letters. The child would come at Christmas, and all would be well, she wanted to reassure me as to that, because both of us were good people, and it would come out that way, she knew it, no matter what the world might think. Not that things were easy. She had grown larger. She had got away with it when she'd met her cousin at the Strand Palace but only just. She'd bandaged herself tightly and several times during dinner had almost passed out. "Are you sure you're all right?" her cousin had kept asking and she had pleaded migraine. What was worse was his jollity in the early evening, hand on her knee, "Now tell me what is it really like to be a citizen of the big smoke?" She had got through it, and she didn't think she'd aroused suspicion, but she'd not take that risk again. Anyhow her condition was obvious now.

And she often found herself crying. She'd put out hands for me and found them empty, but even in the darkest valleys she knew we were travelling towards the sun. The angels were watching above us with outspread wings. Example followed example to prove it.

The two homosexuals did not take kindly to her pregnancy. She saw their suspicions and told them. They were decent enough about it but they asked her to find another room as soon as she could. They'd explained that for them a great part of the charm of their present setup was its short-circuiting of the mother and the womb. It brought memories of suffocation. O boy, it was a queer world, and there sure were some queer people in it, she sang, but the angels were there too, she couldn't go on except for the angels.

And the angels were still there. She'd met this Irish couple, the Kavanaghs, who had four children, and a large Victorian house they'd bought cheap near the Archway, and they had renovated it themselves. He drove a tower crane on the buildings and she was a nurse in the Highgate Hospital. Because of the children the wife worked nights. The house was so big that they had spare rooms even with the four children. They knew our story and they felt that we had done the right thing. The very sound of the word abortion made Michael angry. And she was able to be of real use to Nora Kavanagh. She made Michael and the children's supper whenever Nora was working nights. She got the children out for school and let Nora early to bed when she got home, "They were dying off like flies last night," Nora'd say some mornings and she'd babysit any time Michael and Nora wanted to go out. Often they'd bring back beers and the three of them would sit and talk in front of the TV. She knew I'd like the Kavanaghs and they thought I'd acted well in the whole business and wanted to meet me. She felt completely taken care of. She loved the children and the house. She'd said to Michael that she'd be willing to change places with their sheepdog if it meant being able to stay on in the house and they'd both collapsed laughing. She'd difficulty getting them to take the small rent and they gave it back and more in presents. They wanted her to give up her job at the Tottenham yard but the work was so easy that she'd keep it on up to the last.

She felt as if she was in a train. The doors were locked and it was moving fast. All the faces about her in the carriage were happy and smiling. The train had passed all the early stations and was now racing through the night. In a very short time it'd stop. She'd get out at Christmas to the child and she knew the angels would be watching.

The first plan was to have the child in the house. Then it was decided that it was safer, because of her age, to have the child in the hospital. Michael's wife was able to arrange a bed in a semi-private ward in her own hospital.

She gave up work in the Tottenham yard two weeks before Christmas and asked for the money I'd earlier offered. Papers arrived for me to sign. The train was still beautifully on course, all the doors locked, though it now seemed probable that it would carry past Christmas and possibly into the New Year. Would I come to London for Christmas? London was the most exciting place in the world at Christmas.

While these letters brought me near a winter that was happening elsewhere, her bells for good cheer were for me a

217

simple cause of gloom. I met the black-haired girl casually, but often saw her coats and dresses, now so familiar to me, in a crowd. They had become the envelopes of a quiet love.

"It's bloody awful," I complained at the end of a week in which not a day had gone by without a letter of glad tidings from London.

"There's nothing you can do about it," she said.

"I suppose it's just vanity on my part. You imagine you control your life, and then something comes along like this and blows it wide open."

"It is vanity."

"To realize that doesn't seem to make it any better."

"You seem to me to have behaved well. What are you to do? Marry the woman, for God's sake?"

"O, I behaved well enough, all right. I know that. But I behaved well as much out of cowardice as anything else. It's safer to behave well. It's more protection than behaving badly."

"Well, it's done now," she said, and at the bus stop where we usually parted, she said, "You might as well leave me back tonight."

"Are you sure?"

"Are you sure?" she smiled, and without thinking I closed my grip on her arm.

As we went between the two lighted globes above the hospital gates I felt invaded by a fragility, a spiritual lightness that had nothing to do with the hospital or dark in the hospital. I had no sense at all of the misery and suffering and even exaltation that may have been going on in that darkened ward. The same fragility I had felt entering rooms of strange people at their ease or walking up to the door of a building the morning of taking up a new job. I was entering a new life. I was being questioned, and I had no longer the power to turn away, nor the confidence to say yes, only that I could try and try with all that I knew, the rash heart given its rashness, but given it by watchfulness and care, knowing they could not know where it might lead but determined to be its shadow everywhere.

It seems we must be beaten twice, by the love that we inflict and then by the infliction of being loved, before we have the humility to look and take whatever agreeable plant that we have never seen before, because of it being all around our feet, and take it and watch it grow, choosing the lesser truth because it's all that we'll ever know.

We went straight to her room, more cell than room, the black cross on its white bare wall, careful even of our breathing between its paper walls.

In the morning when I rang for the taxi I was about to turn to her to say that the hospital seemed to have fewer night visitors in winter, when down the corridor doors started to open softly and footsteps come towards us. We kissed quickly and I could feel her laugh by my side as we heard, "Can we share the taxi into the city?" I had seen none of the sharers before, the sauce chef was not there, and we drove into the sleeping city in a drowsed silence.

I was too tired to read or work the next day, but did not want to sleep, as if by sleeping I'd consign the night casually to some section of animal desire, like any night, as if it was necessary to keep a wilful vigil. In spite of this, I must have fallen asleep in the cane chair, for I was startled by the bell. I had no idea what time it was. The fire had gone out.

A telegram, I thought as I went downstairs. From London or the country. A birth or death or, I stirred guiltily, a death in giving birth, but when I opened the door it was my uncle who was standing there.

"It was the last ring I was going to give," he said petulantly. "I thought there was no one in. I was just about to powder off with myself."

"Is she gone or what?" I asked too quickly out of surprise.

"No, but it'd be a blessing for the poor thing if she was. She's back in the hospital. She collapsed. I'd to come up in the ambulance," he was undismayed.

219

"Is she conscious?"

"She is," he said but I could tell by his answer that he did not know the meaning of the word.

"Has she her senses about her?"

"Not at all. She's just collapsed. She never moved or spoke a word all the way up. She's like a dead person but she's not dead."

I grew aware that we were standing all that time in the doorway, "Come in." As we climbed the stairs I saw that he was practically immobile between self-importance and self-pity.

"You haven't been down," he accused. "That woman was expecting you a lot of the time."

"I'm sorry. I meant to, several times, but I didn't."

"There's been big changes."

"What changes?"

"Well, I bought a place," he announced.

"What place?"

"McKennas." I shuffled through the local names until I came on a big farmhouse with orchards and sheds between the saw mill and the town.

"But that's a farm. What do you want with land?"

"Won't it make money even if it was only left lying there?" he began to laugh, which continued after I asked how much he'd paid for it. "Guess," he chuckled and I knew I'd have to draw out the game to the last trick, and settled on a figure I knew to be too high but not outrageously so.

"You must be joking," he laughed with pure pleasure.

"You mean to say you had to pay more than that?"

"You must be daft. Not half it."

After we'd tortuously reached the right figure, which I'd to tell him was so low he should have been up for swindling, he wiped tears of pleasure away with the backs of fists.

"That'll do you," he laughed as he scolded. "That's enough."

"You must admit you got it cheap."

220

"Well, it wasn't too dear. I'll admit that much. I could have made a profit on it since anyhow."

"You know you were welcome to use my house. In fact I was hoping that you would. It needs living in."

"I know that but sure you'll live in it yourself. It's coming to the time when I believe if a man hasn't his own house he has nothing."

His own state had always been the ideal state, the proper centre of aspiration for everyman.

"I thought you weren't going to leave while she was ill," I reminded him.

"Well, I haven't left yet."

"Does she know that you bought the place?"

He grimaced with hurt as he told, "She said I was a fierce eejit, that at my age a one-roomed hut close to a church would be more in my line. But then she's sick. That woman hasn't been herself for a long time. She's not been minding her business for ages. And things has been going from bad to worse between me and Cyril."

"What happened?"

"Well, it got so bad, one evening he had the drink to do the talking for him and he was going on about me being in the place and not paying, when I always paid far more than I took. Anyhow I took the key out of my pocket and threw it on the floor. 'Pick it up,' I said, 'and only one of us will walk out that door.' After that," he chuckled blackly, "It was about time I thought of looking for my own place."

"Why didn't Cyril come with her?"

"Why didn't Cyril do a lot of things? Cyril'll not stir himself now, as long as there's anybody in the world left able to move."

"What are you going to do now?"

"I'm going to go home on the train. I want you to ring for Jim to meet me off the train. He can take the big car or the truck. If he's not around someone will get word to him. Then

221

you better go in to see if that woman has come round," he was all orders.

"What happened to her?"

"She just fell. At the top of the stairs. She was lucky she didn't roll down. She was supposed to go into hospital a few days before that and didn't. Lucky the ambulance was there and able to take her. I came with her in the ambulance."

"Have you eaten?"

"No. I haven't had a bite. I'm starved."

We had a mixed grill in the North Star across from the station, and I saw him to the train, using the fact that I'd to phone ahead for Jim to meet him in order to avoid the awkwardness of those minutes that wait for the train to go.

"I don't suppose it'll be long until I have to be down now," I referred to the impending funeral.

"No," he said confidently, as if some certainty was a matter of rejoicing. "It won't be long, but you will go in to see her?"

"I'll go in as soon as I make the call," and he was satisfied, making a careless gesture of dismissal. How confident and full of well-being he was compared to the small shaken figure that had got off the train that sunny day in early spring to visit her in the hospital. Death had been well reduced from beauty as well as terror. It happened to people who were foolish enough to cease minding their business.

He had exaggerated her state. I thought I'd find her in a coma but she was completely conscious though very weak.

"Is your uncle gone home?" was her only question and when I nodded she smiled before she let her face fall. She recovered her strength so rapidly in the next few days that I thought I'd resume the normal visits. I took her in a bottle of brandy.

"God bless you but I don't need that any more. It's cost you enough already, all those old bottles."

"There's lots more bottles," I protested.

"No. I'm taking the pills. You don't need anything while you're taking the pills."

222

"I thought you didn't trust the pills," with every fumbling sentence I was losing ground in the face of her calm.

"I trust the pills good enough—for what I have to do. When you take them you don't feel anything. In a few days I'll be out of this old place. I won't be coming back. I've fought long enough and hard enough and it's beaten me, bad luck to it," she even laughed.

"You can't say that."

"I can say that because it's the bitter truth and I've earned it. I'm not worried. I was just thinking that there's already far more people that I've been close to in my lifetime on the other side than on this side now. There's some good stories now I'll have to tell them. I'm afraid there's many a laugh we'll have to have over most of the stories," her eyes were shining. "I'll have to start looking to see if that uncle of yours can be given extra space up there as soon as I arrive, for no doubt he'll want to bring that bloody old saw mill with him, not to talk of this doting farm he's just bought."

I'd to turn away, "I'll be in early tomorrow."

"You might as well ring your uncle. To tell him to come up for me the day after tomorrow. That I'm going home," I heard her add. "Anyhow we can settle it tomorrow."

I hate tears, hate that impotent rage against the whole fated end of life they turn to, and when I fought them back I was embarrassed by the bottle of brandy still in my hands, like a coat I'd been given to hold by someone who had forgotten to come back.

Two days later I helped her into the big car outside the hospital and drove her and my uncle out of the city. She was practically gay, harassing my uncle's stolidity with sharp wit. He was well insulated against all suffering, wearing a coat of embarrassed righteousness far thicker than his black crombie which seemed to proclaim, "You see the compromising sort of situations people who insist on being stupid, who do not mind their business force you into." As before, at Maynooth I left them to get the bus back into the city. As I kissed her frailty our silence seemed to acknowledge that we'd never see one another again. Her coldness shook me, her perfect mastery. It was if he she'd completely taken leave of life, and any movement back was just another useless chore, and everything—me, my uncle, I doubted if Cyril could even light her eyes now—had become boringly equal.

"My aunt was in the hospital and is gone home," I told her when we met, unable to keep from touching her black hair.

"I know. Some of the doctors were annoyed that she was brought to us when she collapsed. She should have been taken to a local hospital. There's nothing we can do for her any more."

"She has money. You know what influence is in a small place. They'd think the Dublin hospital would be better, and she'd have to go to the best. Anyhow she'll not be back. It's all neat enough. There's only two telegrams to wait for now. A birth and a death."

"Maybe she'll not send word about the child."

"You think she might land on the doorstep?"

"No. That she'd think her own interests would be best served by staying separate. That she could do anything she wants with the child."

"She'll be able to do that anyhow."

I gave her the letters to read. She read them, but very reluctantly.

"What do you think of her and the whole business?" I asked.

"What does it matter what I think? No matter what I think it's useless," she refused to be drawn.

The telegram came five days after Christmas, announcing the birth. I just waited.

A rapturous letter followed. She had had a dangerous and difficult confinement, but the child was worth it all. The child was beautiful. All his little features were replicas of my own, except the ears. We can't all be perfect, she quoted from her favourite movie. I should hear him crow.

I wrote restating my old position in what I thought were the clearest possible terms, which she described as brutal and hurtful.

All right, we could give up the child for adoption, but on these conditions. I'd have to come to London and live at Kavanagh's and take care of the child for a whole week. Feed it, change it, wash it. She'd move out for that time. If, at the end of the week, I could be heartless enough to give it away for ever, then she'd consent to the adoption, but there was no other way she'd consent.

I just repeated my position, saying whether I took care of the child for a day or a month could make no difference.

The next letter did not come by return and was more cautious. Would I come to London?

I hesitated for some days before writing that I would go to London. I'd see her to talk about what she intended to do, but under no circumstance would I agree to see the child. It had the echo of negotiating a deal of sale. I might be prepared to go ten thousand but under no circumstances would I consider fifteen or anything close to it.

I took the plane with the feeling of being flushed from one city to the other, that there should be a chain to pull. I rang her from London Airport.

"It's great to hear your voice," she said. "If you'd rung a half-hour earlier you'd have heard the little man crowing. But he's sound asleep again. You'll have to wait till you get here. Where are you ringing from?"

"The airport."

"Why don't you get the tube? It's quicker at this time. I'll meet you outside Archway Station. And we can walk here."

"I'm not going to the house."

"But you're expected. Everybody's looking forward to meeting you. There's food and drink. Michael and Nora have been talking about little else but meeting you for days."

"I'm sorry but I'm not going to the house," I found myself trembling with nervousness. "I don't intend to see the child."

225

When she was silent I said, "I'm keeping to my end of the bargain. Meet me at ten in The Bell at the bottom of Fleet Street. That's if you want to meet me."

"But everybody's expecting you. And don't you want to see your child at least once?"

"No. And I'm sorry. Meet me at ten in The Bell if you want to meet me."

As I'd plenty of time, I walked from Cromwell Road across London to the pub. Walking in a city where a great deal of time has been spent is like walking with several half-tangible, fugitive images that make up your disappearing life. There had been snow and there was packed ice along the edges of the pavement. I loved the glow of the night-lights. If one could be free of this clinging burden of tension it would be a lovely place to walk in, asking nothing but to be free to walk and look and see, hunch shoulders against the cold. Except I was too old not to know that it was by virtue of this very tension that it took on the apparel of happiness.

She came through the door on Fleet Street just before ten, with a man in his forties, red hair thinning, his powerful body managing to look awkward and ill at ease in his blue suit and shirt and tie. He was plainly Irish, from a line of men who had been performing feats of strength to the amazement of an infantile countryside for the past hundred years, adrift in London now, pressing buttons on a tower crane, and I knew at once he was Michael Kavanagh.

"I wanted to come on my own," she said in a low pleading voice, "but Michael insisted on driving me. He's been wanting to meet you for a long time."

"That's fine with me. I'm glad to meet you," and he reluctantly gave me his hand. That he was raging with uneasiness showed in his every movement.

"What'll you have to drink?"

"A light and bitter," he said and she had a glass of lager.

With the warm brown wood of the bar, the white mantles hanging from the gas lamps, the governor in his long shirtsleeves behind the solid counter, it could have been a very pleasant place to talk and drink.

"Well, what are you going to do?" Kavanagh was going to sort me out quickly.

"I don't know," I said and watched him finish the pint, order another round from the bar. She was worn and looked as if she'd been through a severe illness. The grey in her hair showed much more. I found myself completely indifferent to her, as if we'd both journeyed out past touching. Kavanagh drank the second pint more slowly.

"How do you mean you don't know?" he pursued.

"What is there to do now? Either the child is adopted or kept."

"And it's no concern of yours, like?"

"It is some concern."

"Some concern . . . after all you've put this poor girl through. It'd make stones bleed."

"I'd prefer if the child could be adopted. That way it'd have two proper parents. . . ."

"I couldn't give the child away. I don't know how anybody that even saw him could give him away," she said. But I hardly looked at her. It was with Kavanagh I'd have to contend.

"Well, you better come back to the house and see your good handiwork anyhow. That's all the girl says that she wants. Many a man would go on his bended knees at the very thought that such a girl should even think of marrying him. And all she wants from you is to go back to the house for an hour. That's all she says she wants. And if that's the way you are, in my humble opinion, she's well rid of you."

"Come back with us to the house," she put her hand on my arm. "That's all I ask. If you want you can walk out of the house after that, and be as free as you want to be."

"I'm not going back to the house. And I'm not seeing the child."

"What did you come to London for, then? Why didn't you

227

skulk with the rest of the craw thumpers back in good old holy Ireland that never puts a foot wrong?"

"I'm leaving," I said. Time had been called several minutes before. And we were attracting the governor's eye. Twice he had come out from behind the counter and lifted our glasses.

"Goodnight. Thanks," I said to him and turned to go out by the back way, towards St Brides. I had just let the door swing when Kavanagh caught me and pulled me against the wall, "Are you coming or not?"

"No," I pushed against his arms but it was like pushing against trees.

"Are you coming or not?" and he started to shake me. I had no fear, feeling apologetic in the face of my own coldness, having the bad taste to remember a Civil War joke, "Who're you for?" the man with the gun was asking the drunk outside the pub : "I'm for yous."

"Are you coming or not?"

"No."

"Well, you'll be took," he started to drag me. At that, strength came to me, and I managed to free one arm, and strike and kick. Then I was spun completely free, and I could feel the blows come so fast that I could not be certain where they were coming from, and the hardness of the wall. I must have been falling, for the last I remember was striking out at her as she came towards me with outstretched hands. I must have lost consciousness for moments only, for they were quarrelling nearby when I woke. "What did you want to do that for?" she was crying. "You've gone and ruined everything."

"Leave him there and to hell with him. To hell with both of you and all stupid women."

I was at the bottom of steps. Quickly I pulled off shoes, and rose, holding the shoes in my hand, and stole round by the church.

"He's gone," I heard, and I tried to hurry but I wasn't able.

228

There was a deep doorway in a lane somewhere off the church whose gates hadn't been locked across and I went in and sat on the innermost steps.

I heard them searching for me but they never came quite my way. Only once did they get close enough for me to hear their voices and then I couldn't be sure of the words, "I told you he's done a skunk. He was only faking being hurt. There's no need to worry over that gentleman. I'm telling you that cunt will take good care of himself."

Soon there was no one near, the spasmodic jerky sound of the distant night traffic, some aeroplanes, their landing lights flashing as they came in over the Thames. I felt the cold and it was painful to move my lips and my face seemed numb, one eye was closed; and I was extraordinarily happy, the whole night and its lights and sounds passing in an amazing clarity that was yet completely calm, as if a beautiful incision had been made that separated me from the world and still left me at pure ease in its still centre. I could walk except for a dragging foot, but I hesitated to feel my ribs and face. When I did manage to bring myself to look closely by the light of a street-lamp in a barber's window, I knew I'd have to be very careful not to run into any policeman on the beat.

A milk bar saw me through till morning. I sat in a corner with a newspaper and let the coffee go cold. Using the newspaper as a screen I was able to examine my face in a far mirror but wouldn't have recognized it except by moving my hands and the newspaper's angle. The one cut that would need stitches was across the upper lip where the blow had cut it right across against the teeth. For a while everything had that same ethereal clarity, but that went too, in tiredness and stiffness and some pain. As soon as it was light I took a taxi to the airport. At such times, it is a great blessing to have money. It was now extremely painful for me to make the slightest facial movement. One or two people did make gestures towards my appearance in the airport that made me laugh, but the laughing too was painful so that I had to turn and lean against the wall.

Now it was a luxury to be flushed from one end to the other and I got a taxi to a doctor who stitched the lip. He thought there were no bones broken but wanted me to go for X-rays. He said he thought it'd be three weeks or so before I was presentable.

My luck seemed to be holding. There was no telegram waiting for me on the glass-topped table when I got in.

She has lived so long, I thought, let her live for three weeks more. I thought I'd never make the last steps of the stairs once I saw the door. I had just the one simple, fixed idea—to crawl to the bed and sleep. There is nothing that can stand against an overwhelming desire for sleep. It is as strong as death.

I slept late, but my aunt did not wait for my appearance to heal.

Mrs O'Doherty died at four, the telegram said.

I knew by the formality of the name that my uncle had sent the telegram. I watched the coarse paper start to shake in my hand and tried to say, backing away from the emotion I could not fight down, that I had known for a long time she would not get better, and it would be like her to pick this most inconvenient time to go, when my appearance was guaranteed to cause general mirth and head-wagging all over the small countryside : "Did you see the appearance of your man carrying the coffin? He *was* a sight"; but still emotion kept rising treacherously : her sturdy independence, her caustic laugh, her anger and her kindness, her person, the body of all life, growing, fighting, joying, weeping, falling, and now gone; and suddenly it beat me. I broke, and far off I could hear the wildness in my crying. Guard the human person well even in all its meanness, in its open hand, spite, venom, horror, beauty —profane sacredness, horrible contradiction.

I was so disturbed I needed to tell some person and walked to the end of the road and rang Maloney. I was surprised by my own matter-of-factness as I told him that I'd be out of the city for some days because of my aunt's death. He received the news with formal gravity. He even asked me her name and where she was likely to be buried.

When I rang my uncle I could tell even on the phone that he was practically unable to move with the sense of his own importance in the importance of the occasion. He insisted that he meet me off the train and when I glimpsed him as the train pulled into the small station he had taken up the most prominent position on the platform, iron-clad in the security of his role.

"Well," he was coming comfortably towards me with some profundity like *She's gone* or an equally swollen silence, when my appearance brought him to a quick check. First I saw disbelief, then outrage, and in a voice that clearly accused me of having done it all to embarrass him, he said, "I take it that the other fella is at least dead."

"I'm sorry," I found the laughing painful but couldn't stop it.

"Well what's happened?" he cleared his throat, his face an exaggerated version of hurt, and I decided not to lie. His focus was now so sharp that he'd probably be able to tell if I was lying.

"I got beaten up," I said.

"Tell me more news," he interposed sarcastically. "You'll be a wonderful addition for the next few days. You might even make the papers."

"Anybody can get beaten up. Somebody just turned on me. It wasn't my fault. There wasn't even a fight," but I saw the question did not go from his eyes but held steady. "Yes, there was a woman mixed up in it. It hurts like hell to have to talk."

"You'll never learn sense," he said.

He had brought the big car to the station. After about a mile of silence I said, "It's done now and I'm sorry. I was hoping she wouldn't go so soon. The question is what am I to say?"

"Say what?"

231

"How it happened. I don't suppose I should tell the truth."

"Are you joking?" the way he said it I knew all was well. That great institution, the family, was closing ranks.

"Well, what will I say?"

"Didn't you go to school long enough to think something up?"

"It's not all that easy when yourself is at the centre of the trouble."

"Well, why don't you say"—he cleared his throat, sounding like a sudden change of faulty gears—"Why can't you say you were in a car crash?"

"Will they believe it though?"

"What do you care whether they believe it or not? As long as they have no way of finding out!"

There were several cars in front of the house. Inside the house all the doors were open.

"I'm sorry," I shook Cyril's hand in the hallway.

"I know that."

"I'm sorry to look like this. I was in a car crash."

"You're sure you're able to be up?" he asked.

"I'm all right. It just looks bad."

Several people shook my hand, "I'm sorry for the trouble."

"I know that indeed," the response had been fashioned for me long years ago. I climbed the stairs to her room. There were four people sitting about the bed on chairs, two women and two men. I knelt at the foot of the bed. I looked at her face, her form beneath the raised sheet, the beads twined through her fingers. What a little heap of grey flesh the many coloured leaping flame burns down to. The two men were drinking whiskey with a chaser of beer. There was port or sherry in the women's glasses. One of the men was remembering her when she first came to the town as a young girl to work in Maguire's shop, and how young she was still when she opened her first shop, in this very house, above which she was now lying. They mustn't have been used to ashtrays, for one of the men pushed his cigarette end into the neck of the beer bottle between his feet where it began to hiss. When I rose from my knees the four people shook my hands and one of the men offered me his chair which I was able to refuse.

My uncle was waiting for me at the foot of the stairs, clearing his throat before saying loudly, "We better go now and see that man about the car insurance." Some people stopped me to shake my hands as I followed him out in an uncaring numbness.

"She looks good," he said as we got into the big car.

"Who laid her out?" and he named two women.

"They did a nice job. What men do we have to see about the insurance?"

"No man," he laughed. "It was an excuse to get you out. Haven't you been in a car crash! We won't need to go back now till the removal. And I thought we might as well dawnder out to my place. That's where you'll be staying tonight. There's a room made up."

"What happened in the end?" I asked.

"I'll tell you in a minute," he said as he suddenly turned up the avenue to his new house. "I'll tell you in the house."

It was a big slated nineteenth-century farmhouse, five front windows and a solid hall door looking confidently down on the road. We drove round by the cobbled back and parked in the yard, which was completely enclosed by out offices, their red iron roofs dull with rain. It was very warm in the kitchen, and the first thing he did was to shake down the Stanley and pile in more coal. Blue and white mugs hung from hooks on the deal dresser, and an oilcloth in blue and white squares covered the big deal table. Wedding and baptism photos, even one ordination group, hung with the religious pictures around the tall walls. I found it very lovely.

His old face was as excited as a boy's as he searched my battered face to see his excitement mirrored.

"Well, what do you think?" his voice was nervous.

"I think it's lovely."

"I threw in a few extra hundred and they agreed to leave

233

everything as it was. Tables, chairs, beds, dresser—everything."

"You got away with murder."

"I'd say, safely—with two murders. You wouldn't be started till you'd see a thousand pounds in this room, and there are ten rooms."

"Some woman must have been fond of blue," I said.

"What do I care what they were fond of?" he chuckled so deep he shook, "It's ours now!"

I had to turn away because the laughing hurt. He thought I was laughing with him, and he was partly right; for he showed me the rest of the house in such an extravagance of delight that the tears streamed down his face.

"What have you done with the land?"

"It's stocked, with bullocks. They don't need much minding."

"Well, tell me what happened?" I said in an old armchair one side of the Stanley.

"What'll you have first?"

"I'm all right."

"You'll have to have something. It's your first time in the house."

"Whiskey, then."

He opened a cupboard across from the dresser. "Are you sure you wouldn't sooner something different?" to show that the cupboard was bursting with drinks. The same bottles would probably be there at the same level next Christmas.

"No. Just whiskey," and he poured me a large tumblerful, turning his back to pour only the minutest nip for himself.

"Well, tell me what happened?" I said, the whiskey making the inside of my mouth smart like hell.

"Well, Cyril will never forget it," he began powerfully. "She left him everything. And I don't begrudge him a penny. In the end he earned it, down to the last farthing."

"How?"

"Well, as soon as she got home she sent for Delehunty and made her will. They spent a long time making it and then she sent for me. She told me straight out that she was leaving everything to Cyril. She'd have left me something but she said she knew I had enough," his voice thickened and grew hesitant. He had obviously been hurt.

"And you have, of course. You have more than enough."

"O I told her that. And in no uncertain terms. And I told her as far as I was concerned she could fire her money and houses out into the street, for all I cared."

"She can't have taken too kindly to that."

"No," he crowed. "She told me to shut up, that she always knew I was an eejit. I told her whether I was an eejit or not she'd never find me giving my money to strangers. She mentioned you, that she was thankful, and all that, and that she'd thought of you, but that you were young and had an education as well as your own place."

"So Cyril got everything. I'm not surprised."

"Wait," he laughed. "The best is on its way. She then sent for Cyril. She told him that she was leaving him everything but that it was on condition he never tried to see her again. He had only bothered with her when she was well and wanting something off her. He hadn't come near her since she'd got badly sick. And now she didn't want him at the end."

"How did you find out this?"

"The poor fella was so upset that he came out here and cried it all out."

"What did you say?"

"What do you expect? I told him of course that the woman wasn't in her right mind," he chuckled. "When it was about the only time she *was* in her right mind lately."

"Who took care of her?"

"The nurse was in. And she didn't even want the nurse. There was an invitation too to a wedding, far out cousins of ours from the mountains, the Meehans. One of the girls was getting married. She sent them a present. But she said that she'd not be at the wedding, that she had a much harder thing to do, and that she wished them as much joy and fun from the wedding as they could get, for one day they'd have to do the same hard thing that she had to do now."

"Did you see her again?"

"Yesterday morning. I went in to tell her that I had given the Meehans the present, when who did I meet scrubbing the stairs but those two Donnelly sisters. One of them is a friend of Cyril's. Did you ever notice that when things are rightly bad there'll always be some stupid woman to be found who'll have started scrubbing or tidying?"

"What did you do?"

"I ran them."

"Did she have any idea of this?"

"Not at all. If she was even half right they wouldn't get within a mile of the place. The nurse was there when I went in and the room was in half darkness. I thought at first that she was talking to the nurse, but then I saw she wasn't talking to the nurse at all. Her voice was so low that it was hard to hear it, but I think she was talking to your mother, God rest her. Whatever it was it must have been funny for she seemed to be laughing a great deal or it was like as if she was laughing."

"Was she talking all the time?"

"No. She'd talk and then go quiet as if listening. It's in those times that she'd start to laugh. Then she'd start up talking again. I suppose the poor thing was going out of her mind in the finish."

"Did you say anything?"

"No. The nurse told me there was no use. In about five hours after that she went."

"I'll miss her. But with the way she was it was an ease."

"We'll all miss her. But things have been going wrong with her for a long time. I don't think they were ever right since the day she married. That was the real turning point."

"I suppose you'll close down for the whole of the week?"

"For the whole week, are you joking! There's enough gone wrong without us going the same way. Jim too was thinking we

236

mightn't start up for the week but he got a land. We'll be starting first thing the morning after the funeral."

Before we left, he shook down the Stanley again and heaped in more coal. "Coal is the only thing that gets up a real heat. I bought five tons back there. Wood is all right but only for getting the fire going. You'll find the place will be roasting when we get back."

"You were very lucky to get this place," I felt I had to praise it again.

"It's only once in a lifetime a place like this comes on the market. And the man and the money was waiting. Wouldn't I be in a nice fix now if I'd gone on depending on other people?"

"The man with the money," I echoed to tease. "I'll be round with the hat any one of these days."

"That'll do you now," he shook with pleasure. "That'll do you now."

The house was so crowded when we got back that it was hard to get through the hallway and I was so tired that I no longer cared how my appearance was taken, but enquiries had been made, and the car crash was in general circulation. People sympathized with me over the accident in the same tone as over my aunt's death.

Then a murmur ran through the house that the hearse was outside, and all except the close relatives, and a few people asked to stay, filtered silently out, some glancing furtively back as they went. The coffin was brought in, eased up the narrow stairs, lifted across the banister, turned sideways in the door, put on chairs alongside the bed. There was no priest in the house, and the only four people in the room were the undertaker, his assistant, myself, my uncle.

"Is there any more that wants to come up?" the undertaker asked, and I marvelled at the tact that omitted *to look on her a last time in the world*.

When there was no answer he asked in a whisper, "Does Cyril want to come up?"

My uncle went out on the stairs, and in some silent, mysterious way the question was conveyed down below. When my uncle came back to the room he said, "No. He doesn't want," in a voice clear with self-righteousness.

"I suppose we can begin," the undertaker said and looked around, "Let one of the women come up."

For what? startled across my mind when the undertaker said again, "Let some of the women come up to see that everything is done right," as if he'd heard my silent enquiry. Was the division between men and women so great, the simple facts of sex so tabernacled, that a woman had to be chaperoned between deathbed and coffin? In the same mysterious way as word had been conveyed to Cyril it went down to the "women" and none of them wanted to come up.

"It's all right. We can go ahead," the undertaker said. He drew back the sheet. Silently we took hold of her and lifted her from the bed. Her lightness amazed me, like a starved bird. The undertaker arranged her head on the small pillow, and looked at us in turn, and when we nodded he put the lid in place, turning the silver screws that were in the shapes of crosses. There was a brown stain in the centre of the snow-white undersheet where she had lain.

The superstitious, the poetic, the religious are all made safe within the social, given a tangible form. The darkness is pushed out. All things become interrelated. We learn sequence and precedence, grown anxious about our own position in the scheme, shutting out the larger anxiety of the darkness. There's nothing can be done about it. There's good form and bad form. All is outside.

At heartsease we can roll about in laughter at all divergences from the scheme of the world. We master the darkness with ceremonies : of delight at being taken from the darkness into this light, of regret on the inevitable leaving of the light, hope as founded on the social and as firm as the theological rock.

"It is nothing. It's not what we struggled towards in all the days and nights of longing. We better look at it again in case

238

we've missed something we find at the end of each arrival. But then many see that they've arrived in the longing of eyes that used to be their own."

"It's always this way," an old voice says. "Everything. Sex, money, houses. Death will be the same way too, except this time you won't even realize it. You will be nothing."

"Since it's this way it's still better to pretend. It makes it easier, for yourself and others. And it's kinder."

"But I don't need kindness."

"You will," a ghostly voice said. "You will. We all will before we'll need nothing."

Outside, the large crowd waited across the road for the coffin to come out of the blinded house. They had already parked their cars and would follow the slow hearse the hundred yards or so on foot to the church where the old and some women and children had already taken their places. The crowd stood on the tarmac where the stone wall once ran to the railway gates, the three blackened and malformed fir trees, the two carriages and the square guard's van waiting to go to Drumshambo. Behind the mourners, the large water-pipe that looked like an elephant's trunk was missing from the sky. Those images of day that greeted her every morning when she went out to lift the shutters from the shop windows had proved even more impermanent than she.

My uncle asked me to drive the big car at the funeral.

"I can only see properly out of one eye."

"It'll be still better than my two. I can't manage slow driving, and we'll be right behind the hearse. It's the distance between that beats me."

"All right," I was secretly glad to have the driving. I was in more pain now than the day after the beating, and was glad of anything that forced me to concentrate elsewhere. My uncle handed me the car keys as soon as we left the house, "You might as well get the feel of it now," to drive to the church for the High Mass. The hearse was parked in front of the church gates, its carriage door raised like an open mouth; and

239

I parked the big car behind it. The first thing I noticed as I got out was Maloney standing on the tallest step between the gate and door. He was dressed all in black, and the wide-brimmed black hat made him look more like an ageing dance-band personality than a mourner. I detached myself from my uncle to go to meet him. "What are you doing here?"

"Paying my last respects."

"How did you know about the Mass?"

"I read the papers. And ye put it in de papers. And I'm pleased to see that you're properly turned out for the occasion. Yes," he grinned from ear to ear beneath the big hat, mimicking a Negro blues accent, "very pleased, to see you formally turned out for the occasion, in black and blue."

"This is all we need," I said before I realized that my uncle was standing close, and I introduced them.

"I've put up at the Commercial," he said, gesturing to the hotel just across the road from the church.

"I'll see you there later, then," I saw that my uncle was impatient at the interruption.

After the High Mass she was wheeled from the altar on a shining new trolley not unlike the trolleys used to gather in trays and used dishes in big wayside cafeterias, and we carried her on shoulders down the steps to the open back of the hearse. The hearse crawled slowly through the small town, stopped for a few moments outside the blinded house, but as soon as it passed the town-sign it gathered speed. Soon we were climbing into the mountains, passing abandoned houses, their roofs fallen in, water trickling from the steep sides onto the road, the brown of sulphur on the rocks. We drove immediately behind Cyril's car; and as we climbed, the coffin, in its glass case, seemed to rise continually in air above us.

"It's a big funeral," my uncle said with satisfaction as he looked back on a whole mile-long stretch of road below us still covered with cars. "That Mr Maloney that was at the church," he cleared his throat. "He's a friend of yours?"

"I do work for him."

240

"Writing work?"

"That's right. What do you think of him?"

"Seemed a bit overdressed for the part," he probed cautiously.

"He's all right. He likes to make a bit of a splash. It's a way of getting attention."

"I could see that end of it," he said.

When we got out of the car onto the hard gravel of the road the whole air felt rainwashed. The slopes were bare. And the urgent, rapid sound of racing water ran between the scrape of shoes on gravel, the haphazard banging of car doors, the subdued murmur of voices. We carried her round to the back of the small church, bare as the slopes on which it stood. On the rain-eaten slab of limestone above the open grave I was able to make out my mother and father's names and my grandmother's name, Rose; but you would need a nail or a knife to follow the illegible lines of the other impressions they were that eaten away. Through the silence of the prayers a robin sang against the race of water somewhere in the bare bushes. After the decade of the Rosary I was waiting for the shovels to start filling in the clay when the undertaker unrolled a green mat of butcher's grass and placed it over the grave. They'd fill in the grave as soon as the churchyard was empty, some barbarous notion of kindness.

Standing around and shaking hands afterwards in the graveyard I introduced Maloney to Cyril, who had been weeping during the prayers; and Cyril seemed as impressed as my uncle had been resolutely unimpressed, and invited Maloney back to the house. Five or six cars drove together back to the house.

"When are you going back to Dublin?" I asked Maloney in the house.

"Whenever you want. I can offer you a lift."

"Would tomorrow morning be too late for you? My uncle sort of expects me to stay that long."

"Not at all, dear boy. I'd like to look over the town. It reminds me of our old *Echo* days. I'd like to view the quality

241

of the local blooms, the small-town Helens. I have a room in the Commercial. We can leave round lunchtime."

"Earlier than that."

"Whenever you want. I'm at your service."

Cyril heard us and came over. He'd bought a headstone and wanted us to see it before we left in the morning. Apprehensively he included my uncle in the invitation, but it was brutally refused. "Some people still have to work. The mill will be going tomorrow."

"It's marble," Cyril said. "It's the best that money could get."

My uncle turned his back. It was crossing and recrossing my mind that the headstone must have been ordered while my aunt was still alive.

"We're being invited to an unveiling," Maloney reminded me coolly.

"All right. I'll be glad to see it," I agreed, and Cyril arranged to collect us in the hotel at ten. I was almost as impatient as my uncle to get out of the house. As we left, I saw Maloney's head bent low to Cyril's, in an exaggeration of listening.

"Where are we going?" I asked my uncle as I handed him back the car keys.

"I suppose we better go out to my place and make tea or something. If we went to a restaurant it'd be all over town that we didn't want to eat anything in the house."

"Or weren't given anything?"

"Or weren't given anything," his laugh was a harsher echo.

He wanted to show me his fields and stock. Perhaps because of my affection, I took pleasure in his pure pleasure, and I didn't have to talk at all. Then he insisted we go over to my place, pointing out things in need of repair or change, past the point when I no longer listened.

"You should stock that land yourself," he said later in the evening. "You shouldn't let it any more when this letting runs out." He'd forgotten that till he'd stocked his own land he was against all stocking. "Nothing but trouble," he used to declare.

"It's a full-time job. Don't say anything more."

"Who'd look after it for me?" I asked tiredly.

"I would—until you'd come yourself. Who's for my place after me but yourself? With everything running well there'd be no stronger men than us round here."

I rose when I heard his alarm go the next morning. He was making breakfast when I got down, rigged out in boots and overalls for the mill.

"You'll think over what I said last night?" he pressed as we ate.

"Sure."

"And you'll be down soon?"

"Or you'll be up," I said without thinking.

"No, I won't be up. Not if I can possibly help it," he half laughed. There were certain places and people to stay clear of, such as hospitals and undertakers.

"All right. I'll be down," I said.

Maloney was at breakfast when I went into the Commercial. He probably had a hangover. He was in a sour mood.

"How did you find the local blooms?" I asked.

"This isn't Grenoble and I'm not Stendhal's uncle. Have some coffee? Tell me how you got your decorations."

"She had the child. I went to see her in London. She had a protector who beat me up."

"And your aunt inconveniently died next day?"

"Right."

"Did this gentleman give any reason for beating you up?"

"He said that I had had my fun and I should pay for it."

"I agree with him. And don't think you're washed clean by the beating. Don't imagine you've been washed in the blood of the lamb or any of those cathartic theories. Don't try to slip out in any of those ways. I know you."

"Haven't I done enough?"

"By no means. We can't have people running round the country with their flies open and all male members at the

243

ready. I'm glad you got beaten up. You'll get beaten up many times. You deserve to get beaten up."

"Why?"

"Because," he used his spoon to point, "you behaved stupidly. People should always get punished for behaving stupidly and they generally do. I always did," and suddenly he shouted, "Here comes the happy widower. All dressed for the unveiling. *He*'s not behaving stupidly," and he let go a long deep groan that could have passed for a poor imitation of a donkey's bray. From the groan and the over-elaborate greeting—florid to the point of insult—I guessed he'd passed the rest of the funeral drinking with Cyril. Cyril noticed nothing. He was clearly impressed with Maloney and greeted us both with extreme affability, exuding the self-satisfaction and sense of anticipation of a man about to show off a racehorse or a girl that he felt reflected flatteringly on himself.

Cyril led us towards the red shop front with its wire grille and as he pushed open the door a warning bell rang. It was a shop I'd loved, and though it had been enlarged, the essential feel of it had hardly changed at all. The long solid counter with its brass measuring yard ran past the wood and smoked glass that partitioned off the bar near its end. Neat rows of boxes stood in line : seeds, nails, bolts, door handles, fishing hooks, a special offer of cartridge. Tools leaned all around the walls. Buckets, wellingtons, bridles hung from the ceiling. A rotavator and a shining copper spraying machine stood side by side in the centre of the floor. The old foreman recognized us and came over. Cyril introduced Maloney, "Mr Maloney . . . down from Dublin . . . for the funeral," in an impressed-with-himself-being-impressed hush of voice.

"I thought those days were gone," Maloney picked up the copper spraying machine by its leather straps.

"You'd be surprised at how many of our customers haven't managed to fit in with the new way of going about things,"

244

Brady, the old foreman, said. "But there's no doubt those days are gone. I suppose ten years at most. But we'll stock them as long as there's a demand and they can be got."

We moved through the partition into the bar. It was very small, two wooden stools at the counter, bare benches around the walls, one table at the back. It was no place for drinking sessions but rather for having a sobering drink while waiting for a large order to be put together in the shop or settling bills or ordering a tombstone or coffin. The door of the bar opened on to another shop and a farther yard where the plastic wreaths were kept and graveclothes and coffins and tombstones and the two hearses.

"Whiskey," Maloney said.

"Whiskey," I said.

"Three whiskeys," Cyril ordered, but Brady nodded to the young girl that the drinks were on the house. I noticed they served Bovril and coffee and fresh sandwiches as well. Black coffee bubbled in a jug beside a tray of sandwiches from which green leaves of lettuce bulged.

"Your good health," Maloney toasted the foreman with suitable gravity. "This is certainly the old style."

"You have to give the people something back," the foreman smiled. "It's not even good business to be taking all the time."

"Is Mr Comiskey about?" Cyril asked.

"He's in his office. He's expecting you. But there's no hurry. Anytime. Enjoy your drinks whatever ye do. I'll show ye up to him after a while."

"Do you still make coffins or do you just order them?" I asked.

"Order them," he answered. "No more than the poor spraying machine the days of making your own coffins is gone. There was a time you just nailed a few deal boards together and that was that. In the thirties, none of yous would remember, when I started here, people couldn't afford to even have the coffins painted. The few bare boards was wrapped in a

245

black sheet and carried to the church and grave covered with the sheet so no one could see the lack of paint or handles. Now it's the opposite : oak and walnut, brass and silver. It'll be gold handles next. People have to be kept back from spending money now. And it all goes down into the ground anyhow. And who can tell the man that wore the ragged jacket?" he quoted expansively.

"Still, I suppose they're expressing their feelings," I said in deference to Cyril's increasing discomfort during the speech.

"People are anxious to do the best they can," Cyril added. Maloney, who had his arms folded, unbuttoned himself enough to take out his spectacles, polish them, put them on, inspect Cyril as if he was some rare botanical specimen for a long minute. Then he went through the same silent show while returning the spectacles to their pocket.

"Apparently it's a sight all together in America," the foreman went on. "The boss was out at a conference in Los Angeles a few months back. Apparently they've gone wild there. The sky's the limit. Apparently the whole talk at the conference was how to interest people again in the plainer type of burial."

"Thanks very much," Maloney put down his glass firmly. "Having thus regaled ourselves we may as well see—is it Mr Comiskey?—about the rest of our business," but if he thought he could march to the office, see the marble slab, and get out, he was wrong. When we opened the bar door two coffins stood on iron trestles and beside them a pair of sleek hearses. The names were already on the nameplates. One had yesterday's date as the date of death; but the second had the day's date. The person, James Malone, had been alive a few hours before. I had never thought of history as so recent. On the shelves were plastic wreaths, and flat brown boxes which must have held the graveclothes.

"They're just ready to go out," the foreman said when he saw us linger.

"I didn't know you could get the information on the nameplate so quickly," I gestured to the day's date.

"It only takes a few minutes. Getting the spelling right is the main thing. Sometimes they don't even have their own names spelled right, but when it's pointed out to them that it's wrong by someone else, they're apt to storm in and kick up one unholy fuss. By that time, of course, the coffin is in the ground. It doesn't happen often. We either know the person or can check. But we always keep the slip they give us just in case."

"This man must have died since midnight?"

"I can answer that in fact," the foreman said proudly. "I took the order myself just after opening the shop. He died at six o'clock this morning; ah, a quiet inoffensive little man, you'd often see him round the town with a hat, very fond of a pint."

"You see," I said to Maloney. "This is as good as your Paris venture. And it's not made up either." I thought I heard him curse, but my ribs and jaw gave warning not to laugh.

"Ah yes," Cyril said sententiously, standing between the pair of coffins and their waiting hearses. "Ah yes, when you think of it, life's a shaky venture," and they did hurt, even more so when I saw Maloney glower at him as if to eat him up, before the foreman led us up the wooden stairs, showed us into the office and withdrew.

Comiskey came out from behind the desk to shake our hands. He had on a worsted blue suit, shiny at the back and elbows, a Pioneer Pin, and an array of fountain pens and biros across the breast pocket to the lapel. His silky brown hair was combed back. It was not that he was very fat, but that the rich covering of flesh, sleek as any of his hearses, seemed to shake inside the cloth, and there was a permanent blush of raw beefsteak on both cheeks.

"We finished everything for you, Cyril, last thing yesterday evening," he said in a tone that managed to be both authoritative and familiar. In a slow jog he led us down the stairs, rubbing his hands and talking as he went. He led us away from the hearses and out into a big yard. He paused at an

247

enormous slab of black marble. "There we are," Comiskey stood to one side.

Beside my aunt's name and dates in gold on the marble was the silhouette of a fashionable young woman. On the base of the marble, in gold too, was Cyril's family name, O'DOHERTY. I looked at Maloney but he lifted his eyes briefly to the sky and then fixed them intently on the points of his shoes.

"It's very nice," I said to break the growing tension of the silence. "It must have cost a lot of money."

"We tried to do the best we could," Cyril said, again in his hushed voice. "She was a fine person. Her generosity to me was abundant. She left me everything she had."

"It's the best," Comiskey said, "It'll look very nice," and if his foreman had all day to discourse he plainly hadn't, and he led us back to the bar, "These gentlemen will have a drink on the house," he said in a lordly way to the girl, shook our hands, and left us. We had whiskeys again.

"Her generosity to me was abundant." I marvelled at the phrase as I looked at Cyril's handsome, dull face and wondered if he'd bought it with the marble.

"What are you going to do with the old limestone?" I asked.

"Well," he said ponderously, "I gave it a good deal of thought, and I didn't like to have to remove it, but there comes a time, just the same as with old houses, when you can't do them up any more. You're throwing good money after bad. You're far better to start from the ground up again. I think the marble will be no insult."

"Quite right," Maloney chorused with alarming fierceness.

The rain had already half eaten many of the names : Rose, Jimmy, Bridie. . . . Soon the limestone would not be able to give them even that worn space. They would be scattered to the mountain air they once breathed. It would be a purer silence.

"You'll have one more drink on me," Cyril pressed.

"No," I said. "We have to be back."

"We're late," Maloney added. We shook hands with the foreman on our way out, with Cyril outside the door.

"You'll be very welcome any time you're down," he said in the first generous flush of his new estate.

"He's your uncle-in-law," Maloney said before Cyril was even out of earshot.

"That's right."

"Well your uncle-in-law is an eejit."

"I concur."

"And by the way that was a cheap crack about the Paris business, and like all cheap cracks full of a little truth, helping it up into a bigger lie. Nobody would pay the slightest attention to you wheeling a baby around in a coffin in this misfortunate country. They'd think you couldn't afford a pram," he said fiercely. "Look at today—isn't the whole country going around in its coffin! But show them a man and a woman making love —and worst of all enjoying it—and the streets are full of 'Fathers of eleven', 'Disgusted' and the rest of them. Haven't I been fighting it for the past several years, and giving hacks like you employment into the bargain. But what'll work here won't necessarily work elsewhere and vice-fucking-versa. That's why I'm not giving up my Paris idea. Every country has their own half-baked version of it and they wave it around like their little flags. It's coffins here. It's class in England. It's something stupid or fucking other everywhere."

"That's a speech for this time of morning!" I said sarcastically.

"But is it any wonder that the lowest common denominator rules," he ignored. "There's hardly any fixed people around at any given time. They're all either dead or growing up or growing down or standing like your Early York out in the back garden."

"What are we to do now?"

"Oh you're all right. You're our Renaissance man, a true sophist. Inflaming people and fathering children which you later disown. Let me tell you this, sir. We're not letting you off the hook. You've lowered the moral average all around. And you're making us all feel good."

"Will we go to the car?"

"The car's here," he pointed to a shining new car across the road that I hadn't seen him with before.

"We'll go," I said. "We'll go by the saw mill. It's the shortest way."

I could hear the singing of the saws above the purring motor before we reached the mill. Maloney let the car go slow so that we had a clear sight of the mill for several seconds.

My uncle was at the big saw, an enormous trunk of beech on the rollers. You could only see him when the saw was still. Once he set it screaming he was hidden by its streaming dust. Jim was farther back but he was not sawing. He seemed to be setting up or oiling one of the minor saws.

After the strain of greedy watching, knowing it would all be soon lost from sight, I was partly grateful when the thick whitethorns shut it out; and I had no wish to stop or to go back. It would only idly prolong what had to be ended and my uncle had even more need of his own space than when he'd come up the long platform, the raincoat over his arm, to see her that first day in hospital. Today was after all the formal beginning of his new life without her, a marrying of it to the old. He'd fill it now for the forever that it was.

"There's one man who knows he's going everywhere by staying put," Maloney said. It was impossible to tell from the tone whether it was intended as a cosmic joke or a simple breath of admiration.

"I'm thinking of proposing marriage to a woman and coming back here," I said suddenly.

"You're what?" Maloney swung the wheel so violently that I had to shout to watch the road. "You're returning? So that the cattle can have the privilege of saying loo to you. You can start to see God in the bushes, not to speak of a bank manager. All that caper?"

"I don't know. There comes a time when you either run

250

amok completely or try to make a go of it. I'm going to try to make a go of it."

"Embedded first in the warm womb, of course, and then hold hands and listen to the dawn choir. O sweet suffering Switzerland. We must talk about it. There's a good hotel in Kells, if I can be seen with you so close to Dublin. Your outer aspects reflect accurately what must be an appalling inner moral condition. I don't like people starting to do things I was doing ten years ago. Anyhow she may well turn you down."

"It won't matter."

"How do you mean it won't matter? Has this beating softened your brain as well?"

"The life has to be lived afterwards anyhow, no matter what the answer. Won't it be even more difficult if the answer is yes?"

"What if she does say *No*?" he shouted.

"The world won't stop. There'd be a chance of a real adventure lost. I'd be sorry," and I was beginning to be sorry I had spoken.

"O you're some lover, I tell you. But fortunately I know you. Blacken day with night. Tell the nodding plants they'll grow just as well in shade as sun. It's all in the sweet quality of the mind, so forget the fucking circumstances, brother."

The rain had started, the powerful wipers sweeping it imperiously aside as soon as it spotted the shining arcs, sweeping and sweeping.

"You'd have seen me if you had been paying attention," she'd once said to me, the night she came towards me across the floor of the Metropole. By not attending, by thinking any one thing was as worth doing as any other, by sleeping with anybody who'd agree, I had been the cause of as much pain and confusion and evil as if I had actively set out to do it. I had not attended properly. I had found the energy to choose too painful. Broken in love, I had turned back, let the light of imagination almost out. Now my hands were ice.

We had to leave the road of reason because we needed to

251

go farther. Not to have a reason is a greater reason still to follow the instinct for the true, to follow it with all the force we have, in all the seeing and the final blindness.

"Have you gone dumb or is there nothing you have left to say for yourself or what?" Maloney had taken his eyes off the road to look me full in the face. His scant white hair spilled out from under the wide rim of the black hat. He looked definitely more danceband now than funeral. I gritted my teeth to try to stop the fit of laughter because it hurt so much, but the very pain was making it all the more impossible to stop.

What I wanted to say was that I had a fierce need to pray, for myself, Maloney, my uncle, the girl, the whole shoot. The prayers could not be answered, but prayers that cannot be answered need to be the more completely said, being their own beginning as well as end.

What I did say was, "Why don't you watch the road?"

"I've been watching the bloody road all my life, and it tells me nothing. Yoo-hoo, Road!" he suddenly shouted. "You see! It doesn't answer. It just speeds past. Yoo-hoo, Road!"

"It might get us there if you did."

"It'll get us there anyhow. Yoo-hoo, Road! Yoo-hoo, Road!" he was shouting, driving very fast.

I tried to say something back but couldn't. And in the silence a fragment of another day seemed to linger amid the sweeping wipers, and grow : the small round figure of my uncle getting out of the train away down the platform, childishly looking around, the raincoat over his arm, at the beginning of the journey—if beginning it ever had—that had brought each to where we were, in the now and the forever.

"Yoo-hoo, Road. Yoo-hoo, Road. Yoo-hoo, Road. Yoo-hoo. . . ."

252